Also by A.J. Pine

THE MURPHYS OF MEADOW VALLEY
Holding Out for a Cowboy

HEART OF SUMMERTOWN
The Second Chance Garden

FINALLY FOUND *my* COWBOY

A. J. PINE

sourcebooks casablanca

Published by Sourcebooks Casablanca, an imprint of Sourcebooks
P.O. Box 4410, Naperville, Illinois 60567-4410
(630) 961-3900
sourcebooks.com

Printed and bound in the United States of America.
OPM 10 9 8 7 6 5 4 3 2 1

For the dreamers…

Chapter 1

ELI MURPHY STARED AT HIS YOUNGER BROTHER Boone. At thirty-six and thirty-one respectively, four and a half years lay between them, yet there were times like this when Eli felt like a father trying to rein in his overly eager son.

"I thought we were taking this slow, *one* horse at a time."

Boone clapped Eli on the shoulder. "We *are*, big bro. We are." He flicked the brim of Eli's cattleman, and a small growl escaped the older Murphy brother's lips.

"If you're trying to get on my good side," Eli began, "you're doing it *wrong*."

Boone laughed as if Eli had been kidding. But Eli didn't joke about ranching or horses. He narrowed his eyes at the elephant in the room, which was actually the trailer attached to Boone's truck on which his brother now leaned. The *horse*-filled trailer.

Eli pointed at the barn. "You've got Cirrus in there who is nowhere close to being done with his rehabilitation. He may be good with you and Casey, but his anxiety with new riders needs further treatment."

At least that was the best excuse Eli could come up with on short notice. Scratch that. *No* notice. Boone had given him zero warning that he was showing up with a new resident for the barn. And now he expected Eli to, what, smile and nod like this was everything he'd always wanted? What Eli *wanted* was to forget he'd agreed to reopen the Murphy family's ranch and just go back to his quiet life as a quiet veterinarian who minded his own quiet business one quiet day at a time. Did he mention he liked quiet?

"I'm still in treatment for my own anxiety," Boone replied, unaware that his brother's inner monologue was scrambling for any excuse to shut…this…*down*. "Hell," he continued, "probably will be for life, but you still let *me* out of the barn every now and then." Boone crossed his arms and flashed Eli his best shit-eating grin.

Eli sighed and briefly lifted his hat. He ran a hand through his hair, somehow hoping the gesture would buy him time to think. He knew Boone wasn't giving up until he pleaded his entire case. And even then, the younger Murphy would poke and prod the grumpy bear he likely viewed his older brother to be until Eli relented. One way or another, Boone Murphy always got his way. That was how it had been with their parents, and it became the dynamic between the brothers as well.

"What's his story?" Eli finally asked, nodding toward the trailer.

"*Her* story," Boone corrected. "Name's Midnight. Picked her up in Sacramento from a family that didn't find her useful anymore if she couldn't compete. Can you believe that? Assholes."

Eli narrowed his eyes. "What's her *story*, Boone?"

Eli's brother squinted toward the sun as if he had to ask the sky for the answer. Finally, he met Eli's gaze again. "She...uh...she fractured her radius... On the left side." He winced.

"Christ, Boone." Eli pressed the heels of his hands to his eyes. "That's a hell of an injury. Was she a show horse?"

Boone nodded. "At least they wanted her to be. But I think they worked her too hard, had her trying things she wasn't ready for, because she's a little skittish with—um—people."

Eli threw his hands in the air. "Didn't we just establish that we already have *one* skittish horse to deal with? Now we've got a seriously *injured* skittish mare?"

"She already had surgery," Boone assured him. "Fully recuperated. But the owners can't be bothered to rehab her. Said they have three other horses, though none as pretty as this one if you ask me." Boone waggled his brows, but Eli wasn't about to encourage him. Finally, Boone sighed, his expression growing serious. "Eli, the owner flat out said they don't have time to deal with a mare who limps." He leaned forward and whispered, "They were gonna euthanize her. Caught wind of it from a trainer I know in town, and I just…I couldn't leave her when I knew we could help her."

Dammit. Of course he wasn't going to let a perfectly healthy mare be euthanized. Eli shook his head and muttered, "Assholes."

Midnight whinnied from inside the trailer, seemingly aware that she was the topic of conversation.

Boone straightened and pivoted toward the trailer. "It's okay, girl. I think we convinced him."

"It's called manipulation," Eli grumbled. "You got her papers?"

His brother laughed, gave the trailer a gentle pat, then turned back to face him.

"I have the record of sale, but the owners said they trashed her passport prior to euthanizing. Decided since she wasn't competition worthy anymore that neither was the record of the few things she'd already accomplished before her injury."

Eli clenched his jaw. "Record of *sale*? They charged you for her?"

Boone shook his head with incredulity and let out a bitter laugh. "Oh yeah. This guy Morrison is a real piece of work. *He* thought she was worthless but decided if I found value in her, it was only fair I compensate him for that value. Went on and on about how her breed is scarce in these parts, that she'd be worth a pretty penny if she wasn't lame. Do you believe that shit? Charged me twice as much as he'd have paid to put her down. What was I supposed to do?"

Find another vet, Eli wanted to tell him. *Stop spending money our one-horse ranch doesn't actually have.* He had plenty of comebacks for his little brother, but none of them would have saved the mare like Boone had. None of them would have put that proud smile on Boone's face like showing up with a horse in need had. Eli tried to imagine what he would have done had he been in Sacramento rather than Boone. Would he have saved the mare of his own volition? Or would he have made every excuse to himself not to, just to protect himself from reopening doors to his past?

He was pretty sure he knew the answer, which meant he was also pretty sure Midnight's former owners weren't the only assholes Boone had come across this week.

"How the hell do you look so damned—"

"Happy?" Boone interrupted.

Eli shook his head. "I was gonna say—"

"Ass-over-elbow in love with my wife and my new baby girl?"

Eli groaned. "Can you shut the hell up for a second? You won. Midnight's staying, but that's *it*. This place hasn't been a ranch for years, and I'm still…" He blew out a breath. "I'm still wrapping my head around having horses on the property again. But you look so—"

He stopped short, waiting for Boone to cut him off again, but to his credit, the younger Murphy was still listening.

"So *sure*," Eli finally said. "How do you look so damned *sure*?"

And *young*, he wanted to say. Eli never thought much of the few strands of silver running through his dark hair or the fine lines at the corners of his eyes. But sometimes he simply felt weathered, like life had put him on the fast track to world-weary and wise, except the wise part hadn't yet set in.

"Sure of what?" Boone asked. "Being able to rehab Midnight?"

Eli shook his head. "Of *everything*."

Boone took a step toward his brother and slung an arm over his shoulder.

"Dr. Eli Fucking Murphy. Are you asking me for advice on living your best life? Because if so, I've got two words for you...therapy and *knitting*."

Eli sighed. "I did the therapy thing for a year after losing Tess. And I'm okay on the knitting front, but feel free to make me another scarf for Christmas this year."

Boone let his brother go and held out his arms, slowly turning in a circle as he took in the red barn they'd repainted this summer, the new fence they'd installed around the arena, and the chicken coop they set up on the land behind Eli's veterinary clinic so they could move Jenna's chickens out of the barn in order to make room for more horses.

"You forget how much you loved this place when it was Mom and Dad's, when raising horses was it for us." He stopped when he was facing Eli again. "Tess's accident was awful, and I won't pretend to know what it was like to lose her…and Fury. But we can do this, Eli. *You* can do this. I promise not to push you too hard. So we'll start with Cirrus and Midnight, and we'll take it from there. Okay?"

Eli's throat tightened. He'd already said yes to Boone getting the ranch up and running again, this time as a rehab facility. But they'd barely had Cirrus a year.

Eli had done the labor. He'd readied the property to be what it once was when the Murphy name was synonymous with horses. He just hadn't yet readied himself. And now *she* was here. Midnight.

"You want to meet her before I get her set up in her stall?" Boone added. "Maybe that will help."

Midnight whinnied again, pressing her dark nose against a slat in the red trailer. Eli couldn't see much else, and right now he didn't want to. Still, his hand flinched as if it wanted to reach for the mare with a long-buried instinct he didn't realize still existed.

He'd seen Boone on Cirrus, watched his brother on the skittish white stallion as they circled the arena and even jumped a few barrels.

"When's the last time Cirrus tossed you?" he asked, skirting the subject.

Boone groaned. "We're doing all right, Eli." He rolled the shoulder he dislocated all those months before. "See? Good as new, thanks to a certain vet I know who put me back together."

Eli opened his mouth to respond, but Boone shook his head.

"I'm not hiding anything from you, okay? We hit a few bumps in the road every now and then, but Cirrus trusts me, and I need you to trust *both* of us to keep each other safe. Come on." He motioned toward the back of the trailer. "Come say hello. She's been dying to meet you."

Eli cleared his throat and shook his head. "Delaney just called. Something about Nolan and an earache. She's stuck at the pediatrician, so I'm heading out to pick her sister up at the airport. Least I can do for my new office manager, right?"

Boone shrugged and redirected, heading back to the driver's side of the truck. "She'll be here when you get back." Then he hopped back behind the wheel, pulling the door closed through the opened window. "This is going to be good for you, big bro. I can just feel it. New mare, new person to run the office... Who'd have thought you'd go from loner to *two* new women in your life, huh?" Boone laughed. He didn't wait for Eli to respond and simply drove off the rest of the way toward the barn.

Eli clenched and unclenched his fists, then rolled his head from side to side. He wasn't averse to change, but that didn't mean he had to welcome it with open arms.

He'd rehab the mare and get her placed with a good family or on a proper farm. And Delaney's sister would be an employee. There were no *women* in Eli's life, just *people*, and that was fine by him.

He'd already married—and lost—the love of his life. Now he simply focused on the routine day-to-day of living. Living was enough. It had to be, because despite what anyone else thought, he didn't deserve any more than the safe, comfortable cocoon he'd built over the past three years.

Safe. Comfortable. Predictable.

That was all he had left to protect now.

Chapter 2

"SMILE, MISS," THE PLANE'S CAPTAIN SAID AS SHE stepped onto the Jetway. "You're in the biggest little city in the world."

Beth Spence bristled inside yet obliged. After all, the man did just defy physics for the past ninety minutes and got her there in one piece. She adjusted the tote bag on her shoulder and limped through the passageway and into the Reno-Tahoe International Airport terminal. On the outskirts of the waiting area, a tall, spindly airport attendant stood behind an empty wheelchair.

"Will you be heading to baggage claim, Ms. Spence?" the young, dark-haired man asked.

Beth slowed to a stop, which didn't take much effort considering her lack of speed to begin with, and glanced down at the walking cast on her left leg, then up at the attendant. Before he had a chance to make his own comment about her expression, she flashed him her winningest showgirl smile and waved him off.

"Thank you," she told him, "but I won't be needing any assistance."

"But, Ms. Spence," he pleaded. "The airline

received several calls from a Delaney Callahan insisting—no, *warning*—that if we didn't take you to baggage claim, she would have whoever was responsible drawn and quartered. She even named the four horses who would be up to the task." His Adam's apple bobbed as he swallowed. "If it's all the same to you, I'd prefer to keep my limbs attached to my torso."

Beth laughed. Only Delaney could bring a genuine smile out of her after the month she'd had, and the woman wasn't even here yet. "Consider you and your limbs safe, my friend. My big sis is way more bark than she is bite." She winked at him and then spun on her good heel, continuing on her way.

Her left ankle throbbed, and her throat grew tight. On any other Tuesday, she'd have been thrilled to make the trip from Vegas to Meadow Valley to visit Delaney, Sam, and her adorable niece, Nolan. But this was a pity party disguised as a visit.

"I'm sending you a ticket," Delaney had told her when she called the week before. "All expenses paid, open-ended, stay as long as you like."

"All expenses paid?" Beth had asked dryly. "Like, all forty bucks? Or do I get to check a bag too?"

"Baggage is free," Delaney responded, playing along. Beth could hear the artificial perkiness in her sister's tone. "Up to two checked bags."

"I'm busy," Beth lied, though what was the point? Delaney knew exactly what Beth had been doing since being released from the hospital and what she'd be doing for at least another four to six weeks. Absolutely nothing, unless you counted wallowing. She'd be doing *so* much wallowing. Just because her sister had gotten her out of Vegas didn't mean she'd gotten Beth out of her funk.

"Sam and I will pick you up in Reno and bring you back to Meadow Valley. Ticket's already purchased and in your inbox, so I won't take no for an answer...unless you want to cough up that forty bucks."

So here Beth was, on the day she should have been stepping out of a taxi and into Times Square, finally transitioning from Vegas showgirl to Radio City Rockette. She should have been dancing her way through the company's summer preparatory programs before beginning rehearsals for the Christmas Spectacular in early autumn. Instead, she was headed for Middle of Nowhere, California, on an open-ended ticket, final destination unknown, but it was certainly not the city that never sleeps.

The pain in her ankle increased with each step, a constant reminder that the girl who had been a dancer since the age of four now couldn't make it a few steps without wincing or swearing under her breath. She should have let the guy do what he was asked and take her where she needed to go. But pride was funny like that. It knew what was best for you yet chose the opposite. *If you let yourself believe you can't even walk to baggage claim, the next thing you know, you'll start believing the doctors that your dancing days are over.* That was what the voice in her head told her. Still, Delaney would take one look at her and know she was in pain, and that poor guy who was just doing his job *would* actually get drawn and quartered.

"Sorry, airline guy," Beth mumbled under her breath. "You deserved better."

When she finally made it to the baggage carousel, her rolling suitcase had already been pulled from the belt and placed in a clump of other unclaimed luggage. Had it really taken her that long to get there?

She sighed, lifted and extended the arm of her case, and began rolling it toward the exit.

She expected to find her sister standing inside the doorway, arms waving as she yelled, "Bethy!" Instead, she slowed her approach as she noticed a tall, dark, and clueless…*cowboy?*…looking right, left, and just past her as he held up a piece of white paper with *Beth Spence* scrawled on it in black marker.

"Who are you?" she asked when she was only a few feet away from him. "And please tell me you've got something parked outside that doesn't have four legs and hooves."

He startled, his head dipping so his bright blue eyes met hers.

"Shit," he said softly. "Where'd you come from?"

"Well, that's a hell of a greeting," she answered, letting go of the suitcase handle and crossing her arms as she appraised him. "But I asked *you* first."

He looked at the sign in his hand and then at her. He pulled a phone from the pocket of his jeans and swiped at the screen. Now he was glancing from his phone to her and back to his phone again.

"I guess this is you, right? Beth?" He showed her the photo on his phone, a selfie she and Delaney took years ago at a New Year's Eve party. "You look different," he added.

Beth's pulse quickened. "You mean younger?" The words came out more defensive than she'd intended.

He raised his brows. "No, it's just… You're smiling in the photo, so I wasn't sure if—"

"Ooooh," she interrupted. "So this is the part where you tell me I'm prettier when I smile or that I should be happy to be in the littlest big city…or the biggest littlest city…what the heck did the guy say?"

The stranger held his hands up in surrender, his phone with the picture of her in one and the sign with her name still in the other.

"The biggest little city in the world? And you can smile or not smile. Makes no difference to me. I'm just making sure I have the right person before I take you back home. I don't need your sister having me drawn and quartered for accidentally leaving you stranded at the airport."

Beth sighed. Whoever this guy was, Delaney definitely sent him.

"Sorry," she told him. "I didn't mean to bite your head off. It's just been a day." Or a week...or month.

He crumpled the sign and tossed it into a nearby trash can, slid the phone back in his pocket, and held out his hand.

"Eli Murphy, your ride back to Meadow Valley... in a *truck* with wheels. No legs or hooves."

Beth grabbed his hand, his rough palm warm against hers.

A muscle pulsed along the line of his jaw. A half smile played on his lips. Was she a hypocrite for thinking the guy would be really good-looking if *he* smiled?

Not if she didn't say it out loud.

"Wait, you're the veterinarian who helps Delaney with her rescue shelter?"

Eli nodded.

"So...not a rancher, then?" She nodded up at his hat. Then, because she couldn't help herself, she let her eyes roam down the length of his long, lean, yet decidedly firm build to where a pair of dusty, square-toed cowboy boots poked out from the worn hem of his jeans.

He gave her a single shake of his head. "Not anymore," he replied coolly.

Also not much of a talker, she guessed. What would help make this whole situation less excruciating would be if he wasn't much to look at either. But regardless of the pain she felt with every step and the foul mood that set in every time she realized she was on her way to Meadow Valley instead of Manhattan, Beth's vision was still intact.

She was going to give her sister hell for not only forcing this trip on her and then *not* being the one to pick her up but also for giving her zero warning about the tall, dark, and brooding *not-a-rancher-anymore* vet she sent in her place.

"Beth Spence," she finally added, not able to take another second of silence. "Congratulations on being the second person my sister threatened on my behalf today and on escaping the consequences. I don't know if I can say the same for the guy with the wheelchair at the gate."

Eli winced. "Turned him down, did you?"

"Cold." She dipped her gaze to their still clasped hands and cleared her throat.

Eli loosened his grip.

"If you've got something to prove to yourself or your sister, I'm happy to let you hoof it back to Meadow Valley. You'll probably make it in a day or two, pending traffic and wildlife."

Beth stifled a grin. Brooding with a side of biting wit, huh? "Thanks. I'll take the ride if you promise that's the end of your comedy show."

Eli barked out a laugh, and dammit if she wasn't right about what he looked like when he smiled.

He grabbed the handle of her suitcase and tugged it toward the door.

"Well then, Ms. Spence, your double-parked chariot without hooves awaits."

Beth pulled her phone from her tote and found a message she hadn't seen before she'd disembarked from the plane.

Delaney: Nolan spiked a fever. It's nothing. Just an ear infection, but had to run her to the pediatrician and then pick up antibiotics. Sending my friend Eli to grab you. Warning, he's painfully good-looking and easily spooked, so be nice. 😬 😬

Beth groaned.

"Touché, big sis," she mumbled, then followed Eli through the automatic doors.

———————

"Sorry in advance if Bethy talks your ear off," Delaney had said when she'd called him that morning. So color Eli Murphy relieved when the woman conked out for the entire ninety-minute ride.

"I'm not good at small talk," he'd told Delaney.

"It doesn't have to be small talk. Just steer the

conversation toward something you know, something that makes you feel more comfortable. Beth can talk about anything."

His comfort zone was animals, so if the small talk had veered into personal territory, he'd decided to grab whatever fun animal fact popped into his brain first. Thankfully, he'd had no need to worry because by the time he pulled onto the Murphy property, his passenger was still snoring away.

He put the truck in park and relaxed his shoulders, not realizing they'd been hunched in anticipation the whole ride.

He reached for her arm to nudge her awake, but her sleeveless denim top made him hesitate.

Seriously, Eli? Tess's voice played in his head, and he could see her dark brown eyes rolling as she spoke. *I'm not going to be jealous if you wake a stranger. Hell, I'm not going to be anything, babe, because I'm still dead.*

He knew that. Of course he knew that. It had been three years already. But despite it stating the obvious, her voice was still there. He could still conjure it, remember it, and that was all that mattered, preserving her memory the best he could.

He shook his head and scrubbed a hand across his jaw, then cleared his throat.

Beth didn't stir.

He watched her chest rise and fall, wondering how she could possibly be comfortable with the window as a pillow.

She hummed softly with her next exhale, the sound breathy and sweet—and strangely intimate. He'd met her less than two hours before, and now he knew the noises she made when she slept.

He dipped his head toward the long, tanned legs beneath her army-green shorts, then to the air cast on her left.

She let out a soft snore, and he laughed. She made the sound again, but this time it was punctuated with something that sounded like a whimper.

His head shot up, and he noticed her eyes—her lashes—were damp.

Eli cleared his throat again. "Beth?" he said softly. When she still didn't respond, he spoke louder and finally gave her shoulder a quick shake. "*Beth!*"

She gasped, knocked her head on the glass, then sat bolt upright.

"Shit!" she hissed, rubbing her temple. Then she turned to him, her green eyes wide with tiny gold flecks gleaming in the glint of the sun. "Did I doze off?" she asked with a laugh.

He was probably supposed to say something, but he couldn't look away from her eyes.

"Hellooooo? Eli?" Beth waved a hand in front of his face.

"Huh? Sorry. I was just—"

"Staring?" she interrupted. "Don't worry. They're used to it." She gave her shoulders and chest a little shimmy. "You don't spend your early twenties as a Vegas showgirl without a little ogling."

"What?" he asked, incredulous. "Jesus. *No*. I was *not* staring."

She raised her brows and crossed her arms.

What the hell? This was worse than small talk. This was...

"The female ferret will die if she doesn't mate once she goes into heat!" he blurted.

Good *god*. Could the floor in the truck just open up and let him plunge into the fiery depths of hell? *Please?*

"Oh my god!" Beth stared at *him* now, horrified.

But then she doubled over, laughing. *Squealing* with unbridled giggles. Eli thought he might have even heard a snort.

"Oh my *god*!" she said again, out of breath, shoulders still shaking as she straightened in her seat. "I don't know what to ask first, if that's even true or why it's the first thing that comes to mind when you get flustered." She swiped at the corners of her eyes where tears fell freely, but these were, without a doubt, tears of joy.

Eli couldn't help it. Her laughter was infectious, the momentary joy contagious. Was he mortified beyond recognition? Abso-freaking-lutely. Was he laughing anyway? Yes. Yes, he was.

When they'd both caught their breath and the laughter finally died down, he had to ask.

"So…what are the odds of you keeping my random ferret fact just between the two of us?"

Beth squeezed his forearm and smiled sweetly. "Zero to none, Dr. Murphy. Zero. To. None."

Chapter 3

BETH STARED AT ELI FROM THE PASSENGER SEAT as he stood outside her opened door.

"I…don't understand what's happening here," she told him.

Eli's brows pulled together under the shadow of his cowboy hat. "Hopping down and *out* of the truck is a bit more perilous than climbing in." He nodded at her cast. "Thought you might need a hand."

She shook her head. "I mean, thanks for the chivalry and all, but why would I be getting out of the truck *here*?" She glanced at what looked like a modest ranch home behind him, a combination of light blue siding and a reddish-brown brick. If it wasn't for the sign above the door that read MURPHY VETERINARY CLINIC plain as day, she would have thought it was someone's home. One thing was certain, though. This was *not* Sam and Delaney's home.

Eli still looked perplexed, the crease between his brows seeming to take up permanent residence. "Because this is where the clinic is?" He shoved his hands in the front pockets of his jeans. "And the guesthouse?"

Beth's stomach sank. She didn't know what was happening, but she somehow knew it wasn't good. She picked her tote bag up off the floor in front of her and held it to her chest as if it could protect her from the outcome of this scenario.

Eli's expression morphed from confusion to what looked like realization as his eyes opened wide and he huffed out a laugh.

"She didn't *tell* you. Unbelievable." He mumbled the last word as if it was only meant for himself.

Meanwhile, Beth's palms were starting to sweat, and that sinking thing that her stomach was doing turned into a sort of cartwheel or flip-flop. Maybe with a somersault or two.

"Eli, *where* did my sister tell you to take me?" She squeezed the quilted cotton of her bag, sure that it would leave handprints when she let go.

Eli crossed his arms and raised his brows.

"She told me to give you an hour to get settled into the guesthouse before getting you started at the clinic."

The clinic?

The *clinic*?

Beth didn't remember deciding to do it. She just slid out of her seat and onto the truck's running board, teetering on her right sneaker before hopping onto the dusty drive. She pitched forward, and Eli made a move to catch her, but she held up a firm index finger, keeping him at bay. She righted herself and thanked the universe for letting her keep her pride intact. Then she marched toward him, slowly and with her uneven gait, thanks to the extra height of the cast.

"Do you mean to tell me"—she pointed at him, the tip of her finger grazing his forearm still resting against his chest—"that my sister invited me to stay with her and then pawned me off on you as an unwilling tenant and, what? Animal whisperer? Because I'm not the Spence sister who got that gene."

He dropped his arms, but she was frozen where she stood, finger still pointed in accusation as she ran her conversation with Delaney back and forth in her head.

I'm sending you a ticket.

Beth had joked about the price. Delaney had joked about the luggage.

Oh god.

Delaney *never* said "You'll be staying with us," but why would Beth ever assume otherwise?

"Exactly," she finally said aloud.

"Are you still talking to me?" Eli asked.

Beth startled and stumbled backward. Eli caught her this time with an arm wrapped firmly around her back. She sucked in a breath as she felt the tips of his fingers press against her shirt, though the skin beneath prickled...or tingled. She couldn't exactly tell. All she knew was that her pulse was racing and her head was swimming.

"I'm okay," she finally told him, shifting her weight to her good leg.

"Are you sure?" he asked.

If she'd busted a stiletto dancing in a Vegas club only to be caught by some smarmy tourist, the question would have been laced with innuendo, the expression on the man's face anything from lewd smile to Zoolander-level smolder. She'd seen enough of both. But Eli stared at her with a clenched jaw and hooded eyes that transformed his light blue irises to the darkest of ocean depths.

"Yes," she whispered, her voice nowhere to be found.

"Okay," he responded, his voice rough as he gently let her go.

She brushed her palms down her shirt, smoothing wrinkles that had set in during the drive only for them to reappear once she lowered her hands.

"I'm not a damsel in distress," she muttered, sounding less convincing than she'd hoped. "I can still do all the things I did before *this*." She stuck her booted leg out, the heel kicking up dust in the slight breeze.

"An Achilles tear is often career-ending for a dancer," the surgeon had said. "I've seen it in several other patients. You'll walk just fine, and dancing for exercise or recreation? Sure. You can still do that. But the stress you'd put on the tendon—not to mention other muscles and joints that would try to compensate for the injury—if you tried to go back to dancing full-time would only exacerbate the situation. If you rupture it again—"

"You're wrong," Beth had interrupted. "I mean, you *could* be wrong. Not every patient is the same. You don't know *me* or what *I* can do."

"I didn't say you couldn't," Eli responded, bringing her back to the present. He nodded toward her cast. "But you *are* injured. And when you're hurt, you don't have to bear it in silence or prove you're still you. Just—I don't know—be hurt and accept a helping hand if you need it. There's no shame in that."

She squared her shoulders and stood up straight. "Yeah, well, my *sister*—the one who's supposed to have my back no matter what—obviously doesn't believe I'm still me, or she wouldn't have manipulated me into a trip I didn't want to go on, a guesthouse I have no intention of staying in, and a job I'm certainly not going to take. So I'm sorry if you drove me all the way here for nothing, but I'll just call a cab or a rideshare or something and head back to the airport."

Beth pivoted back toward the truck, dumped her tote on the floor, and attempted to climb back into the cab to fish her suitcase out of the small back seat, but it was too cumbersome to lift it on her own. Not that she was about to admit that to Eli. No, she'd rather stay where she was, on her stomach halfway between the front and back of the cab, legs flailing out of the opened door as she continued to struggle…until her phone rang.

She reached into her tote, rummaging through its contents until she found the device.

She scowled when she saw her sister's name on the screen.

"You tricked me," Beth answered with no other greeting.

"Nolan is okay. Thanks for asking. Her fever came down, and Sam finally got her down for a nap," Delaney responded, fighting one guilt trip with another.

"That's not fair," Beth countered. "For all I know, you made all that stuff up about Nolan being sick as part of your grand plan to—to what? Get me to move to Middle of Nowhere, California, and answer phones for the rest of my life?"

Delaney laughed. *Laughed.* "My grand plan? No. I guess my daughter spiking a fever was just a happy accident. Jeez, Bethy, will you just hear me out?"

What was Beth going to do? She was planking half inside and half outside a truck that wasn't hers with her belongings stuck in the back seat and no clue whether there were any flights heading back to Vegas before the end of the day.

She groaned. "Fine. It's not like I have anything better to do at the moment."

Delaney sighed. "I'm sorry about what happened

at the audition, Bethy. And I know the last month has sucked."

"Understatement of the year," Beth mumbled.

"I know," Delaney said again, and Beth could hear the sincerity in her sister's voice, which made it really hard to stay mad at her…until she remembered the whole manipulation scheme.

"You still tricked me," Beth reminded her.

"You're right." Delaney didn't even attempt to deny it. "But the doctor transitioned you to the walking cast a week ago, and you still hadn't left the apartment."

Beth's mouth fell open, but before she could respond, her sister continued.

"Mom and Dad were worried, so I said I'd get you out of the house for a bit."

Beth dropped her forehead against the leather seat, banging it softly a few times before propping herself back up on her elbows.

"A bit? You set me up in a guesthouse and got me a *job*. Even if you're on the doctor's side and believe my career is over, you're supposed to lie to me and tell me it's not. You're supposed to make me believe that this isn't the end of the road for me so that—I don't know—maybe I'll believe it too. But, Lanes? You're not supposed to sign me up to answer the phone at a vet clinic." Beth's throat grew tight, and her eyes burned.

"Oh, Bethy." Delaney paused. "I believe in you to

the moon and back. Always. But I can't make you believe in yourself. That's all *you*. What I *can* do is give you a change of scenery and a change of pace while you heal, and I mean more than just the foot in the cast."

Beth didn't respond. She didn't know what to say that wouldn't either cause a rift between her and her sister or turn herself into a snotty, blubbering mess. In another month, she'd be out of the cast. And six months down the road, she'd likely have full use of her leg and ankle again. But that couldn't be *it*.

"Look, if you hate the Murphy guesthouse, you are more than welcome to stay here. I just figured you'd appreciate sleeping through the night, but if you want to get up with Nolan at two and sometimes four in the morning, I won't turn you down."

Beth let out something between a whimper and laugh. "She's still not sleeping?"

"Sam and I are crossing our fingers that by the time she turns two, we'll be fully functioning humans again."

"And the job?" she added.

Delaney sighed. "Anything is better than staying holed up in your apartment grieving alone. Stay a month until the cast comes off. Stay until you're done with physical therapy. I'll help you find a great PT, one who specializes in dance injuries. And then, I don't know, back to New York to try again if that's what you want. I'm on your team, Bethy. I promise. But until you're able to live the exact life you want, I thought maybe just *living*—like…having a reason to get out of bed in the morning—might be enough. Plus there's *me*." Beth's sister let out a nervous laugh. "I just want what's best for you, Bethy, but you never would have come to Meadow Valley if I'd laid this all out ahead of time, am I right?"

Beth groaned. "Of course you're right." She let out a long, slow breath. "I can come hang by you and Sam any time I want?"

"Any time you want."

"And this job… It's a *paying* job?"

Delaney snorted. "Of course it is. And Eli? He's a really good guy, you know. Everything he does for the shelter is pro bono. A guy like that's gotta be a pretty decent boss."

"I guess," Beth mumbled.

"Why don't you get settled, let Eli show you around the property, and I'll pop by after dinner."

Dinner. Beth hadn't even had lunch yet.

Her stomach growled in protest.

"Okay," she relented.

"Okay?" Delaney echoed, and Beth could hear the smile in her sister's voice. "You're staying?"

"For now," Beth told her. But the first thing she was doing once she was settled in tomorrow was finding a physical therapist who would do whatever it took to get Beth one more shot at Radio City.

"I'm so happy!" Delaney blew her a kiss through the phone. "I'll see you later tonight. Bye, Bethy."

"Bye, Lanes."

Beth ended the call.

She craned her neck to glance over her shoulder. Eli was still standing where she'd left him, head down as he tapped something out onto his own phone. This was her cue to make her awkward and ungraceful exit from the truck...again.

She slid slowly on her stomach until her right toe touched the ground. She lowered her cast once she found purchase.

When she spun to face Eli, her stomach growled again. For *food*, of course. She needed food.

He held his hat at his side now, tilting his head up so his gaze met hers. "Last flight from Reno to Vegas leaves in fifteen minutes. I hate to break it to you, but you're stuck here at least for the night. I can take you to Delaney's, though, since I know you have no intention of staying here."

Beth had snapped at the man who'd been nothing but helpful since he met her at baggage claim, and now she approached him with her tail between her legs.

"I'm...*sorry*, Eli. This is all between me and my sister. No, it's actually between me and *me*, but we don't need to get into that. I shouldn't have taken the smile comment out on you earlier, and I shouldn't have taken Delaney's little trick out on you either.

I'm actually a pretty pleasant person when I'm not in the middle of a deep emotional crisis, but we don't need to go there right now either. Where I would like to go, if it's okay with you, is the guest-house. Where I'll be staying. Then I'd love to know where I can grab something to eat. And after that, if you'll still have me—*temporarily*—I'd like to see the clinic and hear more about how I can help out while I'm here."

Eli's lips parted, and she was ready for him to tell her that he'd actually had enough of the younger Spence sister and would like nothing more than to pawn her off on Delaney, Sam, and Beth's rarely sleeping niece. Instead, the corners of his mouth turned up, and his eyes crinkled at the corners.

Again her stomach responded, *loudly*, confusing a smile with something it wanted to devour.

"Are you smiling at this turn of events?" she asked, suddenly famished.

"Are you begging for your job back?"

Beth scoffed.

Eli raised an eyebrow.

"Ugh. Fine. *Yes,* I'm *asking* if I can still have the job for, like, a month. Maybe two. Tops."

He crossed his arms and pursed his lips as if mulling the idea over. Finally, he held out his right hand. "Okay, but if you're good at it, I may have a hard time letting you go." His eyes widened. "From the job, I mean."

Beth laughed. "You've got yourself a deal, Dr. Murphy. And trust me, I'm not a big fan of animals and they're not a fan of me. You'll be counting the days until I'm out of your hair."

They shook hands.

Beth's belly waged a war of cartwheels and somersaults the moment his large hand enveloped hers.

"Food!" she blurted, light-headed now. "I. Need. *Food.*"

Chapter 4

ELI WASN'T SURE WHAT MADE HIM MORE UNEASY: the fact that Beth was only going to be temporary help at the clinic or that she'd signed on to stay at all. He might have gotten her from point A to point B like Delaney had asked him to do, but in the grand scheme of what should have been a random spring Tuesday, he'd taken every wrong turn possible when it came to Beth Spence.

He lifted the griddle from the burner, gave it a little shake, and flipped the pancake from one side to the other.

"Well, color me impressed, Dr. Murphy. I've never seen anyone do that in real life."

Eli's head shot up to find the woman in question standing on the opposite side of the L-shaped counter.

Her blond hair lay damp and wavy on her shoulders, the gray cotton of her T-shirt growing dark where the water had soaked through. The left leg of her white joggers was pulled up, resting on top of her cast, while the elastic of her right leg gathered at her ankle.

"Sorry," she added when he didn't speak. "Didn't

mean to sneak up on you like that, but you looked like you were concentrating on what you were doing. I didn't want to interrupt."

Eli was staring, but in his defense, it had been— how long was it?—years since he'd seen a woman in his home fresh from a shower. Okay, so technically this was the guesthouse on the property and not his actual home, but close enough.

"If that's my pancake, Doc, I think it's burning."

"Shit," he hissed, eyes darting back to the griddle. He turned off the burner and slid the giant pancake onto the plate waiting on the counter. "It's a little crispy at the edges, but otherwise it's still in good shape." He lifted the plate and handed it to her. "There's a glass of water, some silverware, and syrup on the table behind you."

Beth grinned and closed her eyes, breathing in the steam rising from the plate. "Oh my god," she said, eyes fluttering open. "It smells like fresh baked banana bread."

The corner of Eli's mouth twitched. "That right there is my world-famous, big-as-your-head, banana bread pancake." And the only thing he knew how to cook, not that he was about to admit that.

Beth set the plate back on the counter, tore off a piece of the pancake, and popped it into her mouth.

"Oh. My. Gaw!" she exclaimed, mouth still partially open to account for the heat of what was still an extremely hot hotcake. She finished chewing and swallowing. "Why would I ruin this with syrup?" She tore off another piece and greedily shoved it into her mouth.

Eli crossed his arms and raised his brows, now staring unapologetically at the woman enjoying his cooking. How could he not when she was smiling from ear to ear with every bite?

"You're welcome to sit down if you want to. This is *your* place after all," he told her, keenly aware of his own grin and realizing that maybe their strange introduction included a couple of right turns after all.

She laughed, then covered her full mouth with her hand as she finished her most recent bite. She glanced from the small but—in Eli's opinion— adequate kitchen to the plush cream sofa overrun with throw pillows to the bedroom door that now hung open on the wall kitty-corner to his right.

"It's not big," he added, attempting to answer the questions in her head. "But it's clean. The fridge is stocked. And it's rent-free."

She turned back to face him. "You're kidding, right? You think I find this place *lacking*? I live in a studio apartment attached to my parents' Vegas motel. And I use the term *apartment* loosely. This place is at least twice the size *and* has both a tub and shower? Dr. Murphy, this is the lap of luxury, and you are quite the decorator."

Eli's smile faltered, but he did his best to paint it back on.

"I can't take credit for the decorating," he admitted. "That was all Tess. But I did install the tub, so I guess I had a little something to do with how the place turned out."

Beth swallowed, but she hadn't been eating anything at that moment. "Tess..." she began. "She was your wife?"

Was your wife. So she already knew.

He blew out a breath. "I guess Delaney told you." He didn't mind when Tess came up. But he tried to avoid having to tell the story again and again. It would be easier if he could just hand every new person he met a sort of press briefing or memo that got the hard part out of the way.

She nodded. "She mentioned it a while back when the shelter was just getting up and running. Horseback riding accident, right? I'm sorry. I wasn't thinking with the decorating comment. I'm sure this is the last thing you intended to talk to me about."

He stepped out of the kitchen area and strode toward the sofa and the chaise longue portion that was covered end to end with pillows. He pivoted to face her, perching on the arm of the chaise.

"The accident? No. I don't really talk about that. But Tess? She designed this place. It was meant for family. Anyone who wanted to visit would always have a place to stay. Her parents had just sold their place and retired to this great little condo village on Lake Tahoe, so it was perfect. But when I lost her..." He let the words hang in the air a moment, waiting to see if they tried to strangle him or buoy him forward. He inhaled, something in Beth's gaze telling him that whichever way this turned, it was okay. "She was an only child. We didn't have any kids." He shrugged. "The place has been kind of empty for a while."

Eli had two brothers, and once upon a time he thought he and Tess would follow in his parents' footsteps—three little horseback-riding rug rats running around the property, the guesthouse always filled with guests. Now it was just *him*. He'd gotten used to the solitude, to not having to worry about anyone other than his patients and himself and occasionally his younger brothers, especially when they sprung new horses on him without warning.

Eli stared at the mess of pillows and shook his head. Then he picked one up and held it to his chest, wearing it like armor. He waited for the tilt of the head or the *Poor Eli* frown. But Beth hopped up onto the counter, one bare foot dangling next to her cast.

"You *hate* those pillows," she said, brows raised.

The laugh rose from his gut and escaped his lips before he registered what happened.

"How did you know?" he asked, incredulous.

Beth nodded toward the pillow he was holding.

"You all but sneered at that poor stuffed piece of fabric. What did it ever do to you other than offer comfort and, no doubt, sincere design aesthetic?"

Eli laughed again. "I didn't sneer. I *don't* sneer."

She narrowed her eyes at him. "Fine. It wasn't a sneer, but it was this look of, like…what's the word I'm looking for?"

Resignation, he thought, just as Beth added, "Oh! *Resignation.* Like, 'You know what, pillow? We're both here, so we might as well make the best of it.'" She gave him a self-satisfied grin.

Well, shit. You might be even more intuitive than Lucy.

"Who's Lucy?" Beth asked.

Eli's eyes grew wide. "I said that out loud?"

She nodded. "Are you okay?"

Yes. *No.* What was happening? He felt fine, only…*off.* Like something in the air had shifted. Maybe a cold front was on its way in and the change in barometric pressure was messing with his head. Or maybe it had just been so long since he'd held a conversation that lasted more than ninety seconds that he'd forgotten the difference between inner monologue and actual spoken words.

"You were talking about someone named Lucy?" she prodded again.

"You mean this nosy girl?"

Eli stood, glancing over Beth's shoulder to where the screen door slammed back against the frame, and a slightly older version of Beth entered...following the matriarch of the Murphy property, Lucy.

Delaney scrambled after the hen, her blond ponytail swishing wildly behind her as she struggled to catch what she must have thought would be a calm little hen.

"Ouch!" Beth yelped before she had a chance to greet her sister. She jerked her bare foot up to the counter and gasped when she saw a speck of blood on her ankle. "That, that, that, that *happy meal waiting to happen* just *bit* me!" She rubbed her ankle, lips pursed in a pout.

Delaney picked the bird up and held it under her arm like a football. "Don't you listen to her, Luce," she cooed. "Bethy's not quite at one with ranch life just yet." She kissed her sister on the cheek and then rolled her eyes as Beth tended to her wound.

Okay, so maybe it was more than a *speck* of blood if Eli could see it from several feet away.

"How'd she get out of the coop?" Eli asked, only mild accusation in his tone as he rounded the counter and headed for the sink. He grabbed the first aid kit from the cabinet above. "Also, it's *not* a ranch," he reminded his friend.

"Why do you automatically blame *me*?" Delaney teased. Looked like she picked up on the accusation. "And you have a barn that houses not one but *two* horses, Eli. If it *looks* like a horse ranch and *acts* like a horse ranch..."

Eli pivoted and exited the kitchen area, pausing briefly to give Delaney's elbow a nudge with his own.

"I also have a chicken coop with all the chickens locked safely inside when I left this morning and when I returned after doing *you* a favor. If it *looks* like you had something to do with the escape and Lucy *acts* like she's trying to evade the person responsible..." He raised his brows, and Delaney responded with an exasperated eye roll.

"Um, hello?" Beth interrupted. "Anyone remember the one who almost got pecked to death?"

Eli cleared his throat, and Delaney sighed.

"I saw her through the fence, and she looked lonely," Delaney admitted. "Thought she and Bethy would have this amazing meet-cute, and Beth would fall in love with her and not be sad about her injury anymore and want to stay in Meadow Valley forever." Delaney turned toward her sister and batted her lashes as she offered Beth a nervous smile.

Beth lifted her hand from her ankle to reveal a small but more significant cut than Eli had thought.

Delaney winced, and Eli slipped between the two women, setting the small plastic box on the counter next to Beth. "Can I see it?" he asked, nodding toward the palm that covered the wound again.

Lucy squawked at Beth.

Beth glared at the hen. He half expected the woman to squawk back.

Eli glanced at Delaney over his shoulder. "I don't think your plan is working. Would you mind tossing her back in the coop? Promise you can try again tomorrow."

"Tomorrow?" Beth cried. "I don't think so."

Delaney sighed. "She's not usually like this, Bethy. I swear. Only when she..."

Eli's shoulders tensed as Delaney trailed off.

"I mean, I'll be right back," she sputtered. "Don't go anywhere."

Beth rolled her eyes. "Where am I going?" she mumbled. "I'm just getting back on my feet in this stupid cast, and now there's a chicken trying to hobble me for good."

"Lucy's harmless," Eli told her as he pulled a chair from the table and sat down in front of her.

"Wait..." she started.

He glanced up at her.

"*That* was Lucy? You were comparing me to a violent chicken?" She raised her brows and set her jaw.

Eli bit back a smile. He noticed himself doing that a lot today, which oddly made the hair prickle on the back of his neck.

"Can you hand me that?" He nodded toward the first aid kit, and she gave it to him with her free hand. "And she's not violent," he continued as he opened the small box and retrieved an antiseptic wipe. "But some folks around here believe she's psychic."

Beth snorted, then covered her mouth with both hands, which was when Eli swooped in. He lowered her foot to his lap, and she hissed in a breath between clenched teeth as he cleaned the small wound.

"Sorry," he told her. "But that's the worst of it." Then he blew softly on the affected area before covering it with a small bandage. "Good as new," he added, then met her eyes as he closed up the kit and set it on the ground.

She was staring at him, mouth open, still like the air before a storm creeping in.

"Are you...*breathing*?" he asked.

She pressed a hand to her chest, and he watched the shallow rise and fall as she did, in fact, circulate air through her lungs.

She nodded.

"Did I hurt you?" he asked.

She shook her head. "But why did you... I mean, how did you know..."

"I'm baa*ack*," Delaney singsonged as she bounded through the door again. She shook out her floral sundress and pulled the elastic from her ponytail, refashioning her hair into a bun atop her head. "When is this heat supposed to let up? I moved to the north for *snow*."

Eli laughed. "Northern California is hardly *the north*, but it's more temperate than Vegas. That's for sure. And you'll get your snow. We always do. But spring is spring, and summer is summer, and you'll have to find a way to survive both before we get our first frost."

Even he could feel the room grow warmer every time Delaney opened and closed the front door. Or was it just that he wasn't used to being this close to another human, to skin-on-skin contact even if it was only a matter of first aid.

Delaney turned to her sister. "I see Dr. Murphy made sure you weren't mortally wounded." She nodded toward the foot that still rested in Eli's lap.

Beth jerked it away almost as fast as Eli tossed it toward the floor and sprang from the chair.

Delaney held up her hands. "Whoa. Not like I caught you two making out under the bleachers. The doctor's allowed to take care of the patient."

Eli cleared his throat and took the first aid kit with him back to the kitchen.

"Did you tell him to blow on it, Bethy, like Mom always did when you were little?"

Eli froze in front of the sink, arm stretched upward and his hand on the cabinet pull.

"Ever since a particularly bad knee scrape when we were kids—if I remember correctly—Bethy's been terrified of injuries that involve any sort of bloodshed, but our mom had the magic touch."

He heard Delaney sigh, and he forced himself to turn around.

Beth hopped off the counter, wobbling on her left foot before steadying herself.

"I'm a big girl now, Lanes," she remarked coolly. "I'm certainly not afraid of a little scratch. Thanks to the pandemic, I made it through surgery and a night in the hospital all by myself." She brushed off her T-shirt even though there was nothing on it. "I'm going to finish drying my hair so Eli can show me around the clinic." She backed toward the bedroom. "Pick me up later for dinner?"

Delaney nodded, and Beth disappeared into the bedroom, closing the door behind her.

Eli tossed the kit back into its cabinet and turned back to Delaney. "She went through the surgery alone?"

Delaney nodded, pivoting to face him.

"And she's a dancer?" He'd been trying to piece it all together without asking. He knew enough from experience not to ask someone about their trauma when it was still so new. If they wanted to talk about it, they would.

Delaney nodded again.

Behind the closed bedroom door, he heard the muffled sound of a hair dryer as Beth turned it on.

Delaney glanced over her shoulder and then moved closer. "This is it, Eli," she whispered even though there was no way Beth could hear them over the sound of the dryer. "The doctor told her that because of her age and the severity of the tear, this is a career-ending injury."

"Age?" Eli asked. If he had to guess, which he *never* would out loud, she couldn't be more than twenty-five.

"Her thirtieth birthday is next month. You know how there's dog years and stuff like that for animals with shorter life spans than humans?"

He nodded.

"Well, the same goes for dancers and the hell they put their bodies through. She was *this* close when…" Delaney held her thumb and index finger an inch apart, but then she trailed off.

Eli crossed his arms. "So Beth was right. You *don't* believe she can come back from this."

Delaney's eyes widened. "*You're* a doctor. Are you telling me I shouldn't trust the medical professional?"

The hairs on the back of his neck stood up again. He *was* a doctor, and he had no idea why he was tossing logic out the window when he was sure Beth's surgeon knew what the hell they were talking about. But Eli tossed it nonetheless.

"Trust the doctor, sure. But it's also okay to trust your sister. I'm not saying I believe in mind-set over science *or* the psychic abilities of chickens…" He raised his brows and glanced toward the front door and the direction of the coop. "But there's something to be said for a patient's attitude and how it contributes to their healing. I've seen horses with leg breaks I thought I could heal who just seemed to give up after the injury, leaving euthanasia as the only option." He scrubbed a hand across his jaw and squeezed his eyes shut, forcing images of Fury out of his head. "All I'm saying is that no matter what the future holds for your sister, don't let her give up on herself. She's got a shit ton of fight in her still, and that's coming from someone who's known her for a matter of hours."

Delaney raised her brows.

Eli slid past her, suddenly needing a change of location.

"I need to check on the new horse Boone brought over this morning. Can you tell your sister to meet me inside the clinic in twenty minutes?"

He was already backing toward the front door.

Delaney crinkled up her nose. "Was someone cooking with bananas? I swear I used to love them before I got pregnant with Nolan. Can't stand them now."

Neither could Tess.

He spun on his heel and called over his shoulder, ignoring her question, "Twenty minutes, okay?"

"Okay," Delaney called back. "Also, I don't care if you don't believe in psychic abilities! You know Lucy is always right, and I think maybe the reason she went vampire on Beth was..."

But he was already out the door, hightailing it to the barn, before he heard the rest.

Chickens weren't psychic.

The pillow thing and the blowing on the wound thing... God, *why* had he done that? It was all coincidence.

You like her! Tess's voice teased in his head as if she was thrilled with the news.

Not that there was news. He'd just met the woman. He knew nothing about her other than she was dealing with a huge setback, and the last place she wanted to be was Meadow Valley, yet here she was.

Also, Beth didn't hate bananas. Still, that was *coincidence*. Most people didn't hate bananas.

Eli made it to the barn, heart hammering in his chest as he passed Cirrus's stall and made his way to the one at the other end.

Midnight whinnied and took a step toward her stall door as soon as he approached, but when she attempted to put weight on her injured leg, she limped back, almost cowering against the wall.

Eli's eyes locked on hers, and his stomach lurched. He had to brace himself against the door. Even for a logical man like himself, this was too much coincidence for one day.

With every hammering beat of his heart, he felt the pounding of hooves beneath the saddle, felt every muscle in his body working in tandem as he rose and fell in rhythm with her gallop. The stagnant summer air vanished, and instead the wind threatened to whip his cattleman from his head. Eli let go of the reins with one hand just in time to catch his hat as he whooped and hollered with an indescribable joy.

Not real, a voice inside his head whispered.

He squeezed his eyes shut, the sudden vertigo making down feel like up and up like down. He'd never experienced anything like it, and he was beginning to think that maybe, if there was some sort of universal higher power, it had chosen today to fuck with Eli Murphy.

When the room seemed to stop spinning, he finally looked up again and straight into the mare's dark and frightened eyes, the familiar pattern of a white star on her black coat splitting the distance between them.

"Fury?" he muttered, his voice hoarse. Then he fell to his knees, emptying the contents of his stomach onto the dusty and gritty floor.

Chapter 5

BETH COULD SEE THE CLINIC FROM THE FRONT door of the guesthouse, so she waited a full twenty minutes and then some before heading over. She didn't want to seem eager by showing up early. This visit was simply a means to an end, a way to appease her sister and—fine—not stay holed up in a tiny apartment wallowing. She was talented enough in the art that she could wallow anywhere.

She found the entry door ajar, but the lights to the reception area were off as she stepped inside.

"Hello?" Beth called warily. In horror movies, this was the part where she got impaled by a pitchfork or some other farming tool. Or maybe because she was in a veterinary clinic, it would be something more like a scalpel. And the audience would of course roll their eyes because who would be clueless enough to enter a building that had its door ajar and no lights on in a place she'd never been, looking for a man she barely knew?

Apparently, Beth Spence was clueless enough, because instead of running back the way she came—or in her case limping—she continued exploring.

"Eli? Delaney told me twenty minutes. I waited twenty-five." She let out a nervous laugh. "Performers like to make an entrance, right?" She ran her hand along the high wooden counter, behind which someone would sit to greet clients and their furry friends.

Oh god. Barring any unfortunate scalpel-related incidents resulting in her even more unfortunate murder, *Beth* would be the person behind that counter. *Ugh.* She wouldn't have to hold any of those furry friends, right?

She continued with her hesitant exploration.

"If you're, like, into pranks and stuff like that…" she called into what felt like an abyss, "I should warn you that I do *not* react kindly to surprises. See, my sister and I have this thing where we don't wish each other happy birthday until it's the actual time of our birth. I was born at 11:58 p.m., and there was this one night that I had a performance, and Delaney wanted to be the first to wish me happy birthday after the show and thought spraying me with confetti the second I walked into an elevator would be a good idea. My first reaction was to spray her right back. With pepper spray. Spoiler alert… It didn't end well for either of us."

Beth's eyes, nose, and throat burned every time she thought of the incident. Even now, she had to fight the urge to cough.

She crept farther into the space, grateful for the natural light pouring in through the windows, especially since there wasn't a light switch to be found. But as she neared the short hallway of exam rooms, the windows disappeared, as did most of the light.

"You know what? On the off chance that you *are* going to impale me with a pitchfork or a scalpel, I think I'll head back to the guesthouse." She put her weight on her right heel, ready to pivot and move as quickly as possible back the way she came, when she finally received a response.

"In here." Eli's voice sounded from a few feet deeper down the hall, hoarse and weary.

Oh no. Maybe she was the hero of the horror film rather than the victim?

"Eli, are *you* impaled by a pitchfork?" she called as she followed the sound and hoped the odds of this scenario *not* playing out like a slasher film were in her favor.

This earned her a laugh, though a bitter one if she was accurately reading his tone.

"No pitchfork. Promise. I just…needed a few minutes to myself."

Sunlight shone through the crack in what she thought would be his office door, but when Beth pushed it open, she found Eli sprawled on his back on an exam table definitely meant for a creature slightly smaller than a human, one knee raised and his arm bent beneath his head.

"Oh my god! Are you hurt?" she asked, her hand finally finding a light switch on the wall.

"Please don't." He waved her off with his free hand. "My head is pounding. The light will only make it worse. I just need a few more minutes of dark and quiet and…and then I can show you around."

Okay, what happened to the extremely capable and upright pancake-chef-slash-wound-tender who left the guesthouse barely thirty minutes before? The man was not going to be up for an office tour after only a few more minutes of dark and quiet.

"Were you, like, partying hard for the last twenty minutes and you forgot to invite me?"

This earned her another laugh. "Not even close," he told her.

"But…" she continued, "I might be going out on a limb here. Were you sick? You know, the kind of sick where you—"

"*Yes*," he interrupted through gritted teeth. "I just upchucked on the floor of the barn. Is that what you want to hear?" He groaned. "I'm sorry. This is not exactly my finest moment."

Beth sighed. "Okaaay… Well, did something happen to bring the headache on?" Because he was fine less than a half hour ago.

She moved to a sink where she found a paper towel dispenser mounted to the wall and an opened tube of toothpaste next to a visibly wet toothbrush on the counter.

"No," he replied coolly.

You lie, Dr. Murphy.

Something made him toss his cookies, and whatever that something was, he wasn't about to share it with her.

"You need water," Beth told him, wetting paper towels under the faucet.

"How do you know that?" he challenged.

She sighed, her back still toward him. "You're a doctor, Eli." She turned off the faucet. A beat of silence filled the room.

"Right," he finally said. "Dehydration."

Well, he was far from an oversharer, but at least he confirmed she was on the right track as far as helping him get back on his feet.

"Do you have a cup or something in here?"

She spun to face him.

He hadn't moved, and his eyes were closed, so she laid one of the two damp towels over his eyelids and the bridge of his nose.

He flinched slightly, but then his whole body relaxed, and he let out a long breath.

She slid her hand beneath his head. The hair at the nape of his neck was damp with sweat. "And another one right here..." She tilted his head forward and then slid the second towel across his neck, patting it in place so that it stuck to his skin.

His breaths evened out, and the muscles in his face softened.

"How'd you know to do that?" he asked, his voice less strained.

Beth smiled to herself, satisfied with her handiwork. "I'm a Vegas showgirl, Dr. Murphy. Sometimes a girl likes to let off a little steam after work." She laughed softly at her own lie. "And sometimes she lets off a little too *much* steam." Beth glanced back at the sink to see if she missed a glass next to the toothbrush and toothpaste, but the counter was otherwise bare. "Now about that drinkware so I can properly tend to my patient?"

Eli huffed out a laugh. "You might find a stainless-steel pet bowl in the cabinet. Many of my canine patients' veterinary anxieties are soothed with a fresh bowl of water."

"And these bowls are clean?" she asked.

The water was already running again when she heard him shift on the table.

"I am not drinking out of a—"

She shut the faucet and spun to face him, bowl in hand and what she hoped was a *don't eff with me* look in her eye. It must have worked, because he stopped short of finishing his protest.

"It's a clean bowl. You need water. I have water right here. You've already lost your argument, haven't you?"

He opened his mouth, then let his teeth sink into his bottom lip.

Beth's throat went dry, and she had the sudden urge to drain the bowl of water herself.

Eli Murphy was handsome. Some might even say hot. But ever since she stepped—or nearly *fell*—out of his truck, she'd forced her initial reaction to him into a nice little inaccessible corner of her mind. *Why?*

Because you were too busy hating being here and somehow blaming him for it.

She growled at the voice in her head.

"What was that?" Eli asked.

Beth cleared her throat. "Nothing. Just... Bottoms up, Doc!" She offered him the bowl, both hands extended.

"Are you always this bossy with your employers?" Eli asked with a lopsided grin.

Okay, now Beth was feeling her own version of hot. Like, the kind of hot that also came with *bothered*.

Cool off. Cool off. Cool off, stupid neglected libido. The man was in crisis, and all she could think was how good he looked—well—crisis-*ing*.

Eli reached for the bowl, and his fingertips overlapped with hers as they made the exchange. They stayed that way—the bowl in both of their palms—for several seconds longer than necessary.

His eyes locked on hers, and he held her there, staring, waiting.

One second was all it took for this sort of handoff.

Maybe less. But this moment felt like it didn't want to end. Right. The *moment* didn't want to end. Because if Beth was the one extending this…this… fingers-touching-fingers thing…

"Um…" Eli said. "Are you gonna let me have it?"

Beth yanked her hands away, then watched in what felt like slow motion as water sloshed over the lip of the bowl and onto Eli's jeans. Yep. She let him have it all right.

"Oh my god!" she cried. "I'm so sorry!"

Eli glanced down at the wet spot blooming on his thigh, and on instinct, Beth began patting and rubbing the area with her bare palm.

"It's not that bad," she continued. "I mean, it wasn't the whole bowl, right?" She continued to pat and rub, pat and rub, as the dark area of denim spread farther and her palm crept up his thigh.

Oh. My. God.

Her hand stilled, and with her heart and dignity in her throat, she tilted her head up, her eyes finally meeting his.

Bright blue irises darkened to something unreadable.

Anger?

Confusion?

Desire?

No. That third one was all Beth, and she had zero right to desire her new boss, let alone rub her palm up his freaking thigh!

Eli held the bowl high above both of their heads. He lowered it slowly, bringing it to his lips and downing what was left in one messy gulp.

"You should go," he said, his voice strained again. Water trickled from the corner of his mouth. He glanced down to where her hand still rested on his inner thigh.

Oh. My. God. Again!

She snatched her hand back. Heat pulsed through her palm, and she pressed it to her chest, willing this strange feeling away.

"Eli," she began, but she didn't recognize her own voice, breathless and full of *something*.

Ugh. What is wrong with me?

"We'll do the tour tomorrow," Eli continued when she couldn't think of what to say next. "The clinic opens at 9:00. Be here at 7:00. I'll show you the reservation system on the computer, and we'll take it from there."

They weren't touching anymore, but barely any space was between them. Still, without really knowing this man at all, Beth was certain he'd somehow drifted a million miles away.

"Eli," she uttered again. "I'm so sorry. I didn't mean to…"

He dropped the bowl beside him and pressed his hands to her shoulders, gently moving her out of the way. Then he slid off the exam table that was way too small for his tall, lean, muscled frame and stood. He met her gaze but also seemed to look past her. *Through* her.

"It's fine," he told her absently.

"I'll see you in the morning?" Beth forced a laugh. "I still have the job?" Though why she cared, when a couple of hours ago she was ready to head right back to Vegas, she wasn't exactly sure.

Eli nodded. "Yeah. Of course. I...uh...I just need to go see a man about a horse."

Beth snort-laughed, but Eli didn't even blink. "Oh. You're *serious*," she added.

Another nod. And then he strode out of the room and into the dark hallway.

She waited a few minutes until she was sure he had left the building.

"Good talk!" Beth called to the empty clinic. Well, it wasn't a horror flick massacre, yet Beth still somehow felt like she'd been gutted. Also, since she'd effectively been blown off, what was she supposed to do now?

She shrugged, then grabbed the stainless steel bowl from the exam table, washed it, and set it back in the cabinet.

"Gonna see a man about a horse, huh?" she mumbled to herself. Well, if she was going to work in a place full of animals, maybe it was time to get to know one or two of them.

Beth made her way back out of the clinic and was accosted by a chorus of squawking. Violent chickens would not be her starting point, so she made a beeline for the only other place she was sure to find an animal when the clinic was closed.

The barn.

————————

"Are you shittin' me?" Eli asked, incredulous.

Boone cupped his hands over the ears of the smiling baby girl he wore strapped to his chest facing her potty-mouthed uncle.

"*Language,* Eli," the younger Murphy brother responded with a wry grin. "My daughter's first word is going to be *Daddy,* not *shittin' me!*" He whispered the last two words. "Isn't that right, my little Kare Bear? Daddy. *Dad-dy.*"

The tiny blond beauty cooed at her father's voice and bounced up and down in her little carrier.

Eli couldn't hold back his grin as he held out his index finger for his niece to grab. She giggled and bounced even more when he tickled her chubby bare foot.

"I thought her name was *Kah*-ra. Like a short 'ah' sound," Eli challenged. "And she looks nothing like you, you know."

Shit. Eli was being an asshole, and he knew it. But he needed somewhere to direct this energy. He needed someone who could take it without batting an eye. And that someone was Boone.

His brother shrugged. "She can still be my

Kare Bear if I want her to." He opened the apartment door wide and silently welcomed his brother inside. "And thank god she got all her looks from her mama. Means I'm living with the two most beautiful girls in the world."

Eli wanted to be happy for his brother, and in theory, he was. But right now he couldn't get past the horse, the water, and the feeling of Beth's hand on his goddamn thigh.

He combed a hand through his hair as he strode inside and began pacing as best he could amid the baby toys littering the floor.

"I still don't get why you and Casey wouldn't take the guesthouse."

Boone closed the door and then half walked, half bounced his way into the main living space.

"*You* built that place," Boone reminded him. "There's room on the property for Casey and me to design our own home when we're ready. But right now, with Casey's salon downstairs and me taking some time off to do this..."

Boone held out both of his index fingers in his daughter's line of sight, and she grabbed each in time for her daddy to dance them around the blue-and-white-checked area rug that lay between the couch and the oversize chair.

Eli crossed his arms. "Time off from fixing cars, sure, but not from the Fury doppelgänger you dropped in my barn." It wasn't a question.

Boone and Kara's dancing stopped, but Eli's brother continued to absently sway side to side as he spoke.

"Come on, Eli. Black horses are a dime a dozen."

Eli shook his head and crossed his arms over his chest. "Not Friesians with a white star between their eyes. You could have said something."

Boone sighed and finally stopped swaying. "You didn't want to meet her when I was there. Figured when you were ready, I'd tell you more about her. Thought you'd be busy enough with your guest today that it could wait till morning. Sorry if seeing her was harder than I anticipated. That's on me."

It sure as hell was on him. Except maybe his brother had things on his mind other than when would be the best time to tell Eli that the new horse they were rehabbing looked exactly like the horse he couldn't save three years ago.

Kara fussed, and Boone began swaying again. The fussing stopped.

"Shit, you're good at this, aren't you?" Eli gave his brother a single nod of approval.

"I know, right?" Boone responded, smiling proudly.

Eli collapsed onto the large overstuffed chair, then flinched as he raised his ass and pulled a pair of knitting needles connected by a few short rows of yarn from beneath him.

"I thought you babyproofed the place," Eli

grumbled, holding the death traps out for his brother.

Boone laughed. "Babyproofed, sure. Guess I forgot to *brother* proof, though. You want to give it a try? It's pretty goddamn soothing, and you look like you need to be soothed."

Eli opened his mouth to respond, but his phone chirped in his pocket with a sound he didn't recognize.

"What the hell is this?" he asked, pulling the phone out and furrowing his brow at the notification on the screen.

Boone and Kara sidled up next to him, and his brother glanced at the screen over his shoulder.

"Shit," Boone whispered, then covered Kara's ears. "That's the stall alarm we hooked up when we refinished the barn. Someone opened Midnight's door."

Chapter 6

ELI LIVED BARELY TWO MILES OUTSIDE TOWN, but the drive from Boone's place to the Murphy property felt interminable.

A frightened horse in unfamiliar territory was one thing. A frightened horse on the *loose* where he'd all but abandoned Beth to her own devices was something else entirely.

An all too familiar scene played out in his head—a late-night storm, Fury's gate opened by folks who'd hoped to steal her, and Tess chasing after her beloved mare in the middle of it all.

"Shit, shit, shit, shit, *shit*," he hissed as he put the pedal to the metal. He didn't even turn the truck off when he skidded to a stop just outside the barn, just threw it in park and ran.

He saw her feet first—a sneaker and an air cast—jutting out from the opened stall door. He didn't have time to process, only to keep running until he hit a wall or he was trampled by a spooked mare.

The wall came first, and he was barely able to stop before barreling into it. And then there she was. No. There *they* were. Midnight lay resting on the ground while Beth reclined on a blanket she must have found in the tack room, her head propped on Midnight's side.

"What's up, Doc?" Beth asked with a soft laugh.

She had the nerve to laugh when he was likely having a heart attack?

Somewhere in his head, Eli knew it was panic and not a vital organ, but he was far beyond searching the recesses of his brain for the logical answer. He doubled over and pressed his hands to his knees, only now realizing he needed air. *Lots* of air. He gulped as much oxygen as his lungs could handle until he no longer felt like he might black out.

When he finally lifted his head, the two females hadn't so much as moved. Beth even had the nerve to look groggy, as if she'd just woken up from a nap.

"Were you *sleeping*?" he asked, incredulous.

Beth blinked and stretched her arms.

Midnight blew out a breath through her nose, but other than that, the mare barely stirred.

Eli's head, though, swam.

"I might have been starting to doze, but I'm up now." She yawned. "Are you feeling better? Did you see that man about a horse? And what's with the sprinting? I thought those boots were made for walkin'. Or better yet, ridin'." She grinned.

Eli flew to the barn in a full-blown panic, and Beth *yawned*. She yawned and casually asked about his day and had the audacity to *tease* him as if she napped on strange horses in strange barns on a stranger's property all the damned time.

"I don't understand." He rose to his full height and scratched the back of his head. "You're not an animal person, which—now that I'm saying that out loud—makes me wonder why the hell I hired you to work at a veterinary clinic. But that's beside the point. What the hell are you doing in Midnight's stall? *Dozing?*"

Beth bolted upright, eyes wide. "*Midnight!*" She spun to give the mare an affectionate pat on the nose. "So *that's* her name!"

Eli braced a palm against the wall. "How did you know she was a *she*? And that she wouldn't bite you? And…and…you're the only one in here? No one else opened her stall?" He started pacing. Again.

Beth climbed awkwardly to her feet, and he stepped into the stall to reach out a hand, albeit seconds too late.

Too late. What if he'd found a different scene at the barn? What if Midnight had been more like Cirrus when the stallion had first arrived—skittish and prone to kicking up his hind legs in defense? Hadn't Boone described her as such? Yet here she was, reclining in her new stall, letting Beth recline on *her*.

"Did I do something wrong?" Beth asked, interrupting his thoughts. "Also, how did you even know I was here?"

Her blond hair was dry now, and it hung in loose waves against her shoulders. He suddenly remembered her hand on his thigh, and his pulse raced with an unfamiliar longing for the second time that day.

Eli swallowed. "The stall doors have sensors."

"You mean like an alarm?" she asked, moving close to the door to inspect it.

Instinct made him take a step back as he nodded.

She pressed the pad of her thumb over the almost imperceptible device affixed to the top corner of the door.

Eli imagined that thumb doing the same thing to his leg.

Jesus, what was wrong with him? She was Delaney's sister. And his employee. His *reckless* employee.

"What, do people steal horses right off the ranch?" Beth continued with a disbelieving laugh.

He nodded again. "During a goddamn storm under the cover of rain and thunder, not expecting a docile mare to lose her shit at a little bit of weather—or her defiant rider to chase after them."

Beth's head tilted up, and her wide green eyes met his. She asked nothing, but somehow she knew the rest of the story ended with him losing Fury... and Tess.

"Why not lock her door? Or the barn itself?" she asked.

Eli blew out a shaky breath. "In case of a barn fire. Animals have great instincts when it comes to escaping danger, but if they're locked in…"

Beth's hand flew over her opened mouth, and she gasped. "Oh my god. That's terrifying. So you have these animals on your property, and there's nothing you can do to keep them safe other than a silent alarm on their doors?"

Eli nodded. "I don't think such a thing as safe really exists. But we do the best we can."

But sometimes his best wasn't good enough, and that was the part Eli still couldn't get past.

"Is she hurt?" Beth asked. "Midnight? She seems to be favoring her left front leg."

Maybe Beth wasn't an animal person, but she was perceptive.

"Yeah. She broke her left radius," Eli told her. "Which is basically her elbow. She's recuperated from the surgery, but she's out of practice walking on it." He scratched the back of his head. "I'm also guessing she's a little scared to do it. I'm going to rehab her and find her a new home."

Sooner rather than later, he hoped. He wasn't sure how long he could look at Fury's twin before it erased all the progress he might have made in the past three years.

"Will she take a rider again?" Beth's brow furrowed with worry Eli hadn't expected.

"That's the plan," he explained. "She was bred as a

show horse, but her owners didn't have much use for her once she got injured. Best Boone or I can probably do is get her to a good home that cares more about her company than what she can actually do."

As if knowing she was the current topic of conversation, Midnight carefully rose from where she reclined. She nudged Beth's shoulder with her nose, and Beth laughed. Then, because the door was still open, the mare took another small step forward so she stood face-to-face with Eli.

He felt her warm breath on his cheek. He briefly squeezed his eyes shut before daring to glance at the white star between her eyes, the one that made her look so much like Fury.

He opened his eyes again, cautiously, waiting for his stomach to protest like it had earlier that day. But his body didn't react. Not to Midnight at least. But he found a warm hand suddenly clasped in his and realized he'd either grabbed Beth's hand without thinking or she'd grabbed his.

"I'm sorry, Eli," she said softly. "I hope I didn't overstep. You just looked like you needed it."

That was when it hit him. He hadn't raced to the barn because he was worried only about the horse. He'd blown out of Boone and Casey's apartment without so much as a goodbye because he'd also been worried about *her*. Beth. A woman he'd only met that day. But for too many reasons to count, his *worry* could not go any further than this.

He gently freed his hand from hers.

He should have thanked her. He should have asked her how the hell she could read him so well. Instead, he told her a partial truth.

"I guess you're more of an animal person than you knew. And you'll be just as good with their respective humans. That—I guess—is why I hired you." He clenched and unclenched the fist of the hand she'd been holding. "Sorry about that comment earlier about not understanding why I agreed to the whole working in the clinic situation. You're obviously a natural at this, and I'm obviously a dick."

The corner of her mouth twitched into a smile, but Eli swore he read a note of disappointment before it did. The same disappointment that he had already buried somewhere he hoped was deep enough not to find.

"Thank you," Beth replied. She held out her hand to shake but seemingly thought better of it and dropped it back to her side. "Though I have a request...something I'd like to add to my position at the clinic."

She wanted to do more work? After him being a bit of an ass about her qualifications, he certainly wasn't going to argue with that.

He shrugged. "Sure. Why not?"

Beth squared her shoulders and crossed her arms. "I want to learn to ride a horse...with Midnight."

"She still not talking to you?" Boone asked.

The two men stood at the threshold of the exam room hallway where it met the clinic waiting room.

Eli crossed his arms and nodded as he watched Beth smile at Trudy Davis and her ancient beagle, Frederick, as she checked them in.

"It's been a *week*," Eli told his brother. "She's all smiles for the clients. Maybe a little standoffish to the animals, but me? I'm just *the doctor*. 'The doctor will see you now,' or 'The doctor has your prescription ready,' or even her handing me the phone and saying, 'Of course, the doctor would *love* to talk to you about the new medications you think every veterinary clinic needs,' regardless of me standing right next to the front desk, violently shaking my head *no*."

Boone covered his mouth, but not before Eli heard him snort.

Beth's head shot up as she glanced in their direction, and Eli yanked his brother into an empty exam room, slamming the door behind them.

Boone raised his brows. "Big brother, what did you do?"

Eli shoved his hands into the pockets of his white coat. "You mean other than giving her free room and board plus a job she's wildly unqualified for?" Okay, the second part was a lie, and even

Boone could see that. From the second she stepped behind the desk, the clinic was running more efficiently than it had in years.

Boone mirrored his brother's stance, hands shoved into the front pockets of his jeans.

How different he and Boone were. But then Eli glanced down at the boots peeking out from the scrubs he wore beneath the coat, a shred of his former self that he still couldn't abandon, and he wondered if his brother could still see it too, the man Eli used to be.

"Eli, you are full of more shit than Cirrus's and Midnight's stalls plus the entire chicken coop combined. So tell me what the hell you did to incur the wrath of Delaney's sister, and then get your ass out to the barn and check up on our mare. You're late for our appointment."

Eli sighed and pinched the bridge of his nose. When he squeezed his eyes shut, he could still see the mixture of shock and anger and sadness in Beth's eyes.

"You're not riding *any* horse on this property," he'd told her that afternoon outside the mare's stall. "Least of all Midnight."

Her mouth fell open, but she regained her composure a second later.

"Did you just *forbid* me from riding this sweetheart of an animal?" She nodded her head in Midnight's direction. "And let me clarify that that is the first and probably *only* time I've ever said that about something that walks on four legs." Midnight nudged her shoulder softly. "See?" she added. "We're, like, connected or something. She *wants* me to be the one to rehab her. She needs a rider, right? Why shouldn't it be—"

"Dammit, Beth! It's *not* happening!" Eli snapped, and a split second later, he saw it: Midnight shifting her weight to her hind legs, her head rearing back.

In one swift motion, he wrapped an arm around Beth, swung her out of the way, and yanked the stall door shut with his boot. His whole body shook against the metal frame as Midnight struck it with what he hoped was her good hoof. The fact that she'd even struck metal was a blessing in and of itself considering the door was more of a gate. She could have punched right through Eli's back, and then what? Beth would have to deal with the aftermath?

Beth screamed, her head buried in his chest and her body shaking against his. But when she finally pulled away and set her eyes on him, her gaze threatened to burn him to ash.

She pointed at him, and her voice shook as she spoke. "*You* did that."

He could hear Midnight breathing heavily behind him, but she didn't strike again.

"She could have hurt you," he said evenly. *Or worse.*

"She could have hurt *you*!" Beth lobbed back at him.

On instinct, he reached over his shoulder, massaging the part that had taken the brunt of Midnight's kick.

Beth's expression softened. "She did, didn't she? You're hurt."

Eli rolled his shoulder. "I'm fine." At least physically he was. "I knew what I was doing. But you... You fully admit that you know nothing about animals, yet you crawl into a horse's stall like she's some giant stuffed prize you won at a carnival." He heard the volume of his voice rising again and took a beat to collect himself, for Midnight's sake and for Beth's. "You don't know what you're doing when it comes to creatures like her. I do. Midnight belongs to the Murphy ranch, and I'm a Murphy. So...*yes*. I forbid you to ride her or to enter her stall alone again. As an employee of the Murphy ranch and veterinary clinic, can I trust you to do as I'm asking?"

He hated himself for the way he spoke to her then and hated himself even more as he retold the story to his brother now.

Beth had responded by fisting her hands at her sides, then clearing her throat.

"Yes, Dr. Murphy," she told him with terrifying sweetness. "Whatever you say, Dr. Murphy." Then her gaze moved past him and to the mare still standing behind the stall door.

Beth's eyes grew glassy, and Eli swore under his breath.

"Did you say something?" she asked.

He opened his mouth to respond, to apologize for being the asshole he knew he was being. But instead, he merely replied, "No."

"Then I'll see you at the clinic tomorrow," she'd said flatly before giving Midnight one last pat on the nose and storming out of the barn.

Now, Eli leaned back against the exam room door and let his head fall against it.

Boone reacted to the story with a long whistle followed by an even longer silence.

"Say it," Eli told his brother. "Say whatever it is you're thinking. I might have been a dick, but I saved her life." He hoped rationalizing his behavior to his brother would do the job of rationalizing it to himself. But this was a question with a yes or no answer. *Yes*, Eli had been an ass. *No*, the situation didn't have to go down that way.

Boone shrugged. "Sure. Sure. Yeah. That's one way to look at it."

Eli sighed. "And the other way?" he asked.

"Or...you provoked the mare by threatening the only human she trusts right now."

His younger brother didn't say anything more, but Eli knew what came next.

You are the one who put Beth in harm's way, Eli. Just like you did with Tess.

What if Eli had gone after Fury instead of Tess? What if he'd called the sheriff's department instead of trying to catch the would-be thieves himself? What if Tess had mounted the mare *after* the clap of thunder that shook the earth? And the best one yet... What if he'd told Tess to wait inside the house in the first place?

He at least knew the answer to the last question. Tess would have torn him a new one and still done whatever she thought she could to save her horse. But what if he'd found a way to convince her to wait?

What if? What if? What if?

In his head, he'd replayed that night's sequence of events too many times to count, trying to come up with the scenario where Tess lived, where Fury didn't give up on her will to do the same, and where Eli didn't lose every goddamned thing he held dear.

"Hey..." Boone nudged his shoulder. "Did I lose you?"

"What? No. Sorry." Eli straightened and repositioned the stethoscope hanging around his neck. "Animals with trust issues are volatile," he told his brother. "Beth could have sneezed or hiccupped or...I don't know. She could have done any number of things to set the mare off before I showed up. Bottom line is there's no telling how a scared creature like that will react to *any* sort of new stimuli."

Boone took a step forward and clapped Eli on

the shoulder. "You said it, big brother. Not me. Just remember that humans are animals too." He opened the door, but before striding through it, he called back over his shoulder. "Meet me at Midnight's stall, but maybe consider apologizing to that highly efficient young woman out there before you do."

Apologize? For keeping her safe? Whether or not he provoked Midnight, the important thing was that she was too dangerous to ride, especially for a novice.

"Apologize," he mumbled with a derisive laugh as he spun toward the door to follow Boone out. "Ha."

Except…he'd yelled. At Beth. That wasn't him. Eli had never raised his voice to anyone like that, not even his brothers. But Eli Murphy hadn't been *Eli Murphy* in years. And it was starting to scare him that he might never find his way back.

His phone buzzed in his pocket before he made it all the way to the clinic's reception area. It was a calendar invite. From Boone.

Event: Ranchers who knit shit no one wants
When: Every Saturday, 7 a.m. Trudy's bookshop.
Message: You need this. Say no, and I'll drag your ass there anyway. It's up to you. Also, dress for riding. Trudy likes to take pictures for the website. Says it's good for tourism.

Eli sighed and shoved his phone back in his pocket, ignoring the invite and the brotherly threat. Instead he steeled himself, brushed nonexistent dust or lint or whatever from his coat and scrubs, and made a direct line for the check-in desk.

"Absolutely," Beth was saying into the phone. "We can fit your new cat in for those immunizations tomorrow morning. You're welcome. We'll see you then."

She hung up the phone and finished entering the appointment into the computer. Even though Eli could see she'd completed the reservation, she kept her eyes on the screen and dragged her index finger along the mouse's scroll wheel.

He cleared his throat, and after a brief hesitation, Beth finally looked up.

"What can I do for you, Dr. Murphy?" she asked, all cool professionalism, saccharine sweetness, and none of the warmth he heard her use daily with his clients.

He glanced over his shoulder. The waiting area was empty, which meant she must have already situated Trudy and Frederick in a room.

"You're still pissed at me," he began. Not a question but a statement.

She shrugged and tucked her blond waves behind her ears.

"I don't know what you're talking about, Dr. Murphy. I'm simply your employee who does what's asked of her, whether it's being directed to answer calls and take appointments or being forbidden from riding a horse that needs to learn how to carry a rider again."

And there it was.

Eli huffed out a bitter laugh. "So...*pissed*."

Beth folded her hands in her lap, and he couldn't help but notice how much greener her eyes looked when reflecting her green scrubs, like the forest beyond the Murphy property.

"Did you need something from me, Dr. Murphy? Have I double-booked any clients or failed to properly sanitize a room after an exam?"

He'd really messed up, hadn't he?

Eli rested a hand on top of the counter. "No, Beth. Shit. It's not like that. You're doing an amazing job here. It's me. I wanted to tell you that I'm sorr—"

The door to the exam room directly opposite the desk flew open, and Trudy Davis emerged, tears streaming down her cheeks, her beagle, Frederick, lying limp in her arms.

"Eli! Oh god. Help! I think something's really wrong with Frederick!"

Beth sprang up from her chair. "What do you need me to do?"

His tech, Ryan, was in the middle of a teeth cleaning with an anesthetized cat.

"I don't know," he admitted, already heading

toward his frantic client. "Just grab Frederick's chart, and meet me in the exam room stat!"

Today was only supposed to be a checkup. Maybe an ultrasound to see if the mass in Frederick's abdomen was still stable. But today wasn't goodbye for Trudy and her long-beloved companion.

Not if Eli had a say in the matter. And today, he sure as hell hoped he did.

Chapter 7

BETH HAD ONLY MET TRUDY DAVIS UPON CHECK-ing her in for her appointment, but now she held the woman's shaking hand as they waited for Eli to return after he'd whisked the unconscious yet—thankfully—still breathing dog away.

"He has cancer, you know," Trudy told her with a sniffle.

"Oh" was all Beth could think of to respond. She'd never lost anyone close to her and had never been the pet-loving type. Sure, she'd *temporarily* lost her career and had set aside a sizeable amount of time to wallow, but her injury was a setback, not something to grieve. Yet somehow a knot still formed in her throat, as if Trudy's impending grief was contagious.

A lock of salt-and-pepper hair loosed itself from the other woman's long braid, and Trudy reacted with a tearful laugh as she tucked it back in place.

"He always nips at my hair when this happens." She looked at Beth with watery eyes. "Lost most of his teeth, though, so he never did much damage."

Beth plucked a fresh tissue from the box resting on Trudy's lap and handed it to her. "You really love that little fur ball, huh?" she asked.

Trudy took the tissue, added it to the wad of already used ones in her hand, blew her nose, and nodded. "Humans are great…most of the time. But there's nothing like the connection you make with a pet."

"I'll take your word for it," Beth told her. She wasn't yet ready to admit that she'd snuck out to the barn every night in the past week to visit Midnight. She'd left the stall door closed, of course, so she wouldn't set off the alarm again. But she'd wait up until she saw the lights go out in Eli's residence attached to the clinic, then wait until she was pretty sure that he had gone to sleep. And then she'd meet the mare, who'd reach her nose over the top of the gatelike door to nuzzle Beth's chin. She couldn't explain it, her draw to this creature, let alone her desire to *ride* it. All Beth knew was her loneliness felt a little less—well—*lonely* when she visited her new equine friend.

"You've never had a pet?" Trudy asked.

Beth shook her head. "Not any animal I'd consider my own. I don't really connect with them. Delaney got that gene." Midnight was some weird fluke. They were probably just two lonely beings latching on to one another. As soon as Beth got to know Meadow Valley a bit better, she'd probably forget all about the mare.

"It's a wonderful thing to love an animal and have them love you back," Trudy continued. "But you enter into the contract knowing that—barring any sort of unfortunate accident—you'll likely outlive this creature that you've loved since the moment you met, and it will cause you immeasurable pain and heartbreak." She sniffled and blew her nose again.

Beth shook her head, incredulous. "Then why even do it? Why set yourself up for failure?" It didn't make sense. "If a relationship has an expiration date, what's the point of entering into the 'contract'?" She slipped her hand from Trudy's so she could air quote the last word.

Trudy let out a tearful laugh. "Because if I gave up the possibility of pain, I'd also be giving up the possibility of joy. Years of it, which is what I've had with Frederick."

The only thing that had ever brought Beth joy, *true* joy, was performing. No animal or person could make her feel what she felt when she was onstage. From the time she put on her first pair of tap shoes at four years old all the way through her Vegas debut and even to tearing her Achilles at what should have been her career-making audition...*all* of it was happiness like she never could have imagined.

Until it wasn't. The past five weeks had been the *un*happiest in Beth's life, yet she couldn't help but acknowledge how her evenings in the barn made the unhappy a little less *un*.

Beth narrowed her eyes, suddenly remembering something else Trudy mentioned.

"Did you really fall in love with Frederick the moment you saw him?"

Trudy raised her brows. "You don't believe me? Maybe you and animals don't connect, but has there never been anyone in your life you've simply looked at and thought, 'If you're as sweet as you are adorable, I'm going to fall in love with you before the night is through'?"

Beth laughed. She'd met plenty of men between her teens and now, and none of them had made her believe in love at first sight. Then again, relationships always came secondary to dancing, but still. If there was a man capable of sweeping her off her feet, wouldn't that have shown through regardless of how focused she was on her career?

Her pulse suddenly raced as her body recalled the feeling of Eli scooping her into his arms as he somehow anticipated Midnight's reaction before the mare even made a move. Even now, she could feel the place where the tips of his fingers met the bare skin where her shirt had ridden up.

You're furious with him, she reminded herself. And she was. But it didn't change the way her physiology responded to him then or to the memory of him now.

"No," Beth finally croaked, realizing she hadn't answered Trudy's question. "Can't say that I have."

The other woman dabbed at the corners of her damp eyes with her tissue and smiled. "Very convincing, Ms. Spence. Very convincing indeed."

Eli threw the door open before Beth could call the woman out on her unfounded teasing.

"He's stable, Trudy." He looked right past Beth. "I gave him some intravenous fluids and he let me do the ultrasound without a fuss. But the mass is obstructing the bowels, which explains the vomiting and dehydration. I think—I think you should let me operate."

Beth had been so focused on Trudy while Eli and Frederick were gone. Calm, accepting Trudy. But in Eli's blue eyes, she saw a storm brewing.

Trudy stood and strode the few steps to where Eli filled the space beneath the door's frame.

That was the only way Beth could describe Eli's entrance into the room. He filled the space. He took up presence. Hell, he *was* presence. And despite her anger, she couldn't deny that when Dr. Eli Murphy entered a room, she *felt* him there.

Trudy raised a palm to Eli's cheek and gave him a loving pat.

"We already discussed this," she began calmly, but her voice broke on the last word. "He's too old for surgery. You yourself said he might not survive it—"

"But..." Eli interrupted, yet when Trudy shook her head, he said no more.

Beth watched the helpless resignation set into his features, and her heart broke a little for a man she barely knew, a beagle she'd barely met, and a lovely woman who seemed too wise in the ways of love and loss for this to be her first experience with it.

"Can we do it here, or should we go to him?" Trudy asked.

Eli swallowed, and Trudy lowered her hand.

"He's resting comfortably, so why don't we go to him?"

Trudy nodded, and Eli held the door open for her.

Beth sat frozen, not sure what to do. She suddenly felt out of place, like she was about to be witness to something too intimate, an overstepping of boundaries she wasn't sure she was ready to cross.

"Are you coming?" Eli asked, answering her unspoken question.

"Oh." Beth bolted up from her chair. "Of course."

His blue eyes were now clouded over with gray, and Beth wondered if this happened every time Dr. Murphy had to let an animal go. Didn't both doctors and vets somehow detach from situations like this? If not, how could they possibly continue in such a profession?

Eli pulled the door shut after she exited the room. Then he took the lead and headed toward the imaging lab where Frederick waited.

Trudy grabbed Beth's hand and leaned in close.

"My Frederick was Eli's first patient," she whispered. "I've made my peace, but he's going to need a friend when all is said and done." The other woman nodded toward Eli, who had stilled with his hand on the door to the clinic's imaging room.

This wasn't just any loss for the doctor Beth had secretly marveled at all week. His *first* patient. She couldn't imagine the hurt he must feel, and she didn't know how she would be any help to him when, as Trudy said, all was said and done. But she could do one thing. She could let go of the resentment she'd been hanging on to all week.

So she did. And just like that, all Beth's anger rushed out of her in one epic wave of release.

They followed Eli into the imaging room where Frederick lay drowsily on a towel atop a stainless steel table, an IV tube taped to one of his legs.

Trudy ran to her dog and showered him with pets and kisses.

Eli strode to the other side of the table and began typing a combination onto the keypad of a small safe.

Beth grabbed his free hand, and Eli flinched, but his shoulders relaxed as he pivoted to face her.

"Whatever you need, Eli. I'm here."

The corner of his mouth twitched, as if he was trying to smile. But he didn't. Or more likely, couldn't.

"Thank you" was all he said before getting back to work preparing the medication.

Beth's throat tightened, and her heart ached. For the dog and its human, yes. But when she looked at the doctor—at the man who had to perform the deed himself—she felt awash in a grief she could not explain. All she knew was that this would be the last appointment for the Murphy Veterinary Clinic today.

Eli's phone lit up in his pocket. He glanced down at it, hands gloved as he readied the syringe.

"Can you grab that?" he asked, voice rough as he looked at Beth.

She nodded, then reached into the pocket to retrieve the phone.

"It's a text," she told him. "From Boone."

"Shit," he hissed. "Midnight's appointment."

Behind them, Trudy sang softly to Frederick: "In My Life" by the Beatles.

Beth's chest tightened.

"Unlock it." She tapped on the screen, then held it up to Eli's face without waiting for him to respond. "I'll tell him you need to reschedule."

Eli nodded. "Thank you." His voice was barely above a whisper.

Beth fired off a quick response to Boone, explaining the situation. He responded immediately.

"Should he come inside?" she asked, relaying the younger Murphy's request.

Eli shook his head. "Tell him to head back to his family. I'll call him later."

Beth sent the response, waited for Boone's acknowledgment, and then dropped the phone back into Eli's white coat pocket.

He sighed, set the syringe on a small silver tray, and spun to face Trudy and Frederick.

Eli cleared his throat. "Trudy..." he began, and the unspoken plea in his voice made Beth's throat burn.

Don't cry, she told herself. *These people do not need you blubbering all over their moment. You're a bystander. Possibly even an interloper. But you're here, so keep it together.*

Trudy straightened, her eyes meeting his. "Eli..." she countered. "Even if he survived the surgery, it would only be a temporary fix. The time it would take him to recover would be time enough for the tumor to start growing back. I can't put him through all that suffering just for him to suffer more." She reached a hand across the table and gave his upper arm a squeeze. "It's sooner than we'd hoped, I know..." She trailed off, and a tear ran down her cheek. Still, she pressed her lips into a smile. "Thank you for all you've done for him throughout the years. He is so lucky to have had you to care for him all this time. We both are."

All Eli seemed to be able to do was nod.

"Would you like to hold him?" he asked. "You can sit with him in the chair against the wall."

Wordlessly, Trudy scooped the beagle into her

arms, careful not to tug on the tube taped against his leg.

Frederick perked up long enough to give her a sloppy kiss on the chin.

Trudy laughed, and then Frederick nestled into her arms, his body relaxing as if ready for what was to come.

"It'll be quick," Eli told her. "He won't be in pain anymore." Despite the pain Beth knew *he* was in, Eli's tone was now laced with the comfort his client and patient needed.

He rounded the metal table and set the tray on the side opposite the woman and her canine companion. Then he gently lifted the syringe and knelt in front of the chair.

"Don't tell my other patients," Eli cooed softly to Frederick, "but you've always been my favorite." He scratched the pooch behind the ear, and Frederick simply blinked.

"He's ready," Trudy whispered. "So I guess that means I am too."

———

Beth saw Trudy safely to her car.

"Are you going to be okay?" she asked.

Trudy gave her a teary smile. "I got to love that crazy, toothless rascal for a decade of my life. I will miss him every day from here on out. But I meant what I said before. I wouldn't trade it for anything."

Beth felt a tear trickle out of the corner of her eye, and she quickly swiped it away. "I'm sorry," she explained. "I don't know what came over me. It doesn't make sense. I barely know you *or* Frederick, and I—"

Trudy grabbed her hand and made her stop short. "Sweetie, you don't have to apologize for crying for my Frederick...or *for me* for that matter. This town is one big family, and like it or not, you're a part of it while you're here. Though you might be careful with your claim of not connecting with animals, because I think my little guy got to you." She nodded toward the clinic. "He's taking it harder than it looks. Losing patients is part of the deal for him, but this one might be the exception—other than Fury."

The other woman didn't wait for Beth to ask questions but instead climbed into her vehicle and slowly pulled away.

Beth spun slowly back toward the clinic's front walkway, a sinking feeling in her stomach. How did she comfort someone from such a loss when she didn't understand the first thing about how Eli felt? When she didn't really know him at all? If Delaney was sad, a marathon of nineties Keanu Reeves movies always did the trick. She knew her sister. Knew how to be there for her, to love her. But how did she do that for someone she'd barely spoken to all week?

Ryan, the clinic's tech, had finished with his feline teeth cleaning in time to collect Frederick and prep him for pickup by the crematorium, so she found Eli in his office, white coat on the back of his chair as he sat in only his scrubs, typing away at his laptop, a pen clenched between his teeth.

She knocked softly on the open door. "Hey there. Just wanted to check in. I canceled the rest of the day's appointments and thought I would pop by to see how you were doing."

Pop by? Ugh. Beth was the awkwardest awkward to ever awkward.

Eli's head shot up, his blue eyes alarmingly bright. He grabbed the pen and set it on a stack of papers on the desk.

"Thanks for your help." Eli grinned. "I think Trudy really likes you. I just need to finish up this paperwork for the crematorium, and then I'm going to call it a day, so if you want to clock out and go see your sister or something, feel free." He raised his brows. "I'll still pay you for the day, of course."

Beth took a couple of steps into the room, her brow furrowed. "What is this?" she asked, waggling her index finger at him.

He furrowed his brow right back. "Um... paperwork?"

"No…" She paused, trying to choose her words carefully and also wondering why she wasn't simply clocking out and escaping the situation altogether. "I mean this." She pointed at him again. "The Mr. Chipper, I-didn't-just-say-goodbye-to-my-first-ever-patient thing. I saw you in there, Eli. I know you're not okay. Trudy knows you're not okay."

His smile remained, but a muscle twitched in his jaw.

Eli leaned back in his chair and crossed his arms. "You haven't spoken to me in a week, and now you think you have me all figured out, huh?"

His words stung, but she held her ground. "That's not you talking," she told him. "It's your grief, so I'm not going to play your game." Her pulse quickened. Because she *was* playing just by engaging. Why? He'd already given her an out. Why wasn't she running while she had the chance?

He straightened, his smile faltering now. "I think I remember saying you're dismissed for the day, Ms. Spence."

She shook her head and instead took a few steps closer.

"What are you doing?" He sprang up from his chair.

Beth countered by rounding the desk so she was right in front of him.

"Delaney's working at the shelter today. Nolan's with her grandma. And since I'm not allowed near

Midnight without you as a chaperone, I have no one else to hang with and nowhere else to be." She shrugged. "So I'm not leaving you alone. You can dismiss me and *Ms. Spence* me all you want, but I'm not falling for it, *Dr. Murphy*."

Eli tried to back up, but his chair was already against the wall.

"Why are you doing this?" he asked, and she could hear his resolve begin to crumble.

A single tear leaked from the far corner of his eye, and on instinct she reached for him, her palm landing on his cheek and her thumb wiping it away.

"I don't know," she admitted.

She waited for him to jerk away, but instead he exhaled a shaky breath.

"Don't go," he whispered, and he suddenly looked so much younger than his thirty-six years.

"I won't," she whispered back, her thumb now tracing a soft line across his cheek. She kept telling herself that Trudy's belief in love at first sight only applied to animals. But then, for no reason she could explain, she stood up on her toes—walking cast and all—and pressed her lips to his.

Chapter 8

Eli froze. What the hell was he thinking?

Don't go?

He'd all but asked her to do what she just did, but what the actual—

"Oh my god!" Beth blurted, interrupting his train of thought. She took a quick step back, fingertips pressed against her own lips. "I'm sorry! That was so not professional. I don't know what got into me."

For the few seconds her lips touched his, his brain closed the door on everything else.

Fury and Midnight.

Trudy and Frederick.

Tess.

I'm not supposed to forget about her, though, he thought.

But the second Beth pulled away, thought and anything related to it vanished.

Eli *wanted*. And he hadn't felt that kind of want for longer than he could remember.

"I should go," Beth continued when he still hadn't uttered a word. "I just remembered a thing I have to do. Maybe see a man about a horse?" She released a nervous laugh. "Anyway, I'll just…you know…" She took another step back and stumbled as her foot caught on the leg of the desk.

Eli grabbed her hand, then kept her from falling by wrapping his arm around her back.

She stared at him, eyes wide, her chest rising and falling with trembling breaths.

"Don't. *Go*." His voice came out rough, the words caught somewhere between a plea and a command.

"Are you asking that as my boss or my landlord?" she whispered, her eyes locked on his.

Eli's jaw tightened, and he dropped her hand. But because she wasn't entirely standing upright, he couldn't exactly let go without letting her fall. "Shit, Beth, I didn't mean…"

Her lips parted into a smile before he could finish, and he blew out a relieved breath.

"You're messing with me."

Beth shrugged.

His panic receded.

"I don't even want this job *or* to be living in this middle of nowhere town," she told him. "So I'm hardly worried about the consequences of a kiss." But her breathing hadn't yet returned to normal. She cared about the job, even if she wouldn't admit it.

Eli straightened, bringing her with him so that now her chest was pressed to his.

"You're good at it." His thumb slipped beneath her shirt, skimming the soft skin above her pants.

She sucked in a sharp breath, and his pulse raced at her reaction.

"I know," she said, grinning. "Doesn't mean I like it."

The corner of his mouth twitched. What was it with this woman, making him want to smile when he could so easily let the darkness win?

"You like it a *little*," he teased. "You wouldn't be that good if you didn't."

"I'm a good dancer." She shrugged. "Maybe that means I'm a good actor too."

Maybe she was. And maybe this was all an act as well. It didn't change his reaction to her, his unfaltering need to see this moment through, however it played out.

"And I've liked knowing you're in the guesthouse this week," he admitted. "Even though you've been pissed at me the whole time."

"Aww, Dr. Murphy. If I didn't know any better, I'd say you missed me even though I've been right beside you almost every day since I got here."

Eli had perfected his poker face over the years after losing Tess. He'd learned so well how to hide in plain sight. Yet one week had given Beth the ability countless others lacked. She saw right through it.

Or maybe he wanted her to see.

She pressed a palm to his chest, and Eli's heart hammered against it.

"I'm not mad anymore."

He heard no teasing in her tone.

"Yes," he admitted, his voice rough. "I...missed..."

He couldn't put it into words. It didn't make sense. How could he miss someone he barely knew?

Eli gently lifted her onto the side of his desk. He didn't have the words. But he could show her.

Her mouth fell open in what looked like delight. She raised her brows. "*Dr. Murphy...*" And the teasing was back.

He liked the teasing. He liked her. And Eli Murphy hadn't *liked* in years.

She grabbed the knotted drawstring of his scrubs and tugged him closer.

"I was surprised...*before*," he admitted, referring to the kiss. "But it doesn't mean I didn't like it."

Beth nodded, and her fingers fidgeted with the still tied string.

"Are you surprised now?" she asked.

Her pinky skimmed his more than obvious erection, and Eli let out a soft growl.

"Yes," he whispered. Everything about this woman surprised him, kept him on his toes, yet somehow kept his head out of the fog that hung over this day. "You surprise me at every turn, and I don't know what to do with that."

She thought for a moment. "Is that a good thing?" This time, her thumb swirled around the two thin layers of cotton covering his tip.

"Yes," he whispered again, this time through clenched teeth.

"It's your turn," she told him. "Surprise *me*."

Eli wrapped his hand around hers, not wanting her to stop what she was doing but *needing* her to stop if he was going to give himself a second to think.

All week, he'd been racking his brain, trying to figure out how to apologize for the way he'd behaved when she asked to ride Midnight. Only now did he realize that his bad behavior last week wasn't the only reason Beth had lingered in his thoughts each day, long after the clinic had closed.

"I thought you didn't like surprises," he reminded her, buying himself some time to wrap his head around what was happening—around what was about to happen. "I seem to recall something about pepper spray and maybe a pitchfork?"

Beth pressed her lips together and fought back a grin. Finally she said, "Maybe I just needed someone to change my mind, to prove that surprises could actually be good. What do you think, Doc? Wanna change my mind?"

If he'd been waiting for any clearer permission, she'd just granted it.

And he did. He really wanted to change her mind.

Eli pressed his palms against the desk on either side of her, then dipped his head and brought his mouth to within a breath of hers.

"Would it surprise you if I knocked everything off my desk and laid you out right here?"

She swallowed, her breath hitching when she inhaled. "Yes."

He smiled. "Because I'm not gonna do that. It would make a huge mess that I don't want to clean up later." Though the tremble in her *yes* almost made him ignore his reason. Almost.

Beth barked out a laugh, and he took advantage of the disarming moment and hoisted her onto his hips.

She yelped, then laughed some more as she crossed her legs behind him and wrapped her arms around his neck.

He carried her toward the office door.

"Wait!" she cried, and Eli stopped short, sure that she was going to be the one to call off what they both knew was a very bad idea. Instead she grinned and grabbed the cattleman from where it hung on the hook just inside his door, depositing it onto his head.

"Why?" he asked, knowing full well that whatever they were about to do did not require a hat.

She shrugged. "It suits you," she told him. "Makes you look more…I don't know…*you*."

Eli shook off the uneasy feeling in his gut and reminded himself that he had a beautiful woman in his arms who seemed to want him as much as he wanted her. So he continued their journey, striding back through the clinic, out the door, and straight across the short walkway that led to the guesthouse. He paused for a brief moment at the front door.

"It's unlocked," Beth admitted, breathless. She squeezed her knees against his hips, and Eli had to bite the inside of his cheek to keep from kissing her senseless right here against the door.

"Is that safe?" he ground out between gritted teeth.

She nodded. "It is with you so close by."

Her trusting him enough to keep her door unlocked—especially after learning what happened on the property three years ago—should have made him furious. Not at her but at the situation. At her putting herself in unnecessary danger when it was just as easy not to. Instead, it urged him on, made him want her more for the sheer fact of knowing he made her feel safe.

But had she ever anticipated him getting *this* close? He didn't want to ask, didn't want to know if this was pretend or real or some primal thing in between that he couldn't possibly name. So he pushed the door open and strode through. Neither of them said a word as he piloted her through the kitchen and living area and straight into her bedroom.

He dropped her onto her back on the bed. "Surprise. How'd I do?"

"Good." Her chest heaved. "Really, really good. But you still haven't kissed me back."

Eli hadn't kissed anyone in years for the simple fact that he hadn't wanted to.

Until now.

He toed off his boots and climbed over her.

His chest ached but not the familiar ache of longing for what he used to have. This was something new. *She* was new. And Eli ached for *her*.

"I might be a little rusty," he admitted. "Or a *lot* rusty."

"You'd never know it," she told him with a shy grin. "I mean, you've got some moves, Doctor."

He laughed. She kept doing that, kept bringing out of him a lightness he'd forgotten was there.

"Me too, by the way," she added. "I might be a little rusty too. Are you sure you want to do this? Because it's okay if you're not ready. I'll understand."

He nodded. A lie. Eli wasn't sure about anything beyond this very moment, but he wanted to kiss her. And touch her. Now. And he couldn't think beyond that.

"Are *you* sure you want to do this?" he asked her. Maybe she could decide for both of them.

She answered by fisting his scrubs shirt in her hand and pulling him to her.

Her forehead knocked the cattleman onto the pillow beside her. Their lips collided, and their teeth clacked. It was awkward and clumsy and yes…they were *both* rusty. But then, before either of them could react to the clumsy awkwardness of two people navigating the newness of this mutual want, they'd rolled to their sides, hands tangled in hair, legs entwined, and their lips fitting together like a puzzle piece you have to spin multiple times before finally seeing how it fits before clicking it into place. Soon they found a rhythm he could tell was neither his nor hers but something brand new and all their own.

Eli hiked her knee over his hip. Then his hand slid up the back of her leg, fingertips brushing where her thigh ended and another part of her began.

She bucked slightly, her pelvis tilting against his.

"Just like I said," she whispered through short, sharp breaths. "The rusty doc has got *moves*."

Eli laughed and kissed her and then laughed again.

He helped her wriggle out of her shirt and then her bra.

For several seconds, all he could do was stare.

"What?" Beth asked, but she was smiling. She knew what he saw. But did she really?

"Thank you," he whispered, almost wishing he hadn't said it because now he'd have to explain to this woman what it meant for her to not only see him at the most vulnerable he'd been in years but to somehow have *seen* him through it.

But instead of asking what he meant, all she said was "You're welcome," as he continued to drink her in.

He dipped his head and kissed the soft pale skin of her breast, lips brushing tenderly over her taut, hardened peak.

She gasped, and he smiled against her as she tangled her fingers in his hair.

His hand traveled across her hip and found the space between them, found the loosely tied drawstring of her own scrub pants and pulled it free.

"Is this okay?" he asked, his fingers slipping behind the waistband of both the pants and what lay beneath, skin on skin as his erection strained against his boxer briefs.

"Yes," she whispered, her breath hitching as he slid between her folds, one finger sinking deep inside.

Beth whimpered, and when she called out his name—not her teasing or angrily aloof Doctor Murphy but *Eli*—he swore. She enveloped him in warmth and wonder. All he wanted to do was explore, yet he found himself without a map, without any sort of familiarity to aid in his navigation.

He kissed her hard, and she grabbed his wrist, then her hand moved so her palm fell atop his, guiding his movement, his speed...showing him what she liked.

"Fuck, that is sexy," he growled. "Show me more. Please."

She kissed him, nipped at his bottom lip, and then urged his hand out slowly...so goddamn slowly, until the tip of his slick finger slid over her swollen center.

She cried out, her hand tightening around his wrist as she arched against him.

"More," she pleaded, and this time he knew what to do, knew the pace that kept her right at the edge, knew that he could continue like this for the rest of the afternoon and well into the night if she'd let him.

He propped himself on his elbow as his hand continued to work, patiently, methodically. He watched her chest rise and fall with each inhale and exhale, listened to each soft hum, the occasional sharp intake of breath as he took pleasure in small surprises he was able to pull off by a change in tempo, direction, or holding back on the promise of a touch to tease her closer to the brink.

"*Eli*," she pleaded as he traced a circle around her sensitive core. She writhed and gripped his arm tighter, her fingernails digging into his skin. "*More. Please.*"

She pressed a firm hand over his thin cotton pants—another plea—and for a second, he froze.

Finish this, a voice in his head urged.

So he did.

Beth wanted more, so he gave her more, gave her everything he could with the touch of his hand, his lips on hers.

He savored the sweet taste of vanilla and mint—tea she'd had with breakfast? Something she wore on her lips? Eli wasn't sure, but it might have been the best thing he'd tasted in months. All he knew was that for the time being—however

short-lived—he'd indulge his senses in all things
her.

He watched in rapt wonder as she fell apart, her
fists clenching the bed linens and his palm between
her legs.

Her lips parted in a smile, and once she came
back to herself, her legs fell open, lazy and free and
still trusting the man with his hand inside her.

He slid his fingers free, and she gasped, then
broke into a blissful-sounding laugh.

"I can't remember..." she started. "I mean, that
was..." Her eyes fluttered open and locked on
his. "If that's you out of practice, we might have to
soundproof this place once you consider yourself
fully back in the game." She pushed herself up on
one elbow and yanked the knotted string of his
scrubs, but it wouldn't budge. She pouted. "A little
help here?" she teased. "It's your turn, Dr. Murphy."

His turn. Jesus, what was he doing?

Eli suddenly found it hard to breathe.

"I'm—sorry." He climbed off the bed.

Beth stared at him in...disbelief? Horror?
Another version of the anger or resentment she'd
borne all week? He didn't know, and he didn't
blame her. But also, it didn't matter.

Eli was already back in his boots and out of the
room, his pace quickening as he strode toward
the door.

He barely remembered walking through the

clinic again and into the small home he and Tess had built off the back. He was already naked and in the shower, the bathroom filling with steam as his forehead fell against the cool tile, the hot water beating down on his back.

Eli stroked himself from root to tip, a painful growl rising up and tearing from his lungs.

He didn't deserve to *want*, not when he'd already had—and lost—what some spent entire lifetimes trying to find.

You're still young, your whole life ahead of you. You're going to spend it pining for a woman and her horse who only ever wanted you to be happy?

Tess's laugh rang out in his head along with the imagined accusation.

Eli wasn't pining. That much he knew. He had grieved for his loss and moved on as best he could.

But he still couldn't escape the limbo of *what if.* Would he ever, or was this just where he lived now? He guessed yes, since it had been his home now for over three years.

He slapped a palm against the wet tile as the water coupled with his own firm grip burned away his desire.

His instinct—a thing he used to trust implicitly— had cost Tess and Fury their lives. After knowing Beth for less than twenty-four hours, it had almost cost her *her* life too.

He still wanted her.

Stroke one.

He could still taste her lips on his.

Stroke two.

And like he did with his past, with Beth he would always wonder *what if.*

Three.

But that was as far as this could go.

He worked himself until he found release.

But the ache in his chest held on, relief nowhere in sight.

Chapter 9

BETH LIFTED HER LEFT LEG, THE ADDED WEIGHT of the walking boot making it hard to maintain her center of gravity. But she succeeded—somehow without toppling backward—in gently setting her foot onto the ballet barre.

She exhaled, and her shoulders relaxed.

"I can feel you watching me, you know," she spoke aloud to what was supposed to be an empty carport.

A soft breeze moved through the open space, and Beth breathed in the scent of wild grass and lilac from the fields surrounding her sister's serenely remote home.

"I wasn't trying to hide," Delaney admitted. "Is it wrong for me to want to check out my husband's handiwork…and maybe admire my baby sister's talent?"

Beth lowered into a right plié, attempting to stretch muscles she hadn't used in almost two months. She winced, thankful her sister couldn't see her face. "This only further confirms that this little visit you sprang on me was premeditated. I'm guessing Sam didn't randomly wake up one day

and decide the carport was missing a ballet barre."
She straightened, lifted her right arm into fourth
position, and leaned forward over her elevated leg.

She felt her sister move closer.

"Maybe," Delancy admitted. "But look. You're
working. You're *dancing*...sort of."

Beth reached as far as she could, trying to wrap
her palm around the bottom of the boot, but her
fingers barely scratched the top of it. She groaned.
"It's not enough."

She straightened once more and slowly spun to
face her sister, her left leg following along with the
movement as if it were the hand of a clock. Then
she gingerly lowered it back to the ground.

Delaney's hand was pressed against her chest.
"You're really good, Bethy."

Beth narrowed her eyes. "At stretching?"

"No." Delaney shook her head. "I mean, yes. At
all of it. You just have this grace, you know? It's
beautiful to watch, and I'm just sorry that—"

"Don't say it, Lanes." Beth leaned against the
barre, gripping it tight beside each of her hips.
"Don't tell me how sorry you are that this part
of my life is over. I know you've been biting your
tongue for the past two weeks, but if you wouldn't
mind doing so indefinitely, I'd really appreciate it."

Her sister moved a few paces closer, close
enough to reach out and tuck a lock of Beth's hair
behind her ear.

"Have you talked to the new orthopedic therapist yet?" Delaney asked.

Beth nodded. "Today. I took the afternoon off."

Delaney's expression darkened. "Why didn't you tell me? How did you get there? I could have taken you."

"Trudy Davis drove me. She stopped by to pick up..." Beth cleared her throat. "She had Frederick cremated. Anyway, I asked her about a rideshare, and she told me there is no such thing in Meadow Valley—shocker—so she drove me."

Her throat tightened, but she let go of the barre, shook off the feeling, and squared her shoulders.

"He said given my age and the extent of the injury that dancing for recreation was certainly not out of the picture but that the stress of trying to do it professionally..." She trailed off for a moment before collecting herself again. "It's one person's opinion."

Along with that of her surgeon and the therapist she'd seen in Vegas before Delaney forced her to come *here*.

"There it is." Delaney grabbed Beth's hand and squeezed. "I knew something was up with you this week. I was afraid something happened at the clinic. But you must have been nervous about this appointment, huh? You don't have to keep stuff from me, Bethy. You know that, right? I'm here for you. Despite whether I agree with your doctors or therapists, I'm on your side. So come to me, okay? That's part of my *premeditated* plan." Delaney laughed.

"Okay," Beth relented. "I'll come to you. But only if you mean everything you just said. I'll get through this on my own if I have to, Lanes. But I really don't want to."

She wasn't giving Eli the cold shoulder like she had her first week in town. What happened in the guesthouse was amazing until it wasn't. And she'd told him flat out that if he wasn't ready, that was okay with her. She'd just mistakenly thought once he'd brought her to climax that he was more than okay with whatever it was they were doing.

But Eli got spooked, and Beth wouldn't fault him for that. She'd given him an out, he'd taken it, and she'd had the audacity to let it surprise her. Wasn't that what she wanted, for Eli to change her mind about surprises?

Note to self: For you, Beth Spence, surprises only end in disaster.

She just hadn't anticipated how lonely she'd feel the week following the latest disaster.

The *week*? Scratch that. The past month and a half had been the loneliest of her life. Sure, Delaney could be there for her, but her sister couldn't fix how isolated Beth felt not being able to participate in what had been her world for more than twenty-five years.

Delaney grabbed her sister's hand, bringing her back to the present. "Did you hear me, Bethy?"

"What?" Beth replied. Had her sister been talking to her without her knowledge?

"The clinic," Delaney told her. "I asked if everything at the clinic was okay."

Beth's eyes widened. "The clinic? What? Of course. Everything's fine at the clinic. Perfectly peachy. Why would you think otherwise? Did someone say something? Did Dr. Murphy say something?"

Good god, she needed to shut up. Could the lady protest *more* than too much? Because her physical therapy appointment wasn't the only secret she'd kept from her sister this past week, but there was no way she was touching the Eli thing with a ten-foot pole. It happened. It was over. They'd obviously both succumbed to a moment of weakness after an emotional morning. The end. New story. Chapter One: We're Strictly Professional Now. At least that was how they'd behaved around each other for week two…Eli's choice this time.

Ms. Spence, can you grab so-and-so's chart?

Of course, Dr. Murphy.

Ms. Spence, can you email this prescription to the pharmacy?

Sure, Dr. Murphy.

Hot and cold. That seemed to be how they rolled…with a partial roll in the hay in between.

Delaney's brow furrowed. "Weren't you there when Eli had to euthanize Frederick? You just mentioned Trudy Davis coming to pick up his—um—ashes."

"Right!" Beth responded with entirely too much enthusiasm. "Frederick!" She exhaled a steadying breath. "I mean…*poor* Frederick," she amended, her tone somber this time. "And Trudy too." *And Eli*, she wanted to say. But she kept that part— and any other thoughts she'd had about the complicated doctor—to herself. "I think I get it a little better now, though…how you feel about animals. I only knew Frederick for about an hour, and even I got a little choked up saying goodbye."

Her sister beamed, and Beth couldn't help but smile too. These moments when the two of them connected meant more to Beth now than they had when they were growing up. The physical distance between the two women was one thing. But Delaney had built a whole life here with Sam and Nolan, the ranch, and the animal rescue. It had made the span from Nevada to California—a mere eight-hour drive—feel like traveling from the earth to the moon. If there was any silver lining to her sister's manipulation and—some might say— kidnapping, it was getting to be with Delaney and her family now, seeing her sister in her element as a wife, mother, and rescuer of all animals, great and small.

Okay, so Beth would take her sister's word on the last part. Beth had already taken her baby step into animal interaction by accepting the job at the clinic. She wasn't about to frolic in her sister's petting zoo.

"You're really good too, Lanes. At all the things you do." Beth gave her sister's hand a squeeze. "I'm sorry if I don't tell you that enough."

Delaney sniffled, then fluttered her hand in front of her face to wave off the ensuing tears.

"Oh my goodness! I don't know what's gotten into me," Delaney said. "Maybe I'm ovulating early. I should tell Sam. Might be time to get working on baby number two tonight!" She laughed. "And also, thank you, Bethy. That means a lot. I'll leave you to your stretching. You're staying for dinner, right? I hope you like baked mac and cheese because that's pretty much all Nolan eats these days."

Beth's head jerked at the sound of a loud snort.

"What the hell was *that*?"

Delaney gasped, then covered her mouth. "It was supposed to be a surprise!" The words came out muffled behind her hands.

Beth narrowed her eyes at her big sister. "No. More. Surprises, Lanes. You got me out of Vegas, didn't you? You got me to agree to the job and to staying here until my recuperation is over. What else am I being tricked into doing?" She did the little "Come on" gesture with her hand, like she was

Morpheus challenging Neo to a friendly round of kung fu, knowing her Keanu-obsessed sister would get the reference.

Delaney groaned, then pulled out her phone and fired off a voice text. "You're busted, Sam Callahan!"

After a short pause, Delaney's eyes brightened. She pressed a button on her phone and played the apparent response so Beth could hear.

"Then bring your sister out back so we can do this thing!" It was her brother-in-law Sam's voice.

"Do *what* thing?" Beth asked, now wishing she hadn't pushed the matter. "Remember the pepper spray, Lanes? The pepper spray!" was all she could think to add in order to convey how surprises failed monumentally when Beth was involved.

"Let's go!" Delaney grabbed Beth's hand and gave it a gentle yet excited tug. "There's no confetti, I promise! And unless you're hiding pepper spray inside a bodily orifice, I think we're safe!"

"Ew! Bodily orifice? And what *thing*?" Beth whined as she let her sister lead her out of the carport and along the side of the house.

When they made it to the back porch, they found Sam standing in the grass beyond, patting the withers of a large white horse she knew was *not* Cirrus.

"Bethy," Delaney began, "this is Ace. He and Sam are going to teach you to ride."

Beth stood there, blinking, not sure how to react. She'd wanted to ride *Midnight*, but that prospect was off the table. This horse was a stranger. She could feel a change in the air around them, like the barometric pressure dropping right before a storm. Meeting Midnight for the first time felt different. It felt safe. *Beth* felt safe. But just seeing Ace tied her stomach in knots. It made her dizzy. It made her *scared*.

Delaney led her toward the porch steps that lowered to the grass, and Ace snorted, shook his head, and backed up.

Ace sensed her fear, and he didn't like it.

Beth recognized the feeling she had now. It was the same pit in her stomach she had when Eli lost control in front of Midnight, when Midnight could have seriously hurt either of them or worse.

"Easy, boy," Sam told the gelding in a soothing voice, but Beth felt far from soothed.

"He doesn't like me," she finally said. And Beth was pretty sure the feeling was mutual.

"He's just scared," Delaney told her, trying to inch her forward.

Beth wouldn't budge.

"And so are you," Delaney added.

Beth nodded. "Ya think? Lanes, you're the animal whisperer. Aren't you supposed to ease animals into meeting new humans? I don't know this…this creature, and it doesn't know me. I feel like this isn't following proper horse-greets-new-human protocol."

Ace backed up again, head shaking and breath huffing out from his nostrils.

"Ace is the most-ridden horse on the ranch," Delaney told her. "He's featured on the website. People book trips at Meadow Valley Ranch specifically to meet Ace. This doesn't make any sense."

Beth mirrored the horse's movement and backed toward the house.

"Lanes…" She spoke softly and slowly, all the while keeping her eyes on Ace, who looked like he was ready to charge. Did horses charge? Because Beth sure as hell didn't want to find out.

"Yeah, Bethy?"

Delaney's voice eerily matched her own, as if her sister was finally catching on that *Beth* hadn't traveled to Meadow Valley specifically to meet Ace and that Ace was well aware of that fact.

"I don't trust that horse, Lanes, and I'm pretty sure he doesn't trust me either."

Beth could see her sister nod in her peripheral vision.

"Sam?" Delaney called.

It felt like Ace's eyes were locked on Beth's. She couldn't look away and could no longer back away. She was stuck, unable to make a move unless *he* did.

The horse's front hooves lifted off the ground as he let loose a sound that was anything but friendly.

Sam rubbed Ace's nose and leaned over to whisper something into the gelding's ear. Then in one swift motion, he hooked a boot into one of the stir-rups and jumped onto the horse's back.

Ace reared back, kicking his front legs into the air, and he and Sam took off across the field that separated the house from the Meadow Valley Ranch.

"Back soon!" Sam called over his shoulder. Then he tapped his heels against Ace's sides and yelled, "Yah!" They galloped over a hill, and in mere seconds they were out of sight.

Beth stumbled backward, and her sister caught her by the elbow. Both women blew out a shaky breath.

"What *was* that?" Delaney asked. "I've never seen Ace behave that way before. I swear it, Bethy." She turned her gaze on Beth. "I think he *hated* you."

Beth's mouth fell open, and Delaney burst into a fit of laughter.

"I mean—" Delaney cut herself off, unable to curb her giggles. "He thinks you're the *worst*."

Beth crossed her arms and scoffed. "How can you laugh when we were almost *charged* by that beast? You know, come to think of it, this is twice now that you've brought an animal into my pres-ence and the animal has attacked or at least thought very strongly about *trying* to attack. I'll have you know that every animal that comes into the clinic can't get enough of me, and Midnight would one hundred percent let me ride her if Eli wasn't such a stick-in-the-mud about it."

Delaney's smile fell, and Beth wanted to swallow the words back once she'd said them.

"Ugh," Beth continued. "That sounds so petty and insensitive out loud, doesn't it?"

Delaney grabbed her sister's hand. The early evening breeze made both women shiver.

"Look, I'm sorry about Ace," Delaney told her. "Eli might have mentioned something about you wanting to learn how to ride, so Sam and I just thought... Well, we clearly thought wrong." She sighed. "Horses are always going to be a tough spot for Eli. You get that, right?"

Beth nodded. "But it's better than it *was*, right? I mean, things have gotten better for him since... Tess?" She swallowed a knot in her throat, not prepared for how the name of Eli's late wife would feel on her tongue after what happened last week.

"Yeah, of course." Delaney forced a smile. "Everything gets easier with time. But some things stick with us for the long haul, you know? He's a good man who has been through a lot. If it's hard working with him sometimes, maybe give him a pass or two."

Beth's chest tightened. She didn't want to think about the *long haul*, not for Eli and certainly not for herself. Those words made it sound as if one was living with a burden, with a weight that would always be tough to bear. Agreeing with her sister's assessment felt like an admission, like *Beth* had to bear the weight of some sort of loss for the long haul. Like Eli would never get out from under his grief. But she wasn't conceding to this injury, not before she gave her recovery everything she had. Even then, she wasn't sure she'd be able to admit defeat.

What hit her stronger than she'd anticipated, though, was how much she didn't want to imagine Eli as defeated either. He *was* a good man. She saw that in the way he took care of her the first day she arrived in town, from picking her up at the airport to making her pancakes to dressing her wound when a certain hen went on the attack.

And she saw it in the way he cared for the animals at his clinic and their humans. Watching Trudy lose Frederick wasn't the only thing that brought Beth to tears that day. It was watching Eli—a man experiencing yet another loss—forcing himself to be strong for Trudy when he could have so easily fallen apart himself.

"I guess," Beth finally replied. "But maybe that long haul with the horse thing is something I could help Eli get over if he'd be willing to give me a chance."

Beth realized she meant every word. Riding Midnight would be as much for Eli as it would be for her.

"That's what I'm hoping for," Delaney replied with a mischievous glint in her eye.

"What?" Beth asked. "Why do I feel like you're scheming again?"

Her sister scoffed. "Scheming? Bethy, I don't *scheme*."

Really? How about a plane ticket to Meadow Valley that came with a job she never applied for or a horse Beth never asked to ride showing up in the backyard? But before Beth could further articulate her thoughts, the breeze came again, this time bringing with it the sound of tires on gravel, a vehicle rolling down the quiet, lonely road.

"That must be Barbara Ann and Nolan!" Delaney announced.

"Saved by the toddler," Beth mumbled.

Her sister continued without missing a beat. "They had some grandmother-granddaughter time this afternoon while I toiled away in the kitchen over baked macaroni and cheese." Delaney winked. "Or *maybe* I enjoyed a glass of wine and a bubble bath because I bought the mac and cheese from Pearl over at the Meadow Valley Inn."

"Phew!" Beth replied as the two women spun toward the house. At least whatever scheme her sister had cooked up *didn't* include dinner. "Because your cooking might be something we all should avoid for the *long haul*."

Delaney backhanded her on the shoulder but didn't argue. Laughing again, the two women strode through the back door, making their way through the kitchen and living area before heading out again, this time through the front, to greet Beth's niece and Sam's mother.

But just as Beth was about to let go of the idea that her sister had *more* surprises in store for her today, she spotted a third guest behind the older woman and baby in tow: a man carrying a bottle of wine. A guest she hadn't glimpsed outside the clinic since he carried her from his office to her bedroom a week ago today. A guest whose cowboy hat still hung on the row of key hooks just inside the guesthouse's front door, reminding her that she hadn't imagined the wonderful feeling of his hands on her skin, his lips on hers... or that he'd bolted the second she'd cried out his name.

"You invited *Eli*?" Beth asked through a teeth-gritting smile.

A large, rambunctious dog scurried out of the house from behind them, playfully chased by a three-legged black cat. Both animals darted back and forth across Dr. Murphy's boots until the man finally stopped, laughed, and dropped down to greet the rambunctious fur balls.

"Of course I did. He's Butch Catsidy's favorite human aside from me and Sam. And Scout? She loves everyone. Maybe even *you*." Delaney bopped her sister on the nose with her index finger. "There's my baby girl!" she called, arms out-stretched to the bouncing child in her grandma's arms. "Come on in, everyone." She propped Nolan on her hip. "The wine is already open, and Sam will be back soon."

Chapter 10

ELI SHOULD HAVE SAID NO WHEN SAM OFFERED to top off his wineglass again, but the slight buzz he had going made it increasingly easier to sit across the table from Beth without wanting to both sprint the other way and lean across the short expanse between them and kiss her until they both forgot their own names.

"You're still coming to dinner tonight, right?" Delaney had asked. It had become a standing thing on Friday nights. At first, it had felt like a pity thing... *Let's invite the poor widower for dinner since he'll just hole up at home when everybody else is out.* But now he understood that Delaney and Sam were simply good friends who enjoyed spending time with other good friends. He'd had to cancel the week before when he received an after-hours house call from a cat owner who didn't know her cat was pregnant until it had given birth to a full litter...that afternoon. What confused Eli on this particular Friday was *why* Delaney had to double-check that he was coming, but now he knew.

"Bethy, did you know that any animal, whether

two-legged, four-legged, warm- or cold-blooded, trusts Eli like he's their mama hen?"

Beth had raised her brows, her eyes directly on his. "Is that so?" was all she said in response.

"And, Eli, did you know my sister was a backup dancer for a certain world-famous pop star who had a residency in Vegas?" Delaney dropped to a stage whisper. "She had to sign this really fancy nondisclosure agreement about the experience so I don't think we can mention the name, but basically my sister is kind of a big deal."

Sam Callahan cleared his throat and nudged Eli with his elbow. "You look like you're getting low, Murphy. Let me fill you up."

When Sam's mother had taken Nolan upstairs for a bath and to tuck her in for the night, they'd moved the dinner party to the back porch, where a small outdoor couch was flanked by two chairs.

"Let our guests have the couch, Sam. It's more comfortable."

And Sam took his wife's directive, offering Eli an apologetic smile.

This was a setup. Which meant Delaney either had *no* clue what had transpired between Eli and her sister, or she had *every* clue. Neither option did anything to tamp down his growing anxiety about the situation.

The second Beth sat down on the couch and he attempted to sit next to her, he sprang back up.

"You know, I should probably get going. I have a busy morning tomorrow."

Delaney narrowed her eyes at him. "Tomorrow is Saturday. The clinic is closed on Saturdays."

"House call!" he blurted. It could have been true. That was the reason he left Saturdays open. There was no way she knew he had no appointments as of yet.

But Beth knew. She made the appointments. He couldn't bring himself to sneak a glance at her.

Delaney sighed. "Oh…okay then. But we'll do it again next Friday, right?"

"Right," Eli lied. "Of course." That gave him a week to come up with an excuse to cancel. God, he hated being an asshole. He really did. But he hated even more being so close to Beth without the boundary of office decorum to keep him from thinking thoughts he shouldn't think and wanting to kiss people he shouldn't kiss.

Okay, person. He wanted to kiss *one* person. And he was starting to forget why he shouldn't.

Sam stood to shake Eli's hand, but when Eli took a step toward him, the deck began to sway.

"Whoa, buddy," Sam said, clamping a hand on Eli's shoulder. "How many glasses did you have tonight?"

Eli squeezed his eyes shut and pinched the bridge of his nose. "I don't know," he admitted. "She never let my glass go empty."

He pointed an accusing finger at Delaney. When he opened his eyes to look at her, she smiled sheepishly back at him.

"Guilty." Delaney shrugged. "A good host doesn't wait for her guests' glasses to go empty."

Sam sighed. "Funny how I only got one glass. I'll drive you back. Delaney and Beth can follow in your truck."

"Actually..." Delaney stood, then swayed herself. "I think I'm a little too tipsy myself. But here's an idea! Bethy doesn't drink. Maybe she should drive them both home."

Now Beth stood, her mouth hanging open. "Hello? Anyone notice the super-fashionable cast on my leg?"

Delaney waved her off. "You drive with your *right* leg, sweetie. It's a very short drive. I'm sure you'll be fine."

Eli watched a whole conversation pass between the two women with nothing more than a series of looks. He might have been too inebriated to drive, but he could still tell that Beth was not happy about her sister's apparent schemes. Neither was Eli.

"It's still not entirely safe," he interjected. "I mean, yeah, Beth's right leg is fine, but in case of emergency, her left probably shouldn't be impaired. I could just leave the truck here and somehow get it back tomorrow."

Delaney crossed her arms. "What about your early house call?"

Eli's jaw clenched. Busted. "Right. My house call."

"I'm on call at the ranch early too," Sam told him. "You're welcome to spend the night on the couch."

Beth groaned. "Fine. I'll do it. I'll drive us home. I don't want to be stuck here. I mean, I appreciate your hospitality, guys, but I want to sleep in my own bed, and I'm sure Eli does too. It's a five-minute ride. I'm sure we'll be okay. And if we're not, I'd like it printed on my headstone that my sister sent me to my peril all in the name of her misguided schemes."

Eli bit back a grin. At least he and Beth were both on to Delaney and neither of them were having it.

She likes you. And I like her.

Tess's voice sounded in his head as Eli waited by the driver's side door while Beth said good night to her niece.

Eli normally would have silently argued with the voice, but tonight he felt…buzzed. And buzzed seemed to be changing the blueprint of the evening in more ways than one.

I like her too, he thought, wondering if the voice could hear.

Of course I can, silly. I'm not really me. I'm you.

Eli knew that. Of course he knew. But his projection of Tess was all he had left. The pain of losing her had receded to a dull ache that would always be there, but he knew now he could live with it. It was how it all happened he couldn't seem to shake.

If you're me, tell me I'm not allowed to be happy then. Tell me I should have been able to save you and *Fury, but instead I lost you both. That's not a guy who gets to be happy again.*

He imagined Tess's sigh. *So serious,* she'd say. *So ready to take on the burden of the world and make everything your responsibility. When are you going to cut yourself some slack?*

Maybe he should crawl into the passenger seat and pretend to fall asleep before Beth returned. No. That would be extra-shitty. Especially since she'd never driven his truck before. She'd need help adjusting the seat and the steering wheel and likely navigating back to his property if she was still getting the lay of the land.

Eli was lost in his head, trying to get Tess to talk him out of how he felt, when someone poked his shoulder.

"Hey," Beth said as he spun to face her.

"Hey," he replied. "You snuck up on me."

"I didn't sneak. This is the driver's side door. Why are *you* here? I thought *I* was driving," she added, then crossed her arms over her chest.

She was so unassuming in her purple zip-up

hoodie, a tank underneath, and matching leggings. Yet the questioning look in her eyes seemed to ask so much more than *Why are you here?* Eli wished like hell he had the answer.

For several seconds, he simply stared. What *was* he doing? And why did he feel so out of his depth whenever she was near?

"Are you okay?" Beth continued, brows pulled together.

Eli cleared his throat. "Yeah," he lied. "I just wasn't sure if you needed help getting into the truck." He held his hands up. "I know. I know. You're perfectly capable. But I wasn't going to be a total dick and plop my ass down in the passenger seat to let you fend for yourself if you did, on the off chance, need a hand."

The corner of her mouth twitched, and Eli's own lips parted into a smile.

"Wait. Is that a smile? Did I just make you smile? That means I did good, doesn't it?" he asked.

Beth groaned and rolled her eyes.

"So...not good then?" he corrected.

"Come *on*." Beth fisted her hands at her sides. "You have to know how maddening it is to have you be this charming and then to...to..."

"To run hot and cold on you like I've been because of how much I like you and how much it kinda freaks me out that I do?" He leaned back against the driver's side door.

Beth's eyes widened.

Eli laughed. He wanted to turn off this feeling of lightness that had to be a mix of the wine and the nearness of her. He wanted to run as fast and as far as he could from this *like* he had for her. But he couldn't seem to put enough distance between them. She just kept catching up, and Eli couldn't deny that he wanted her to.

"Guess your sister got enough wine in me to at least turn off my filter." He'd probably regret letting the truth fly out like that in the morning, but right now, he *wanted* her to know.

Her mouth opened, but nothing came out.

He raised a brow. "Charming or maddening, me saying what I said? Or maybe a little bit of both?"

"I…" Beth finally uttered. Then she fisted her hands at her sides. "I mean *you*…" She blew out a long breath, then held out her right hand. "Maybe you should give me the keys and see if I actually get us home safely before I go admitting how I feel about you saying what you said."

Eli pulled his key fob from his pocket and dropped it into her outstretched palm.

"An admission, huh?" he teased. "Must be some big feelings."

She scoffed and closed her fist around the offering.

He had no idea where this playfulness was coming from. It wasn't him. From what he could

remember, it had never been him. But with Beth—
and a little too much wine—it *was*.

She nodded toward where he stood. "You're
kind of in my way."

Right. The door.

Eli pushed himself off from the side of the vehicle, opened the door for his driver, then held out
his hand.

Beth glanced from his hand to the running board
and sighed. She tossed the key fob onto the driver's
seat and then grabbed his palm.

The second her skin met his, Eli had to fight the
urge to pull her *to* him rather than hoist her into
the truck. In the clinic, he had no problem being
Dr. Murphy and *only* Dr. Murphy. But tonight?
He didn't want to be her boss or her landlord. He
didn't want to be the widower who couldn't forgive
himself for what he'd lost. And he didn't want to
pretend like he wasn't feeling things he hadn't felt
in years. Eli just wanted to *be*, but he somehow
couldn't remember how.

"Um, Eli?" Beth glanced down at him from the
driver's seat. "I kind of need to close the door."

Because again he was standing there, lost in his
head, wanting what he didn't think he deserved.

"Right. Sorry about that." He pivoted away and
rounded the back of the truck, swearing under his
breath.

Once he was in the passenger seat, Beth pressed

the ignition button and brought the truck to life. She grabbed the gear shift, and he grabbed her wrist.

"You do know how to drive, right?" he asked, realizing this tiny detail should have been established before they left Sam and Delaney's backyard.

She rolled her eyes. "Of course I do. And my right foot is fine, so it shouldn't be an issue, right? I just assumed it was kind of an unwritten rule that you didn't drive when you were… Whatever. I'm perfectly capable of getting us home."

She just hadn't wanted to. She hadn't wanted to be in this situation with him, period. He knew that. Yet despite Delaney's less than subtle agenda for the evening, Eli was happy he was next to her now, even if it was only for a five-minute ride home.

He loosened his grip, but he wasn't ready to let go.

"I know you are perfectly capable of doing this," he told her. "I trust you. I'm pretty sure, cast or not, you could do any damn thing you wanted if you set your mind to it."

Her cheeks flushed, and he let her go, not bothering to hide his grin.

———

They made it home without incident. Eli wasn't sure why that disappointed him, but it might have had something to do with the five-minute ride feeling more like five seconds.

Beth turned off the ignition but made no move to exit the vehicle. Her hands still gripped the steering wheel, and she stared straight ahead as if a long road stretched out before her.

"It freaks me out too, you know," she finally said...to the windshield.

Eli scratched the back of his neck. "You're going to have to be more specific than that. *What* freaks you out? Spiders? A citywide blackout that might elicit a purge? Me saying how much I like you?"

Beth spun abruptly to face him. "That!" She pointed at him. "Well, all three, actually, but the last part scares me the most."

He narrowed his eyes. "So just to be clear, how I feel about you freaks you out *more* than an impending purge?"

Beth laughed, but then her expression grew serious. She shook her head. "Do you know why I'm not half in the bag and speaking without a filter?"

Eli opened his mouth to respond, but she didn't give him a chance.

"Because I don't drink." She threw up her hands. "I don't drink. I don't date. I don't do *anything*...except dance. And it's not because anyone forced me to give those things up, by the way. My mom wasn't, like, one of those dance moms you see on TV. Every path I've traveled has always been my choice. I simply chose single-minded focus on dancing until I achieved my goal." She pressed her lips together, waiting for his response.

"What about all that stuff you said about letting off a little steam? About knowing what to do when I had my dehydration *situation*?"

She shrugged. "Saw it in a movie, I think. The point is, this?" She motioned between them. "I'm as clueless about it as you seem to be. I'm not supposed to want anything other than getting back on my own two feet and rehabbing this stupid injury so I can audition again. Yet here I am, freaking out about how much I might like you with the added fear of knowing that you most likely aren't ready to like someone like we…um…might like each other." She winced.

He stared at her, every goddamn emotion warring in his head and his heart. All he wanted to do was silence the noise.

All he wanted was *her*.

He clicked open his seat belt, then hers, and leaned across the center console. She didn't move, only stared back, chest rising and falling with each shaky breath.

He cupped her cheeks in his palms, her flesh molten against his.

"Unless you tell me not to, Tiny Dancer, I'm going to do something I've been wanting to do ever since the last time I did it."

Her throat bobbed.

"I might be smaller than you, but I'm five foot five. That's the minimum height for a Rockette, I'll have you know. But...I'm mighty," she whispered.

"The mightiest," he whispered back.

She skimmed her teeth over her bottom lip, and it took everything in his crumbling will to keep from nipping at it himself.

"Tell me we shouldn't," he continued.

"We shouldn't."

"Tell me this won't end well."

She nodded. "I never wanted to be here in the first place. I'll be running back to the Big Apple the first chance I get."

Eli's chest squeezed. Whatever happened between them, this part was inescapable. Beth Spence didn't belong in Meadow Valley. She was all bright lights, big city, and equally big dreams. This *would* end badly simply because it would end. But none of that mattered when his lips were this close to hers.

"But you're not running now," he told her, softly brushing her cheeks with each thumb.

She closed her eyes and hummed a soft sigh.

"Couldn't even if I wanted to. But...I don't want to. Not now."

Tell me to stop, he willed her to say as he dipped his head, his mouth dangerously close to hers. But she didn't move.

His bottom lip brushed hers.

"Wait!" Beth slapped her palm against his chest.

Eli threw himself against the passenger door. *Shit.* He'd misread the signs. Or maybe there were no signs at all. How would he know? He hadn't done this in years, hadn't *wanted* to in just as long. And shit, he was tipsy. Maybe everything he'd been feeling had all been in his head and his head alone.

But she'd said she liked him, didn't she? Hell, his inner monologue was apparently twelve years old.

He opened his mouth to apologize but stopped short when he realized she was smiling.

Eli pinched the bridge of his nose. "Jesus, Beth! Did I fuck up or not?"

She gasped, hand flying to her chest. "Oh god. No! Sorry! I only wanted…I mean, before we kiss—and I *do* want you to kiss me—I need to lay out one condition of our agreement."

"Our kissing agreement?" Eli was so confused.

Beth nodded. "You may kiss me and *only* kiss me since I'm not taking advantage of a man while he's drunk." She hesitated but then added, "I kind of already feel like I took advantage of you being slightly vulnerable after Trudy and Frederick and—"

"Wait…" Eli interrupted her. "If you are trying to up the sexiness of the moment by bringing up dead animals I wish I could have saved, let me run into the clinic and grab you a few more charts."

Beth groaned. "Ugh. *No.* I didn't mean it like

that. But if it happens between us, like *really* happens, I want us both to be in a good place here..."
She pressed a palm over his heart. "And here..." She leaned forward and pressed her lips to his forehead.

Well, shit. That was sweet as hell.

"*And...*" she continued, straightening so her eyes met his, "in the morning when you *don't* have a house call, unless you somehow booked one after we closed the clinic this afternoon, you're teaching me how to ride. With Midnight."

She pressed her lips together and raised her chin.

A challenge and an ultimatum all wrapped up in one.

Eli needed that mare rehabbed and off his property, which meant the mare needed a rider. Midnight clearly didn't trust him. That much he knew. But for some reason, she and Beth had forged a connection on their first day in town.

"You're not going to let this go, are you?" he asked, resignation already seeping in.

She shook her head. "Nope."

Eli sighed, but he didn't get a chance to respond.

"Wait!" Beth pulled the brakes again.

He held his hands up, assuring her he wasn't making any moves.

"I won't push you into anything you're not ready for," Beth began. "So if tonight's too soon for this..." She motioned between them again. "Or I'm rushing you to put me on the horse tomorrow, I can wait. Not forever, but I'll do it on your timetable. This is a big deal for you, and I should have been more sensitive to that from the beginning. But Midnight does need to be ridden again, and I want that rider to be me."

Eli slowly lowered his hands.

"Beth?"

"Eli?"

"Are you done freaking me out every time I'm ready to kiss you?"

She pressed her lips together and nodded.

"Fine. Wait there a second." And before she could respond, he opened his door and hopped out. On his way around the truck, he unlatched the tailgate and then strode up to her door, which was already hanging open.

"What are you doing?" she asked.

He held out a hand, but instead of helping her to the ground, he lifted her off the running board and hiked her legs over his hips.

Beth yelped and burst into a fit of laughter until he made his way back to the truck bed and deposited her on the edge. He pushed her knees open just enough so he could stand between them.

"Oh!" she said.

"Now we're eye to eye," he told her.

"And nose to nose." She leaned her forehead against his, and the tips of their noses brushed.

"Lemme just show you the last part." He tilted

his head to the side and softly nipped her bottom lip just like he'd wanted to moments before. He hesitated then, savoring the familiar taste of vanilla and mint, this time sure it wasn't morning tea.

"Lip balm," she whispered, somehow reading his thoughts. "I hope it doesn't bother you."

He kissed her once, then licked his own lips with a grin.

"I don't think I've ever tasted anything sweeter."

He kissed her again, hands moving up her back as she hooked her knees over his hips, squeezing him tight.

"You sure about that just kissing deal?" he asked, his lips traveling down her neck and to the soft skin exposed above her tank top.

"No?" Her knees squeezed him again. "But yes?"

He understood. She wanted him in the right headspace for this to go any further, and he wanted to *be* in the right headspace for her. He wanted to believe he deserved what she was willing to give. Until then, he'd give her whatever she was willing to receive.

"Should I only kiss you here?" he teased, lips brushing hers once more.

"Maybe," she whispered. Then, "But maybe other places too."

"How about here?" He unzipped her hoodie and kissed the hardened peak of her nipple beneath the fitted cotton.

"Mm-hmm," she acquiesced.

Just kissing, he reminded himself, but there were so many places to kiss.

He moved to her right side, giving equal attention to her other breast.

Her back arched. Eli lowered her slowly so her head rested on the truck bed.

"Nothing below the belly button," she told him. "Or I won't be able to stop, and I want the next time I—I want to do it together."

Eli nodded, hooked his fingers under the hem of her tank, and lifted it over her breasts. He growled when he found them bare, no bra separating him from her soft, pink flesh.

"Also small but mighty," she teased, rising up on her elbows. "Means sometimes nothing more than a supportive tank is necessary to hold the girls in place."

He laughed. "If you don't mind, I'm having a moment with *the girls*."

And bending the rules as much as she'd let him, he kissed and nipped and tasted until they were both dangerously close to a point of no return.

Beth lay breathless, hands white-knuckling the tailgate's edge.

Eli throbbed against the prison of his jeans.

"We have to stop." His words came out hoarse.

"I know," she lamented. "Why do we have to be so mature about this when we could be having wild, crazy sex in a truck? Outside? Are we making a huge mistake by *not* just getting jiggy with it?"

Eli threw his head back and laughed.

Hell, this woman was funny. And beautiful. And headstrong. And smart. And, of course, mighty.

As much as he wanted to bury himself inside her right here in the bed of his truck, he'd hate himself for it in the morning, probably pull a selfish disappearing act again, and then Beth would hate him too. If they were going to go down whatever road this was, Eli was going to figure out how to do it right...or as right as he could given the past baggage they both brought to the table and the future they didn't have.

He readjusted her tank, then pulled her so she was sitting again.

"I will be thinking about you all night, *Mighty* Dancer."

She smiled, and her green eyes shone in the moonlight.

"You'd better be," she teased.

She kissed him once more, then let him help her to the ground so they could both pivot and go their separate ways. But just as he was about to head toward the clinic, she grabbed his wrist. "Wait," she said softly, for once not freaking him out that he'd done something terribly wrong.

So he waited, not daring to take another step toward the guesthouse for fear neither of them would be strong enough to stop themselves.

Eli watched her stride toward the front door, grateful for a reason to keep his eyes on her, if only for a few moments more. She'd barely stepped inside before she turned back to face him, his cattleman in her hand.

His stomach clenched at the reminder of why she had it, but then he remembered what she'd just told him.

"I can wait. Not forever, but I'll do it on your timetable."

Beth meant more than just her riding Midnight, and the realization made him dizzy.

When she stood before him again, she reached up and dropped the hat back on his head.

"There," she told him. "There's the Eli I've missed all week." She kissed the tips of her fingers and then pressed them to his lips. And then she left him standing there, a smile tugging at his mouth as he unapologetically watched her walk away until the door closed behind her and she was safely inside.

Tess didn't talk to him anymore that night. Instead, the entirety of his thoughts overflowed with images of a woman who lived just across the yard. If he ever fell asleep that night, he knew his dreams would be only of *her*.

Chapter 11

BETH SHOULD HAVE KNOWN BETTER.

She groaned. No, this was a growl because she… was… *mad*. How could he go back on his word after last night? After the way he kissed her, the things he said?

"I'll be right back, okay, girl?"

Beth patted Midnight on the nose, and the mare snorted in response.

Then, as best she could with the boot still slowing her down, Beth stormed out of the empty, Dr. Murphy-less barn.

She mumbled under her breath all the way to the clinic about waking up early and letting Eli be a distraction when she knew she should be focusing solely on her recovery. But she'd googled it. Horseback riding was great for strengthening her core. It promoted stability and flexibility, both of which were really hard to work on with limited mobility. Riding would keep her from having to bear weight on her left leg and would keep her in shape for when she could actually start dancing again. All she had to do was not fall off.

Actually, all she had to do was get *on* the horse,

but without her MIA riding instructor, that wasn't happening.

When she found the clinic door locked, she hesitated. She'd never been inside Eli's house or apartment or whatever he called the living space attached to the back of the clinic. Two weeks of working with the man and living on his property, and he hadn't so much as invited her over for a cup of coffee. Storming up to his front door—or was it technically a back door?—somehow felt like a violation.

Then she heard it, the squawking.

"It's just a chicken," she reminded herself aloud as she walked along the side of the clinic to the fenced-in yard—and chicken coop—that lay beyond.

The squawking grew louder.

"She's *not* going to peck your eyes out," Beth continued through gritted teeth.

Beth paused at the gate and squinted as the morning sun glared back at her. She swore she saw an un-chicken-like figure sitting in the grass outside the coop, but the sun in her eyes made her second-guess whether it was a human, an unusually short scarecrow, or possibly another animal that might see her as the enemy like Lucy and Ace had.

She steadied herself with a calming breath, unlatched the gate, strode hesitantly through, and then relatched it behind her.

Using her hand as a visor, she slowly made her way across the grass and toward the coop, waiting for a hen to attack with each step.

Another squawk sounded as she approached, but the closer she got, the more she also heard... chirping.

Beth stopped short of a pair of cowboy boots that were crossed, one ankle over the other. As her vision cleared, she followed the long denim-clad legs up to where they met Eli's broad torso. In his lap paced a half dozen baby chicks. Another roamed in circles around the upturned cowboy hat sitting in the grass, and one more sat on Eli's shoulder, pecking at his ear as he threw his head back and laughed.

Good god, that smile. And he was covered in chicks. Baby. Chicks. How the hell was Beth supposed to muster anger at being stood up when *this* sort of sight lay before her? It was like a page out of a Twelve Hunky Cowboys calendar. The best page.

Still not having been noticed, Beth cleared her throat. She crossed her arms and tapped her foot, attempting the most defiant expression she could muster while her palms grew clammy and her throat dry.

"Good morning, sunshine," Eli crooned, his infectious smile audible in the words. "Am I late? Jenna... The chicks and the coop belong to her. She dropped the chicks off yesterday afternoon.

They were part of some library egg-hatching experiment, and she'd offered to take the females. Came out to check on them and…well…" He gave her a one-shoulder shrug, careful not to jostle the chick on his other one. "Got a little carried away."

Beth opened her mouth to give him a piece of her mind about being inconsiderate and making her think he'd pulled a disappearing act again, but then she realized Eli had done nothing of the sort. He'd simply been distracted by unexpected happiness, which looked *really* good on him.

"Squawk!"

Beth startled, taking a couple of steps back. Her gaze darted left and right, looking for her assailant.

"Lucy's inside the coop," Eli assured her. "She likes to boss the younger hens around early in the morning. I just wanted to give these little ladies some time in the sun." He gently picked up the chick that was on his shoulder and cupped her in his palms. "You want to hold one before I put them back into their brooder?"

She worried her bottom lip between her teeth. "I'll admit I've been getting better with the animals in the clinic. You know…the ones that are already domesticated? But these are brand-new *wild* creatures. They are living on pure instinct right now, and most of that instinct says that I am the enemy."

Eli narrowed his eyes. "And Midnight? She's about as wild as they come, yet you want to hop on her back and let her decide whether she thinks it's a good idea *after* the fact."

"That four-legged beast is an anomaly." Beth nodded in the direction of the barn. "I can't explain why, but I trust her, and I'm pretty sure she trusts me."

Eli nuzzled the chick on the top of its head, then deposited it onto his lap with the others. He patted an empty swath of grass beside him. "Come on. I promise it's safe." He held out his hand to help her if she needed.

She fisted her hands at her sides. "Do you promise to sacrifice yourself if they turn into baby chick zombies that want to devour my internal organs?"

To his credit, Eli didn't miss a beat. He crossed his heart and said, "If it buys you a few minutes of safety before they finish me off and come for you, it would be my honor."

Beth groaned. No man had the right to be this charming this early in the morning.

She took his hand and clumsily lowered herself to the grass, scooting up beside him until her hip knocked into his. *Oops.*

"This is purely for protection," she lied, explaining the lack of space between them.

"That's too bad," Eli said, twisting to face her. "Because I was going to do this."

He slid his fingers into her hair and urged her close enough to sweep his lips over hers. For the first time, Beth was grateful she couldn't find a hair tie before heading to the barn. His touch sent tingles down her spine and butterflies dancing in her belly.

"Oh," she whispered, definitely *not* feeling stood-up anymore.

"Oh," Eli repeated, then kissed her again to the soundtrack of tiny chirps and cheeps.

Beth's head swam with thoughts that had little to do with hopping on the back of a horse, until a loud squawk interrupted her fantasy.

"Ah!" she cried. Then she flinched and glanced over her shoulder to find a large white hen staring back at her from behind the chicken coop screen.

"Luuuucyy," Eli warned, brows raised.

Beth's heart hammered against her rib cage, but she wasn't sure if it was a result of Eli's kiss or another near-death experience with her poultry assailant.

"Maybe she *is* psychic," Eli continued. "And she wants to warn you about taking a chance on Midnight."

This was enough to bring Beth back to herself and her goal for the morning.

"And here I took you for a man of science." Beth stared at him, unblinking.

He sighed. "It was worth a shot at trying one last time to dissuade you." He picked up a fuzzy brown chick from his lap and held his cupped hands out to her.

Beth leaned back, holding her hands up as if to block him.

"You really want me to *hold* it? What if—"

Eli gently plopped the small creature into her lap, and the tiny chicken claws barely registered on her skin through her jeans.

She grinned, but her hands were still in the air.

"See?" Eli told her. "Not only are they harmless when they're little babies like this, but they're also pretty damned cute, aren't they?"

The little fluff ball paced excitedly from one thigh to another. Beth was so caught up in watching it that she didn't notice Eli's hands on her wrists, lowering her arms. By the time she was holding the chick, it was too late to object.

"Oh my god! Ohmygod, ohmygod, ohmygod! I'm holding it!" she exclaimed.

"You sure are," Eli said.

"And it's not poking my eyes out or eating my brain!" Beth added. She laughed as its downy soft feathers tickled her skin.

"Nope." He nudged her knee with his own, careful not to jostle the rest of the chicks piled in his lap. "Maybe *wild* animal instinct is not to identify you as the enemy after all. If *you* don't see yourself as the bad guy, chances are they won't either."

Beth lifted the small creature in front of her face so they were eye to eye.

"Tweet," Beth spoke softly.

"*Chirp,*" the chick replied.

She gasped, a strange warmth pulsing through her. "Is this why you do what you do?" The question was for Eli, but her gaze stayed fixed on the chick. "Because of how good it feels when they actually like you?"

Eli chuckled, and out of the corner of her eye, she caught him lifting one of his chicks just like she had.

"I like 'em…the animals, I mean. And sure, I get attached to some…"

"Like Frederick?" she asked hesitantly.

"Like Frederick," Eli admitted. "But it's not about the affection," he continued. "That's just an added perk, I guess."

She turned her gaze to him. "Perk to what?"

He kept his eyes trained on the chick. "To animals being easier to be around than people."

Something in her heart tugged, or maybe the feeling was more of a reach.

"You don't really believe that, do you?" Beth bumped her elbow against his.

"Have you seen me around town when you're not at work?"

Her brows drew together. "Well…no, but I've heard you go to the tavern every now and then." She squeezed her eyes shut, having inadvertently admitted she'd been asking around about him.

"Because everyone there lets me enjoy a pint in peace. My barstool is like sacred ground."

"And you're great with your patients and their owners. You have dinner parties with Delaney and Sam. And...and there's Boone."

He let out a soft laugh and finally turned to face her.

"You just listed people I either have to interact with because of work or because we're related. Two friends I've known for a few years basically because I do pro bono work for Delaney's shelter, my brother, plus my patients and their humans." He leaned closer and whispered. "The animals aren't big fans of being owned. Especially the cats."

Beth snorted, then resisted the urge to cover her mouth so she didn't accidentally eat a live chick. "You're funny and charming and..."

And a little too easy on the eyes.

"And what?" he asked, one brow quirked.

"And...and there's no way a species other than humans can appreciate what Dr. Eli Murphy, cowboy veterinarian extraordinaire, has to offer." She deposited her chick back into her lap and crossed her arms. "You charmed *me*, okay? There. I said what I said, and I meant it."

Okay, so he blew hot and cold and then hot again, but Eli Murphy was still undeniably attractive and charming. He couldn't turn it off if he tried.

Shit. How much did she like this guy? How much more would she like him if they continued like this?

A muscle in his jaw pulsed. "I don't know why it's so easy with you for me to..."

Beth thought they were flirting, but the pained look in his eyes said otherwise.

"To what?" she asked.

"To *be*. With you it's easy to just *be*."

She cupped his face in her palms and answered her own question in her head.

How much did Beth like him? She was already in too deep to even think about walking away.

Shit.

"Then *be*," she told him.

She kissed him, feeling the tension leave his body as she did.

"But when you're done being," she added, her lips parting into a smile against his, "let's get the chicks back in the coop and get me on the damned horse already."

She felt him smile too.

"Five more minutes," he bargained.

"Nah," Beth replied. "Let's make it ten."

Chapter 12

ELI HADN'T MEANT TO BE LATE, NOT CONsciously at least. The chicks would have been fine if he'd waited until after Beth's riding lesson to check on them, but he knew now when he stood in front of Midnight's stall that he'd been looking for reasons to delay the inevitable—putting Beth on the back of a horse.

"Good morning again, beautiful girl," Beth said as she patted Midnight's nose.

The mare responded with a gentle snort, but Eli's gut was still tied in knots.

"Did a doctor clear you to do this?" he asked, it finally dawning on him that he may actually have a way out. "I know you think you're just sitting on the back of a horse, but riding is a weight-bearing sport for both legs, both ankles, both feet."

Beth pivoted away from the mare and turned to look at him. No, glare.

"Doctors are not in charge of me," she snapped.

Eli sighed. "Technically, when you're under a doctor's care, they *are* in charge of your health. And yes, you are your own person and are entitled to make your own decisions, but as a medical professional myself, I would like to know if you at least floated this by your surgeon or physical therapist or whatever."

Beth cleared her throat and put her hands on her hips.

Eli tried to ignore how good she looked in a plain white T-shirt and a pair of jeans, one leg rolled up above her cast, the other with a lone sneaker poking out from the slightly frayed bottom.

Think like a doctor and not like a teen with a monster crush.

"I don't need to float it by my PT because I'm not going to bear weight on my left leg. I read a few online articles and posts about amputees who ride with one leg, and the biggest issue to overcome is balance. But it's not impossible. Plus so much of dancing relies on balance, so I've got that part down." She smiled and shrugged. "So I don't need to 'float' anything"—she made sure to put finger quotes around *float* this time—"by anyone."

Eli knew he'd promised he'd do this for her. He also knew it wasn't the best idea, medically speaking.

"She needs a rider, Eli. You said it yourself."

Eli did say that. He gritted his teeth. This was Boone's doing. Boone should be here dealing with the mare himself and leaving Eli and Beth out of it. Did having a baby and wanting to be a good father really take precedent? Of course it did, but that didn't make Eli any less pissed at the position his brother had ultimately put him in.

Beth dropped her hands from her hips and then placed her palms gently on his chest. "I'm not insensitive to the fact that this whole situation is bringing up some stuff for you that you'd probably rather it didn't. But maybe this could be healing for both of us."

Midnight whinnied over her shoulder, and Beth laughed.

"Sorry!" she called to the mare. "For all *three* of us."

Eli lifted his cattleman and scrubbed his hand back and forth over his hair. Then he set the hat back on his head and sighed.

He wasn't sure how this would be healing for him, but it felt like Boone and Beth were both pushing him in the same direction, and he was losing the will to push back.

"I call the shots," he began, closing his hands around her wrists. "While we're out there, I'm your riding instructor, your doctor, and your..." He stopped himself before another word slipped out because he didn't know what the hell that word was supposed to be.

Beth pressed her lips together, holding back a grin.

"My...boss?" she asked, feigning innocence.

Eli clenched his jaw. "No." He groaned. "Yes, I'm your boss, but that's only when we're in the clinic."

She nodded and stepped closer. As he loosened his grip on her wrists, she slid her arms around his waist.

"But you're my whatever-that-word-might-be?" She tilted her head up and looked at him with such earnestness in her green eyes that he didn't know if she was mocking him or sincere.

He swallowed, his throat dry, and Beth smiled at him sweetly.

"Don't worry, cowboy. This is brand new. We don't need to name it. But if it makes you feel any better, from here on out you can be my whatever."

Whatever.

Such a throwaway word that meant nothing, yet he was hers. He hadn't been anyone's anything in the years since Tess, and until now he'd thought his work, his few close friends, and his brother had been not only enough but all that he deserved.

But maybe Beth and Midnight falling into his life on the same damned day was some sort of message from the universe. If he could give both her and the mare what they needed to heal, then maybe Eli would heal something in himself as well.

"When I said I was rusty at all this *whatever*, that was an understatement." he told her.

She nodded. "We'll figure it out together. But can we keep this just between us? For now at least? I don't want to get my sister's hopes up that I'm staying in Meadow Valley for good. We both know that we're just taking this day by day, right?"

Eli cleared his throat. "Right. Of course. I'm not a big talker anyway. No reason for me to say anything to your sister about what doesn't concern her." It didn't matter that every part of that promise caused crack after crack in his carefully constructed facade. He already knew it would hurt like hell to watch Beth leave, but he'd endured the worst a man could go through already. He'd somehow make it through. He just had to remind himself that for now, she was *his* whatever, which was already more than he ever expected.

———

With Beth by his side, Midnight had let Eli attach the lead to her halter, but when he tried to get her to follow him out of the stall, she wouldn't budge.

"What's wrong?" Beth asked.

"She's scared," he replied. "I'm not sure how she was treated by her previous owners. I only know that they found her worthless after her injury and were ready to—"

"Don't say it," she interrupted. "I don't want Midnight to hear what they were going to do to her."

"She doesn't know what we're saying." He gave a soft tug on her lead, but the horse still held her ground.

Beth petted the mare gently between the eyes, fingers brushing over her white star.

"You don't know that," she insisted. "When I talk to her, it feels like she understands. Just like I know if her snorts mean she's content or agitated."

Eli narrowed his eyes. "How is the Spence sister without the animal whispering gene suddenly a horse whisperer?"

"I'm not," she replied in the sweet affectation reserved for speaking with a beloved animal. "But somehow, I'm *her* whisperer. I can't explain it."

Eli offered her the lead.

"Wait, what are you doing?" Beth asked. "I can talk to her, but I don't know how to handle her yet."

He motioned again for her to take it. "Why don't we test that theory? Maybe you're wrong."

She stopped petting the horse and extended a hesitant hand toward the blue woven lead rope.

"I'm scared, Eli," she said softly. "This is getting real now."

On how many levels did that ring true? She could be talking about the horse, the *whatever* he and she were becoming, or even what it might mean if riding was yet another thing her injury would keep her from doing. All three scared the hell out of him too, but they had to push forward because he was so damned tired of being stuck.

"I'm here," he assured her. "Every step of the way."

Her fingers brushed his as she took hold of the

lead and he let it go. A fleeting warmth passed through him but was gone as quickly as it came.

"Come on, girl," Beth cooed softly to the mare, putting slight pressure on the lead.

Midnight still didn't budge.

"Seriously?" Beth blew out an exasperated breath. "This was supposed to be our big moment," she told the horse. "We were going to wow the cowboy over there who thinks we're clueless..." She stage-whispered to the mare: "Spoiler alert...I *am* clueless. But come *on*, girl. Show me this thing going on between us isn't all in my head, that we're actually connecting here." She pressed both hands to the sides of Midnight's nose and kissed her right on top of it. "Now let's go." Beth spoke with an unexpected yet confident authority. "It's a beautiful morning, and you're missing it."

She turned toward the opened stall door, applied pressure to the lead, and took a step forward past where Eli stood. Then another. And then one more.

Midnight followed. When Beth paused, the mare paused.

Holy shit.

Beth turned back toward Eli, her green eyes glistening with tears. *Happy* tears.

"Did I really do it?" she asked, voice breaking even as a smile bloomed across her face.

"You did it, Mighty." He nodded, then tipped his cattleman before placing it back on his head.

He watched as she continued down the row of empty stalls until she passed Cirrus. The stallion merely stuck his nose over his own gate to sniff the mare, but he paid her no mind, and Midnight did the same, seemingly spellbound by the woman leading her out of the barn.

Eli knew the feeling. He stood frozen in place, waiting for that spell to wear off. He waited for the agony as his chest would tighten. He waited for his brain to kick into gear to remind him of all the things that could go wrong. He waited for the crippling fear.

None of it came. Instead, he felt himself following Beth and Midnight's path, the anticipation building as a feeling he hadn't expected snuck up and socked him right in the gut.

Joy.

When he made it out to the sunlit arena, the two women—one human, one equine—were slowly making a loop, Beth slowed by her cast and Midnight by her own healing leg.

The way Midnight followed without so much as a shake against her lead showed the animal was not only content but also trusting of the woman in front of her.

Eli leaned against the arena fence, arms crossed and hat tilted down over his eyebrows to block the glare of the sun. He could have stood there for hours watching them, Beth smiling from ear to ear in as much awe of herself as Eli was of her. But today he would play the part of teacher, though he was pretty sure Beth and Midnight might teach him a thing or two along the way.

"Can you believe what we just did?" Beth asked as she and Midnight finally approached. "I mean, I know we're a little slow, but she let me lead her the whole way around. No questions asked. *Me*." She pressed a palm to her chest with her free hand, the other still holding the lead.

Eli nodded, pushed himself off the fence, and picked up the grooming kit he'd set out earlier before checking on the baby chicks.

"Okay," he began. "Lesson number one is grooming your horse."

Beth's expression faltered, but then her smile returned.

"Sure," she said. "So, what? I, like, brush her and then hop on? Are you going to grab the saddle while I make her all pretty?"

Eli set the grooming kit down at the fence post next to where Beth and Midnight stood.

"May I?" he asked, gesturing for the lead.

Beth handed it over, suspicion in her narrow gaze.

Eli tied off the lead around the post and gave Midnight a quick rub between the eyes. Surprisingly, she nuzzled her nose against his palm, and for a second he forgot what he was going to say.

"Eli?" Beth asked when he still hadn't turned away from the horse.

"Right," he answered, coming back to himself and pivoting to face her. "I'll walk you through using the hoof pick," he told her. "Show you where to stand to stay safe in case something spooks her and she kicks. Then we'll get to currying and using the body brush. While you're finishing up with the mane and tail, I'll grab a bucket of warm water, some sponges, and some mane and tail conditioner if we have any."

Beth's mouth fell open. "You're messing with me, right?"

Eli took his hat off his head and dropped it onto hers. Then he kissed her on the cheek.

"I think after the past couple of weeks, you know me well enough to know I'm not really into *messing* with people."

"But—" she started.

"But you've never ridden, and she hasn't had a rider since before her accident. She may trust you to take her on a little walk, but I can't just toss you up on her. You've had a couple of moments in and outside the stall, but this is where you *really* get to know her and where she gets to know you. You two make it through the next hour or two unscathed? *Then* it's time to saddle up."

Chapter 13

BETH WAS SWEATING, AND HER JEANS WERE soaked with the water Midnight shook off when she wrung the giant sponge out on her mane. Twice. Once to wet it to apply the conditioner and once to do the same to rinse it out.

According to Google, which she consulted after Midnight kept protesting the water, most horses don't mind water at all but some are not fans. Looked like she'd gotten one of the latter.

She squinted under the brim of Eli's cowboy hat, the sun high and bright now. He'd disappeared as soon as she'd listened to his short tutorial and gotten the hang of the hoof pick. To spite him for his bait and switch, she refused the stool he brought her to sit on and opted to squat instead. Despite being permitted to bear weight on her injury, her ankle ached, as did every other muscle in her body from stretching to reach Midnight's upper mane— the horse was *tall*—and squatting to deal with the lower extremities. Beth had contorted her body in ways she never had before, and regardless of the shape she thought she was in from continued barre exercises, she hurt. *Everywhere*.

Yeah, she sure showed *him*.

"I don't think he has any intention of ever letting us ride. Do you, girl?"

Midnight snorted as Beth brushed the final wet snarl from her mane.

"Yeah," Beth continued, raising her voice as she caught a glimpse of a figure approaching from the gate. "I totally agree he's being a self-righteous know-it-all who doesn't care how much we need this."

She felt Eli stride up behind her as she dropped the brush back into the bucket of grooming supplies.

"I'm guessing you're not interested in something cold to drink then," he teased over her shoulder. "Wouldn't want to seem like a know-it-all assuming you might be a little parched."

Beth straightened and swallowed, her mouth suddenly feeling like cotton.

She hesitated for a millisecond, but her thirst won out, and she whirled on him, almost knocking the mason jar out of his hand.

Lemonade sloshed over the lip of the jar. Beth licked her lips and reached for it, but Eli brought it to his own mouth instead.

Beth's jaw dropped, and Eli barked out a laugh.

"Oh, so you *do* want—" he started, but Beth's greedy hands snatched the jar out of his grasp. To Eli's credit, he didn't actually resist.

She guzzled the entire jar, not stopping to breathe for fear he might snatch it right back and finish it off.

When she finished, she found him pulling a huge chunk of carrot out of his pocket and offering it to Midnight. The mare accepted and gently took it from his palm.

"She trusts me more now that she saw you take the lemonade." He was still facing the horse as he spoke, stroking the white star between her eyes, the spot Beth was starting to think was her favorite. "Of course, *she* has better manners."

Beth scoffed. "Look at me, Eli! I'm hot, I'm a mess, I hurt *everywhere*, and you promised me I'd ride. But instead, you put me to work." She whimpered, actual tears filling her eyes.

He did look at her, brow furrowed as he sized her up.

"A horse should always be groomed before and after a ride. It's good for her coat and for the relationship between her and her rider."

Beth's throat tightened. "So if I *do* ride, I have to do this all over again when we're done?"

The corner of Eli's mouth twitched, but other than that, his expression remained impassive. "Well, yeah," he said. "But for most folks, it only takes about ten or twenty minutes, which is good because some horses like a good roll in the dirt after a long ride. It's like getting a full body scratch.

But then it's up to the rider to brush all that dirt out. You'll get the hang of it. The sponge bath and mane conditioning can be cut down to just once a week, but I wanted you to get a feel for the whole process."

Ten or twenty *minutes*? Get a feel for the *whole* process? Beth had been out there for at least two hours.

She stared at him, mouth hanging open. He grabbed the empty mason jar and set it on the ground. When he straightened, he tilted her hat so she had no choice but to meet his beautiful blue-eyed gaze.

"Where does it hurt?" he asked.

Beth clamped her jaw shut, crossed her arms, and lifted her chin.

"I believe I said *everywhere*."

Eli laughed softly. "Like here?" He kissed the tip of her defiant chin, and despite the heat, chills ran down her spine.

"Yeah," she sighed. "I guess it hurts there...a little."

He moved on to her neck, whispering as he peppered her skin with feather-soft brushes of his lips. "And here?"

She squeaked out a breathy "Yes," and Eli kissed another trail to her ear, nipping at her lobe. Beth held her breath.

"Too much to go for your first ride? Because I

pulled all her tack. You did such a good job that we just need to let her get a quick drink of water, and then we can saddle up and go."

She leaned back and grabbed him by the shoulders, heart hammering in her chest.

"Really?" her voice trembled. "You're not messing with me or tricking me into cleaning out her stall or something like that?"

If someone had asked Beth a month ago if she wanted to hop on the back of a horse, she'd have had some pretty choice words in response, none of them approaching the affirmative. But the prospect of hopping on Midnight's back somehow felt right, like the rightest thing she'd thought of doing in a really long time.

Eli nodded. The corner of his mouth quirked into what was getting to be—for Beth at least—a heart-stopping grin.

"Yes, really. And no, I'm not tricking you. Like I said, *not* a tricker or messer or whatever you want to call it. I'm gonna make Boone clean out the stall this week, hers *and* Cirrus's."

She glanced down at her dirt- and sweat-stained T-shirt, at her damp jeans.

"I look like that character from Peanuts who's always walking around in a cloud of dirt."

Eli shook his head and gave her hat a playful twist back and forth on her head.

"You look like a cowgirl who trusts her horse,

and that mare most definitely trusts you. Only thing to find out now is how she feels bearing some extra weight on *her* bum leg, but something tells me once she realizes it's you, she'll be ready to give it a go. You're her rider, Beth. For whatever reason, on that very first day you met, she chose you and you chose her."

Beth threw her arms around his neck and rose on the tippiest tip of her right toes, pulling him into a tight yet decidedly off-balance hug.

For a long moment, she simply held him until she worked up the nerve to speak.

"I choose you too, Eli," she whispered in his ear, even though those five words scared her far more than saddling up and finally embarking on her first ride.

————

For two weeks, Beth had risen at dawn to have her time alone with Midnight, making a ritual of grooming the mare—which Beth had whittled down to ten minutes—and leading her around the arena. And for two weeks, Eli showed up in the tack room with a thermos of coffee and two mugs, sharing a quiet moment before he helped her into the saddle and watched her learn to balance with one foot in one stirrup, watched Midnight learn to carry a rider despite her own uneven gait, until they both no longer needed Eli to walk beside them as they made loop after loop along the trodden path.

Except on *this* morning, Beth barely made it out of the guesthouse's front door without barreling into her sister.

"Lanes!" she shouted, stopping short as her sister stumbled back, raising both hands in the air so as not to spill the two coffee tumblers she was holding. "What are you doing here?"

Delaney stood frozen for several seconds, looked above her at the still right-side-up tumblers, and finally lowered her arms.

"Here." Delaney handed her sister one of the coffee cups. "An Americano with steamed almond milk and salted caramel syrup. You're welcome."

Beth's eyes widened, and a smile spread across her face. She hadn't minded Eli's drip coffee with the basic fixings, plain old milk and sugar, though she avoided the former. But this was a treat.

"You remembered? Even the almond milk?" Beth carefully unscrewed the lid and breathed in the bittersweet aroma.

Delaney raised her brows. "You think I'd forget that my baby sister gets a little gassy if she has too much lactose?"

"Shhh!" Beth hissed, then ushered her sister inside. "That happened, like, *once*. I just think the almond milk tastes better."

"Mm-hmm," Delaney replied, striding past Beth and into the house.

Beth screwed the lid back on to her tumbler and followed her sister back in, hoping she'd still have time alone with Midnight once Delaney got on her way.

"While the coffee is much appreciated, you still haven't explained why you're here so early on a Saturday morning."

Delaney stood at the breakfast bar portion of the counter, sipping from her own tumbler.

"Sam took Nolan to his Saturday morning coffee thing with the boys at Trudy's bookstore, and I figured you needed a ride to your appointment if Eli was joining them."

Beth's brows drew together. "Eli's where?" She glanced toward the front door where the clinic and Eli's home lay beyond. "And what appointment?"

Her stomach was in knots before Delaney responded.

Her sister waved her off. "Something about getting Eli to join their little boys' club. Honestly, I have no idea what they do other than drink coffee and knit these atrocious scarves, but Sam hasn't missed a Saturday since Nolan was born. And the appointment"—Delaney bopped her sister on the nose with the tip of her index finger—"is the one you tried to cancel. You know...the one where you get to ditch that air cast for an actual shoe. Ring any bells?"

Beth's mouth fell open, and her cheeks burned

with heat. "How did you… I mean, I *did* cancel. I left a voicemail, so I don't understand…"

Delaney sighed. She unclasped Beth's hands from her tumbler and held them gently in her own. "The orthopedist's office responded to your voicemail by calling back to confirm the cancellation. Looks like they called your emergency contact instead of you. So of course I told them it was a mistake and that we'd be there at eight sharp!"

Beth's jaw clenched as anger began to replace her surprise. "That wasn't your decision to make, Lanes."

Delaney squeezed her sister's hands. "It's okay to be scared, Bethy. But you don't have to be scared alone."

Beth yanked her hands out of Delaney's. "I'm not scared. I'm… I'm still in pain, so that obviously means I should wear the boot for a little while longer."

She wanted to storm away, but where could she go other than the one bedroom or back out the front door again? Delaney had no right to make this decision for her. It was Beth's injury, Beth's medical care, and Beth's choice to wait—or put it off indefinitely.

Beth crossed her arms over her chest and stared down at the now-familiar accessory that had been a part of her life since her surgery eight weeks ago.

"Bethy…" Delaney said gently. "I spoke to the doctor. You could do *more* damage if you keep the cast on longer than necessary. Your range of motion might be drastically reduced if you don't start the next phase of physical therapy. And walking—"

"I know!" Beth blurted, heart hammering and the threat of tears stinging her eyes. "You don't think I *know* all that?" She blew out a shaky breath. "Me and my big words. *I'm going to make a full recovery. I'm going to get a second chance at that audition. I'm going to do all the things I did before despite doctors and therapists and their stupid professional opinions and—*"

"Opinions!" Delaney interrupted. "Opinions, Bethy. No one knows anything for sure, so the best they can do is make the most educated guess. But if you don't even *try* to do all those things you said you can do?" She shrugged. "That has nothing to do with the doctors and everything to do with you. So shut down this damned pity party, and show those silly doctors and therapists who best knows *you* and what you're capable of."

Beth pressed her lips together and nodded. "*I* know me best," she told her sister, albeit with a trembling voice.

Delaney rolled her eyes. "You expect me to believe that?"

Beth threw her hands in the air. "You never believed me in the first place. You've always been on the doctor's side."

Her sister shrugged. "It's just another stupid opinion. Make me believe otherwise."

"*I* know me best," Beth repeated, only slightly louder and with her arms crossed over her chest.

Delaney scoffed and pressed her hands to her hips. "I'm not gullible enough to believe that."

"*I* know me best!" Beth raised her voice.

"What?" her sister asked, holding a hand to her ear.

"I know me *best*!" Beth shouted this time, changing her emphasis to the last word. "I know me best! I know me best! I know me best! Okay? Are you happy now?"

Beth's chest heaved, but the unbearable pressure of *what if* began to lessen, if only for the time being.

"Do you feel better?" Delaney raised her brows.

Beth nodded, still out of breath.

"Are you still scared?" her sister added.

Beth nodded again.

"Good. It's a scary thing to go through. But, Bethy…" Delaney pressed her palms to her baby sister's cheeks. "You are *you* whether you're onstage doing a kick line, running Eli's clinic like the impeccably scheduled ship you've turned it into, or riding Midnight." She shook her head with a laugh. "I swear the last thing I expected when I lured you to Meadow Valley was to see you on the back of a horse, but you always surprise me. And I know you will again."

Beth exhaled a long, steadying breath. "I need to check on Midnight before we leave," she told Delaney.

Her sister glanced at the clock above her head in the kitchen. "We've got time." Delaney lifted her tumbler. "Coffee first. Check on Midnight. Then show the doctor who's boss." She shrugged. "And if you're *really* good, I'll even take you out with the girls for an adult beverage tonight. I hear Boone makes a pretty fabulous virgin daiquiri."

Beth laughed, and her shoulders relaxed as she lifted her own coffee to her lips. She took a long overdue first sip and smiled as her taste buds awoke to the familiar sweetness of the caramel-flavored syrup.

"Are you disappointed Eli's not joining us?" her sister asked, a knowing look in her eye.

Beth scoffed in protest. "Why would I want my boss and landlord to go to the doctor with us?" Because as far as Delaney knew, that was all Eli was to her.

"Oh, Bethy," Delaney replied. "Did you learn that scoff from me? We both know it's my biggest tell when I'm lying." When Beth didn't respond, her sister simply tapped the bottoms of their tumblers together and said, "Cheers, little sis. Everything changes today."

Chapter 14

ELI STARED TRUDY DAVIS RIGHT IN THE EYE AND shook his head. "I can't believe you lied about a new puppy."

Trudy waved him off and slid a to-go cup across the café counter of her bookshop, Storyland.

"I didn't order anything," Eli continued.

"Café rules!" Boone called from the table over Eli's shoulder where he sat with Sam Callahan, Sam's brother Ben, and their buddies Colt and Carter. "We get the place to ourselves from seven to nine until the shop opens, and Trudy gets to try out whatever new caffeinated concoction she's got brewing." Boone pointed at the Stetson on his own head and then nodded toward the similar one that Eli wore. "Glad you remembered the dress code too."

Remembered the dress code? Eli hadn't remembered shit other than dressing for another morning at the barn with Beth. Whatever dress code Boone thought Eli was abiding by, Eli did so against his own free will.

He lifted the cup and took a whiff of the steam pouring from the small spout. "Smells sweet," he grumbled. "I don't like sweet."

Trudy laughed and then shooed him toward the table of men he was meant to join.

"Go on. Boone said he's been trying to get you here for weeks, so I agreed to give you a little nudge. It's not like you had anything else planned this early on a Saturday, right?"

Eli sighed, thinking of Beth alone in the arena with no one to help her onto Midnight's back. He should at least text her that he'd been kidnapped—or lured to the kidnapping site by a willing accomplice he used to trust.

He begrudgingly accepted Trudy's coffee. "Thanks, I guess," he told her and then spun toward the real culprits, his brother and the rest of the lot. "Don't you all have wives and children to spend your weekends with?" he asked accusingly.

Boone didn't bother to look up from whatever monstrosity he was weaving together with two long wooden knitting needles. "Casey gets up with Kara on Saturdays so I can come here, and Sundays I take the early shift so Casey can sleep in."

"Nolan spends Friday nights at the ranch with our mom," Sam added, nudging his brother Ben with his elbow but continuing with an equally hideous design on his own knitting needles. "And Delaney's taking Beth to her doctor's appointment."

"Right," Eli lied. "Her doctor's appointment."

What appointment? Was Beth okay? How did he ask without sounding overly concerned? Wait, he couldn't ask, not now that he'd just made it sound like he knew what the hell was going on. Which he didn't.

Ben at least had the decency to look up and offer Eli one of those bro nods. "Charlotte and I don't have kids yet, and she works Saturday mornings anyway."

"Jenna and our kiddos help with the Saturday morning breakfast run at the ranch," Colt said, referring to his wife and the two teens they were currently fostering.

Finally, Carter looked up from the scarf or blanket or whatever he was working on, but Eli cut him off before he could speak.

"Yeah, yeah. I know. Ivy's not due for another few months."

He finally gave up and strode toward the three small tables pushed together and the empty chair that had apparently been waiting for him.

Eli sat down across from his brother and set his coffee cup next to two knitting needles and a ball of blue yarn.

"What are you all even making?" Eli asked. "And *why*?"

"Nothing," they all said, not quite in unison.

"It's not about the destination…" Boone began, and Eli groaned.

"If you even so much as finish that aphorism, let alone spout one more, I might have to figure out what else these needles can do."

Boone finally met his brother's eyes, holding his needles up in some semblance of surrender.

"We both know you're not a man of violence, but on the off chance that you really are *that* pissed at me, can we call a truce?" Boone asked.

Eli crossed his arms and leaned back in his chair with a groan. "Fine," he responded. "How long am I being held prisoner?"

He knew he was grumpier than he should have been, but Eli was a man of structure and routine. Now that he and Beth had found a rhythm that seemed to be working, he wasn't really a fan of the routine being broken without his consent.

The other men glanced up from their projects with raised brows, looking equally curious for Boone's response.

"This one's Instagram-worthy!" Trudy called from behind the counter, and Eli caught her lowering her phone, which had evidently just captured the moment of *Eli's* capture.

Boone blew out a breath and set his needles and yarn on the table. "We're here until nine. Sometimes we stay past the store opening if we're really going strong. But for you, big bro, I'll give a one-time offer of one hour. Sixty tiny little minutes, and if you're still pissed to be hanging with a few buddies who like to enjoy a little coffee, contemplation, and really ugly scarves, then you're free to go."

Eli glanced around the table at the five other men

who seemed perfectly content to simply be at this table with their too-sweet coffees, their hats that looked ridiculous indoors, their piles of yarn…and each other. This wasn't the tavern where he could sit at the bar with his back to the rest of the world, nursing a beer and disappearing into his own head. If he stayed for even as little as ten minutes, it felt like agreeing to giving up the solitude he'd so grown to enjoy.

Okay, maybe not *enjoy* but *expect*. Comfort came with what was expected.

Sam, who sat to Eli's right, clapped him on the shoulder.

"It's not as bad as it looks," Sam told him. "And one added perk is you don't have my wife trying to set you up with her little sister."

Eli coughed. He tapped his chest and cleared his throat. "Wrong pipe." He picked up his coffee and nodded at the supposed culprit, though he was pretty sure everyone knew he hadn't yet taken a sip.

Sam grabbed the ball of blue yarn and wooden needles in front of Eli. "Come on. I'll get you started."

"What the hell am I making?" Eli asked.

Sam glanced at him with his brows raised.

Eli shook his head and couldn't help but laugh. "Right. It's not about the destination."

Four hours and three salted caramel white choco-
late mochas later (Eli needed the caffeine), Eli had
silently knit the ugliest, most lopsided...*what*? He
couldn't even call it a scarf because that would be
insulting to scarves. But he'd made *something*. He'd
kept his hands busy, his brain focused on his busy
hands, and his ears trained on the conversation
going on around him.

Kara was suddenly doing what Boone called
reverse cycling, which meant she slept all day and
was up all night. He and Casey had been trying to
get her back on track for the past week and were
both exhausted.

"You should talk to Charlotte about that at your
next visit," Ben told him, referring to his pediatrician wife. "I swear I've heard her talk about that
happening with other patients. I bet she has a trick
or two she might be able to share."

Carter and his wife, Ivy, had been working
on her birthing plan. She had the whole delivery
planned out exactly how she wanted it to go, and
Carter couldn't bring himself to tell her how many
babies he or someone else from his company at the
fire station had delivered in barns or on the side of
the road in the back of a truck for parents whose
offspring decided they didn't give a shit about their
plans.

"I sure as hell hope Delaney didn't *plan* to grab
my hand with hulk-like strength and growl during

a contraction, '*You did this to me*,'" Sam joked, but Eli was pretty sure he saw a glimmer of relived fear in the man's eyes.

They all talked like that on and off, periods of verbose conversation followed by stretches of quiet contemplation, all the while the five of them *enjoying the journey* despite the result of their yarn and needles when all was said and done.

Everyone else had filed out in the last half hour or so, leaving just Eli, Boone, and a few actual paying customers in the café.

"It grows on you, doesn't it?" Boone asked, and Eli realized he was still concentrating on his needles, his brows furrowed.

"Not exactly," he replied. "I just feel like...I mean, I perform surgeries on everything from rabbits to Great Danes on a weekly basis. Shouldn't I be better at this than the rest of you a-holes?"

Boone laughed. He reached across the table and grabbed Eli's needles, forcing him to look up.

"It *grows* on you," Eli's brother repeated. "Coming out of hiding for a bit... Am I right?"

Eli sighed. "I guess you know a little about that, huh?" Sometimes Eli forgot that before Boone and Casey reconciled, they'd been estranged since they graduated high school. And that estrangement had cut Boone Murphy off from much of the town, so much so that he once tried to leave it.

"Look," Boone said. "You don't ever have to do

this again. I thought it was just as batshit before I understood it."

Eli brought his coffee cup to his lips and tilted his head back, actual disappointment rushing through him when he realized it was empty. "Understood what?" he asked, setting the cup back down with a sigh.

Boone tapped his own temple. "That sometimes it helps to either get what's in here *out* or to at least focus on something other than whatever it is you're not ready to say." He raised the hours-long trail of stitches he'd been knitting since before Eli even sat down and lifted his brows. "That's all this is, big bro. A diversion? A solution? Maybe something else? Whatever it is, it's been working for the five of us. Thought it might work for you too."

Which begged the question of what Boone thought the problem was that Eli needed to solve. But it was already after eleven, and Eli wasn't sure he was ready to ask.

"Hey. I thought I was supposed to be the wise older brother imparting all my knowledge to *you*," he offered instead.

Boone gave him a self-satisfied grin. "Does this mean you'll be back next week?"

"It means I'll think about it," Eli told him.

"That's not nothin'," Boone replied, crossing his arms and leaning back in his chair. "So I'll take it."

Boone's words kept circling in Eli's head the whole ride home. Actually, it was one word he couldn't let go of—diversion. Was that what this thing was for him with Beth? Was that what *he* was for her?

He wasn't sure why he was trying to define it when whatever *it* was would end the moment she left Meadow Valley. But he was a thirty-six-year-old grown-ass adult, so he supposed he thought more like one than he used to.

He laughed softly to himself as he put his truck in park in front of the clinic, and then he just full on stared. Because there was Beth on Midnight's back, galloping around the arena, both boots in the stirrups.

"What the…"

Eli had given Beth the alarm code to Midnight's stall for her Saturday morning groomings, but she always waited for him to help tack up the mare and get her safely in the saddle. This was so not part of the deal. Yet he couldn't help but marvel at the sight, even as he hopped out of the truck and strode toward the fenced-in arena with every intent to put a swift end to the whole thing.

Except he didn't have to because as soon as he made it to the fence, she caught his eye and slowed the mare to a trot, then a slow walk, and finally a complete stop right in front of him like she'd done it every day of her life.

"Before you go off the deep end..." Beth started, calling down to him from Midnight's back, but Eli shook his head.

"We had a deal, Beth." His words came out hoarse, his throat suddenly dry.

"You weren't here," she added calmly, and he could tell that she was keenly aware of how her emotions affected the large, powerful animal she rode. "And you didn't call or text, so I did what I wanted. I did what I knew I could."

He tried to find the same measured speech, but his heart thumped erratically as he found himself tangled in a mix of awe, dread, and anger, not sure which emotion, if any, he was actually allowed to feel.

Eli cleared his throat and forced his words to come out even, remembering what happened the last time he lost his cool in front of both Midnight and Beth. "I was kidnapped...sort of. And Sam said you were with your sister, so I didn't..." He sighed. "Okay, maybe I should have..." Now he groaned, and Midnight shook her head, taking a couple of steps back. He held up his hands and backed his own couple of steps away from the fence. "I thought I'd be back before you got home. I guess time got away from me." Then he remembered that he wasn't the only one who forgot to communicate. "And it's not like you made any mention of a doctor's appointment." He pinched the bridge of his nose, groaning softly at how childish he knew he sounded.

Beth soothingly stroked Midnight's neck, whispered something into her ear, then hopped down to the ground and tied the mare off on the fence post. His city girl was suddenly a goddamn cowgirl, and he somehow missed it happening right under his nose.

"Well, Dr. Eli Murphy," she began, striding toward the fence and then climbing onto it, swinging her denim-clad legs over the top so her riding boots (when did she get riding boots?) pointed right at him. "Were you worried about me?"

He looked past the boots and the stolen cattleman on her head and finally saw it. Or rather *didn't* see it. The walking cast.

"Your doctor's appointment was to get rid of the cast." It was a statement, not a question. "Why didn't you tell me?"

Beth's chest rose and fell as she seemed to think about her answer. Finally, she shrugged. "Because I had canceled the appointment. I wasn't going to go. Long story short is my sister found out and kept me on the books, then only let me know this morning before pushing my scared little booty out the door." She glanced down at the ground and then back at him. "It's not as high as the horse, but it's a bit more awkward to dismount. Don't think I thought much past how cool I might look if I actually *managed* the whole fence-climbing situation."

Eli bit back a grin, then obliged her indirect request for an assist.

He lifted her off and gently set her feet on the ground, but instead of letting go, his hands stayed pressed to her hips.

"Sounds like you got kidnapped too, huh?" he asked softly.

Beth looked up at him and nodded.

"Why weren't you going to go?" he added.

She pressed her palms to his chest, and he could feel his heartbeat against them, no longer erratic but now calm and steady.

"I thought it was about my career, about the doctor's predictions for my recovery. And it still is. I have a long road ahead if I'm going to make it to next spring's auditions. But I realize now it's more than that."

"Like what?" Eli asked, then held his breath.

Beth took off his hat and pressed it down over his hair. Then she banged her head lightly against his chest. "Like how much this is going to hurt when it ends."

When it ends. Not *if.* Of course not if. Her life and everything she'd been working toward up until a couple of months ago were in New York City. She said it herself that she'd never had time for a real relationship before. Eli wasn't foolish enough to think that either of them could somehow make long distance work.

He could either dwell on the facts or make the best of them. So he hooked a finger under her chin and tilted her head up so her eyes met his.

"Then let's do what we can with the time we have left," he told her before dipping his head and pressing his lips to hers.

She wrapped her arms around him and squeezed him tight, and Eli wondered if he could freeze not the moment but the memory of how he felt in it, something he could recall months or years down the road. He wasn't prepared to lose Tess, and though a part of him would always love her, it was getting harder and harder to recall what that love felt like when he was in it.

Not that this *whatever* was love. After only a month? Not possible. Was it?

The answer didn't matter. All that mattered was knowing his impending loss and figuring out how to bottle up this feeling, *whatever* it was.

"Then I have a request," Beth whispered when they both came up for air.

"Anything, Mighty Dancer," he replied without considering the repercussions.

He should have.

Chapter 15

"It's all about getting back on the horse, right?" Beth asked, hoping he didn't hear the tremor in her voice.

The two of them stared at Cirrus quietly munching hay in his stall.

"Sure," Eli replied absently. "But it's usually a less feral brand of equine."

Beth let out a nervous laugh. "We can't ride Midnight together, can we?"

Eli shook his head, eyes still on the white Arabian in the stall. "She can bear weight, but she's still favoring her healing leg. I think it's too soon to try two riders at once."

She placed a hand gently on his forearm. "Boone's been doing a great job rehabbing him, though, right?" Beth slid her hand down into his, their fingers interlocking. She gave him a reassuring squeeze.

"He trusts Boone," Eli told her. "And *only* Boone." He blew out a long breath and pivoted to face her. "I haven't told you how long it's been...have I?"

"No," she replied. And she hadn't wanted to ask, not him or anyone else in town. If he'd wanted to tell her before now, he would have. But somehow asking someone else to tell *his* story felt like a violation. So she'd buried her curiosity and waited for him to trust her. "And you don't have to," she added. "You don't have to ride either. I just thought maybe…I don't know. I'm not, like, a therapist or anything, but what's been happening with me and Midnight, it feels therapeutic somehow. Maybe it could be for you too."

He let out a nervous laugh. "First my brother and now you, huh?" He scrubbed a hand across his stubbled jaw, and Beth was taken aback by a weariness in his blue eyes she hadn't seen before.

"Forget it," she told him, taking a step back and crossing her arms over her chest. "It was a stupid idea. I'm sorry. I shouldn't have pushed. It's too soon, and…and I can't pretend to know—"

"Three years," he interrupted.

Her breath caught in her throat.

"Three years," Eli said again. "Since I lost Tess and Fury. Haven't been on the back of a horse since. And I saw a therapist. I did, for a full year. Got me through the loss, but it never got me back to riding." He shrugged, not bothering to hide the sadness or disappointment in his eyes. "Figured I was a lost cause when it came to that, so I buried that part of my life with Tess."

Beth swallowed the knot in her throat and sniffed back the threat of tears.

"I'm so sorry, Eli." But her sniffing didn't matter. The corners of both her eyes started to leak. "I shouldn't have asked. I was out of line." She was hugging her own torso now, so out of her depth with what she felt for this man, with how she ached for his loss, one she realized was the only reason she was standing here with him now.

"Hey," he said softly, striding toward her. "You didn't let me finish."

He cupped her face in his hands, and she couldn't help but marvel at how capable and strong he was, not only for the way he took care of his animals and their humans but for being vulnerable with her like this. No one had ever… *She* had never…

"Okay," she sniffled. "Finish."

"I've seen my brother ride Cirrus around that arena hundreds of times. And I've made peace with it. But when I saw you out there on Midnight—"

"You were pissed off?" she mumbled, eyes darting away from his.

He laughed, and she couldn't help but meet his gaze. She'd crossed a line, invaded his boundaries, and he was *laughing*.

"Yeah," he admitted, but his thumbs gently swiped at the damp corners of her eyes. "I was pissed. And scared. And really fucking impressed. But also something else I couldn't name until now." He kissed her forehead, then looked at her with an unexpected smile. "In the few seconds before you saw me, you looked so damned happy out there. And I hated that Midnight got to share that with you and I couldn't."

"What are you saying?" she asked. Beth felt like she was going over the edge of the steepest roller coaster she could imagine, her stomach ready to drop out beneath her.

"I'm saying…" Eli squeezed his eyes shut and blew out a long breath. "I'm saying let's ride."

———

Eli paced in front of Cirrus's stall, surprised at how easy it had been to tack him up and get him ready to ride.

"It's all about looking him in the eye and letting him know who's boss," Boone told him. "Now point the phone toward Cirrus so I can give my boy a quick lecture about how he's supposed to treat his uncle Eli."

Eli rolled his eyes, not because he was ungrateful for his brother's help with the horse but because he had to ask for it at all. Eli, Boone, and the youngest Murphy brother, Ash, used to know the property as nothing other than a horse ranch. The boys could ride before they could walk. At least that was what their father liked to say.

"Eli's something special, though," he'd tell anyone who asked as well as those who didn't.

"There's not a horse he can't whisper…not a one that won't accept him as a rider."

Until an accident cut his father's ranching and riding days short. Sure, he survived, but the Murphy boys became the Murphy men overnight. And that horse whispering Eli could do? It changed overnight as well. He just hadn't known it yet.

"Cirrus?" Boone's voice called gently from the phone screen. "Eli's one of the good ones. You know that, right? He'd never hurt you or let anything happen to you. I trust you'll do the same for him."

Cirrus whinnied and nudged his long nose against the phone.

Boone laughed. "That's right, boy. You love on my big brother just like you're slobbering up his phone right now. Deal?"

Cirrus responded with a snort…*also* on Eli's screen.

Eli wiped the screen on his jeans and turned his brother back to face him.

"I know you think he's not ready for other riders," Boone said. "And maybe I'm partly to blame for that. I've been a little overprotective since he came to us, but it's been more than a year. He sees you every day. He trusts you. And hell, you might have a little bit of salt and pepper going on in that overgrown mop of yours, but you're almost good-looking enough that he might even think you're me."

Boone winked.

Eli groaned. "Goodbye, Boone," he said flatly.

His brother's shit-eating grin softened. "I'm proud of you, big bro. This is a big step. Stop by Midtown tonight for a pint on the house." He paused and raised his brows, then added, "You really like her, huh?"

Eli's mouth fell open. Was his brother talking about the mare? Of course he was talking about the mare...right? But before he could respond, Boone winked again and then ended the call.

Eli stood there for several seconds staring at his phone's lock screen, which was still a candid photo of Tess on Fury, because who could just delete a photo of their late wife from their lock screen?

We're still on your camera roll, her voice echoed in his mind. Or was that Eli's own voice he recognized? He couldn't tell. It had been weeks since she'd talked to him at all. Why was she chiming in now?

"What if I'm starting to forget?" he asked aloud.

You don't have to remember everything.

"I *do*," he countered. "I have to remember what went wrong so it doesn't happen again."

Eli... It was her voice this time. He was sure of it. In his head, she sighed like she always did when she got frustrated with him. *Holding on to the painful stuff is only going to keep you stuck in a past you can't change.*

She'd said those exact words when he'd suggested

she pull back on riding when they started entertaining the idea of expanding their family. "Just to be safe," he'd explained.

He'd thought he was past his father's accident by then. Tess had thought otherwise.

Cirrus nudged the stall door with his nose, and Eli blinked himself back to the present.

"Right," he told the stallion. "We're really doing this."

He dropped his phone in his pocket, then lifted the hat off his head to run a hand through his "overgrown mop." Maybe he'd have to stop by Boone and Casey's so his sister-in-law could give him a trim.

Then he sighed, placed the hat back where it belonged, and opened Cirrus's door so he could lead him outside.

Beth was riding Midnight, the two slow and steady as they rounded the arena when Eli and Cirrus finally emerged.

"I stole your hat," he told her as she and the mare slowed to a stop.

Beth shook her head. "Actually, *I* was just returning what I stole." She tapped the black frame of the sunglasses she now wore and smiled. "This is more my style anyway."

Eli studied her for a moment, still amazed to see her up on the horse like she'd been born a rider. The fact that he'd tried to keep her from it because of his own damned issues made his chest ache.

"That hat suited you," he replied. "We'll just have to get you one of your own."

He gently looped the reins back over Cirrus's head so they were ready for a rider. For *him*.

"You don't have to," Beth told him, sensing his hesitation.

"Yeah," he replied, "I do." He stroked Cirrus's nose, and the stallion nuzzled into it. Eli laughed. "Guess you're more ready for a new rider than we thought you were, huh?" He turned his gaze to Beth. "It's just like riding a horse, right?"

She laughed. "I think the actual saying is *just like riding a bike.*"

Eli shook his head. "Not around here, it isn't." And before he could overthink it any more than he already had, he stuck his left boot in the stirrup and swung his right leg over Cirrus's back, landing square in the saddle as if his three-year absence never existed.

His heart pounded, and his throat tightened. The air thinned. Eli couldn't breathe. Except he *was* breathing. And Cirrus was breathing.

Being on the back of a horse *was* breathing.

"Say something, Eli." Beth's voice sounded from somewhere in the distance. "Are you okay?"

With one hand on the reins and one holding his hat in place, he closed his eyes, tilted his head toward the sun, and truly filled his lungs with oxygen for the first time in years.

When he'd had his fill... *Shit*, he wasn't sure he'd ever have his fill. But when he felt ready, he tapped Cirrus's flanks lightly with his heels, sidled up next to Midnight, and then turned his horse around so the mare and stallion were head to head, so Beth was within arm's reach.

He grabbed her hand and leaned toward her, and she did the same.

She pushed her glasses up onto her head so he could see her emerald eyes shining with tears.

"Why are you crying?" he asked. Wasn't this what she wanted?

She pressed her lips into a smile and reached a hand toward his cheek, her thumb swiping beneath his eye.

He felt the wetness spread across his skin.

"Because I think you're happy," she whispered.

He pressed his palm over her hand. "I think I am too."

He kissed her and kissed her and kissed her, Beth on her mare and he on his stallion.

Eli still wasn't sure if he believed himself deserving of this kind of happiness again in his life. But for some reason, the universe had gifted him with this woman's presence, with this moment he never would have found without her, and Eli couldn't ignore it any longer.

He was falling in love with her. Maybe he already had.

For as long as it was his, he would not waste this gift.

"Can I take you somewhere?" he asked, his lips smiling against hers.

"Anywhere," she told him. "I would go *anywhere*, Eli Murphy, as long as I was with you."

Chapter 16

BETH COULD SEE NOTHING BUT THE TRAIL, ELI and Cirrus in front of her, and trees. Lush green trees in every direction. If she'd been alone, it might have been terrifying. But she wasn't alone.

She was with a man she was never supposed to meet.

She was on the back of a horse she was never meant to ride.

And she was feeling things she'd never intended to feel.

It was too much and not enough all at the same time. She didn't know how to process it other than to simply ride through it and hope she came out on the other side.

"We're almost there!" Eli called over his shoulder. "You still with me?"

"Still with you!" she called back, hoping he mistook the tremor in her voice for a natural reaction to her speaking while riding.

But she wouldn't always be. He wouldn't always be in front of her or beside her. But he was now. And Beth wasn't about to let him out of her sight, especially since she'd be totally lost in the woods if she did.

But then there it was, a clearing. A wide-open space in the middle of the dense wood, save for one giant, gorgeous tree offering shade from the sun.

She followed Eli to the far edge of the clearing. He hopped off Cirrus and pulled two halters from a small pack attached to his saddle.

"We can tie them off to these two trees," he told her, nodding between two identical trees spaced several feet apart, each with a narrow trunk conveniently cleared of branches.

Beth climbed down more gingerly than she had back in the arena, her still-healing ankle sore from her earlier bravado. She gave Midnight's healing leg a soft stroke before leading her to one of the trees.

"You doing okay, girl?" she asked. "That was your first ride off the property. Mine too."

Midnight nudged Beth's shoulder with her nose and let loose a soft snort.

Beth laughed. "I'll take that as a yes."

"Here," Eli began, approaching Midnight with the same type of halter he'd just used for Cirrus. "Put this on over her bridle, and I'll grab the second lead. I packed longer ones so they'll have room to graze if they want."

Together they got Midnight situated at her tree, and the mare took to grazing the second they were done. Then he spun her to face what she guessed was the real reason they were here.

"*That* tree is unbelievable," Beth told him.

"Big-leaf maple," Eli responded. "You should see it when the leaves change color."

She nodded, then added, "Pretty sweet setup you got here. Like it was made for exactly what we're doing. You bring all your lady friends here?" She'd meant to tease him, but she heard the jealousy in her tone and cringed. "You know what? That sounded kinda ick. Let me rephrase."

"It's okay." Eli chuckled, then strode back toward Cirrus, producing a few final surprises from what she was beginning to think was a carpet bag stolen from Mary Poppins. He tucked a rolled-up plaid blanket under his arm and tossed her a cold can of flavored seltzer. "Hope it's one you like. I just grabbed whatever was in the mini fridge in the tack room. It likely belongs to Boone or Casey, so don't tell them it was me who pilfered their stash."

Sparkling apple.

It could have been dirt-flavored for all she cared. Her stomach still performed several backflips and somersaults when the can landed in her palm.

Eli had not only gotten on a horse for the first time in three years, but he'd pretty much planned the most romantic date she'd ever been on…and they were in the *woods*.

He spread the blanket out under the tree, tossed his can onto it, then took off his hat and offered her a dramatic bow. "It's probably a long way from the glitz and whatever that Vegas or New York has to offer, but, Ms. Spence, your table is ready."

Heat filled her cheeks and her belly. The can felt slippery against her palms. She wasn't sure if it was the condensation or her nerves. He needed to stop reading her mind like that, making it feel like he knew her more in a month than most people did in a lifetime.

"Thank you," she replied, curtsying back and then taking his offered hand.

She lowered herself onto the blanket, and Eli followed, dropping his hat on the blanket beside him.

He spared no space between them, his hip nudging hers as he leaned against the trunk that was big enough to accommodate them both.

"Cheers," he said, picking up his drink and tilting the bottom of his can toward hers.

Beth tapped her can against his. "What are we toasting to?"

He sat with one knee raised, his arm resting on it as the unopened can dangled from his fingers.

"Hmm..." he mused, staring up into the canopy of leaves. "To first rides, an amazing woman, and my super-secret childhood hideout known only to two others—Boone and Ash. So to answer your question, I bring *none* of the ladies here." His eyes met hers. "Until now."

She swallowed, realizing now the depth of her teasing question and the real truth it held.

"It's okay, Beth," he told her again. "You can ask."

"Dammit," she muttered. "You *really* have to stop reading my mind." She blew out a shaky breath, squeezed her eyes shut, then set her gaze on his. "Not Tess? She was your wife, Eli. I wouldn't be upset if... I mean, I don't expect you to shield me from the life you had before you met me."

"I'm not shielding you." He shook his head. "Okay, of course some part of me is because I want our firsts to be *ours*. I am up one hell of a creek without a paddle or compass or smartphone or any sort of manual to tell me how I'm supposed to do this." He set his can down and lowered his knee, then slid his hands beneath her calves, tugging her legs over his. "But I got in the boat or on the horse or whatever..." He groaned. "I'm *shit* at metaphors, so let me just say this the best I can. I'm *happy*. Right here. Right now. With you." He pressed a palm to her cheek, his thumb tracing an invisible line across her skin. "And as much as she liked riding, Tess hated picnics. So no, this place wasn't for her."

It was for *Beth*. For *them*.

She swallowed the knot in her throat and whispered, "I think that's a really good toast, Dr. Murphy." Then she cracked open her can, the contents exploding in a cold, apple-scented shower of fizz.

Beth yelped, and Eli swore.

On instinct, she threw the can, then sprang up to...what?

"I don't suppose you have any wet wipes or actual water in that magic bag of yours?"

Eli shook his head and laughed. "I mean, technically, sparkling water *is* water. We just smell like apples now, I guess."

He brushed his splattered T-shirt off with a nonchalance that might have been the sexiest thing she'd ever seen, especially compared to her standing with her arms stretched to either side as if she'd been slimed on a children's game show.

He rose to his feet and took a step toward her. Then he gave both of her hands a gentle nudge, and she dropped them to her sides.

"Are you cold?" he asked. "The sun might have a hard time finding us under here."

Beth glanced down at her own shirt, which leaned more toward soaked than splattered.

"No," she lied, then let out a soft laugh. "Okay. Maybe a little."

She was freezing.

Without warning, he grabbed the hem of his T-shirt and pulled it over his head.

Beth's mouth fell open as she took in his lean but defined frame and the dark dusting of hair that traveled from his belly button down to…

She swallowed. Her skin might have still been cold, but her body now radiated heat from the inside out.

"Here," Eli said, handing her the shirt as though

him standing in front of her *without* a shirt was totally and completely normal. "Take this. You have goose bumps."

Not because she was cold.

She burst out laughing, and Eli's brow furrowed. "Did I say something funny?" he asked.

"Um...no," Beth began. "But seriously? You're just going to stand there looking like...like..."

A mischievous smile played at his lips. "Like what?"

A chill ran up and down her spine, one that had nothing to do with her unfortunate can-opening incident. Every single nerve ending felt like it was simultaneously ice cold and on fire.

"You've *seen* yourself, right?" she asked. "Like, there are mirrors in your home? Because you're a beautiful specimen of a human being, and you should come with a warning label or something, okay?" She crossed her arms haughtily over her chest, wet cotton plastered against her increasingly sensitive skin.

"Beautiful?" he asked with mock confusion. "Can't say anyone's ever called me that before."

He took a step closer, close enough that she could smell *him* mixed with the part of her drink he wore. Close enough to touch him...and for him to touch her.

He was baiting her. She knew it, and he knew she knew it. He was leaving the ball in her court, letting her decide where they went from here.

"Well, you are." She jutted out her chin, trying

still to play at defiance, but what was the point in playing any longer?

Her skin begged to be touched.

Her lips demanded to be kissed.

And her heart? Her stupid, traitorous heart? It needed *him* to be the one to do it all.

"And sexy," she whispered. "God, Eli. I think I might actually explode if you don't kiss me, like, right now."

Beth didn't wait for him to react. Instead she threw her arms around him and took what she needed. And when he pressed his strong hands to her waist, his lips parting to invite her in, she knew right then and there that she was a goner, head over heels in love with this man.

They somehow made it back down onto the blanket, Eli's shirt lost in the shuffle.

She straddled him, her knees pressed against his hips as she kissed his lips, cheeks, nose, eyes, the line of his jaw. She wanted to touch and taste every inch of him, but a tiny voice in the back of her head felt the need to interrupt.

You know you're outside, right? Like, out in the world for all to see?

But could all *really* see?

"Eli?" she asked, her voice breathy as she paused in the middle of kissing his neck.

"Yeah?" His voice came out hoarse.

She stared at him, teeth grazing her bottom lip.

"Does anyone come to this spot other than you and your brothers?"

His devilish grin returned.

"No…and Boone is helping Casey's parents at the tavern this afternoon and evening."

"And your other brother? Ash?"

Eli laughed. "Wherever he is on his tour, which is nowhere near Meadow Valley, I doubt he's even awake yet."

Beth's eyes widened. "On tour? Your brother Ash is *Ash Murphy*?"

Eli groaned. "Yep."

"The country singer," she added, no longer a question.

"That would be him. You worried you chose the wrong Murphy brother now?"

All playfulness left his expression, and she hated she'd made him question how she felt, even for a second.

She rose onto her knees and pulled her wet top over her head, then quickly undid her bra and let it fall to the ground.

She heard his breath catch and couldn't believe that this beautiful man—yes, *beautiful*—could think she possibly wanted anyone on the entire planet other than him.

"Not even a little," she assured him. "I don't even like country music. Just wanted to make sure we are alone."

She lowered herself over him so they were skin to skin, chest to chest.

Eli growled, and Beth's heart pounded against him.

But she hadn't forgotten that day in his office after they said goodbye to Frederick…or the way he hightailed it out of the guesthouse soon after. Was she competing with a ghost? It shouldn't matter. He wasn't hers for the long term, so why couldn't she be satisfied with whatever he could give her while they had time?

"Eli…" Her voice cracked on the second syllable of his name. She rolled off him and onto her side, head propped on her hand. "Are you sure?" *That it's me you want?* "I don't want to be… I mean, it's okay if I'm…" *Your second choice.* Except it so wasn't okay. Beth hadn't waited this long to fall for someone only to have it be under the shadow of his first love.

"Hey." He turned to face her, rising up on one elbow and cupping her cheek in his free hand. "I got spooked that first week, but it's not what you think." He stroked her temple with his thumb. "I see *you*, Beth. Only you." He kissed her. "And yes. I'm sure."

She let loose a shaky breath and smiled.

"I'm sure too," she told him, then reached for his jeans, unbuttoning them in one swift move.

"Shit!" he hissed. "I don't have… It's not like I was planning for us to…"

This time, she was the one with mischief in her smile. "Check my back pocket."

He slid his fingers down her torso, over the swell of her backside, and into the pocket of her jeans.

His eyes widened. "Well, well, *well*, Mighty Dancer. What kind of plans did you have for today?"

Her cheeks flamed. "That's just it. I *didn't* plan. But I wanted it to happen when it was supposed to happen without anything ruining the moment."

He dipped his head and kissed the sensitive skin between her breasts.

Her stomach flipped, and her core tightened as his eyes met hers.

"My hero," he whispered. Then he produced the condom, and she snatched it from his hand.

Beth held the small packet between her teeth. She rolled Eli onto his back and unzipped his jeans, tugging them and his boxer briefs down to his boots, then removing everything and tossing it into the grass.

She opened her mouth and let the condom fall into her palm.

"Seriously, Dr. Murphy. Get yourself a full-length mirror if you don't have one already, because good *lord*, look at what we are working with here."

Eli laughed. He rose up on his elbows. "You better lose those jeans of yours and whatever you've got going on underneath *quick*."

She didn't need to be told twice. In a matter of

seconds, Beth's boots and jeans joined Eli's in the grass, and soon they were back where they'd been before she got spooked and wondered if she'd spook *him* again. Except this time there was nothing between them. No cotton. No denim. No past.

I see you, *Beth. Only you.*

"I hope you like what you see." She hadn't realized she'd spoken the words aloud until Eli answered.

"I love it," he told her. "I love what I see."

And because she didn't think she could utter another word without her voice breaking, she rolled the condom down his length and sank over him, burying him inside her.

Chapter 17

ELI RODE BACK TO THE MURPHY PROPERTY WITH Beth and Midnight beside him and the wind at their back. He couldn't remember the last time he'd been this happy. He couldn't remember a more perfect day, even after being lied to and lured into a sort of knitting-therapy-ambush kind of thing. It hadn't been on his to-do list, but it also hadn't been the worst, not that he'd admit that to Boone.

But Beth had made him take a leap he'd never intended on taking again...with riding...with *her*. He didn't want the day to end, but he was running out of options as to how to make that happen.

This thing between them, this *whatever*, it was *only* between them. So what did it matter that he wanted his tiny little world to know that he had come back to the land of the living, and it was all because of her?

They slowed to a stop at the arena, and they both hopped down off their horses to walk them through the gate.

A strange silence rang out between them as they untacked the stallion and mare and got them situated in their respective stalls. Finally, they stood outside the barn. Eli shoved his hands in his front pockets, and Beth tugged at a hair tie on her wrist.

They were naked under the maple less than an hour before, but it wasn't as if either of them knew what came next.

Beth broke the silence first. "You probably want to get inside and shower. I'm sure you have big plans tonight. It *is* Saturday after all."

He bit back a smile at the way her neck and cheeks flushed pink.

"The biggest plans," he lied. "Huge, really. See, I have this stool at the tavern where I sit by myself and make sure I give off that *Leave me the hell alone* vibe. Then I make my brother serve me pint after pint and ignore everything he says about wanting me to be happy again." He took off his hat and ran his fingers through his already disheveled hair. "Bet I sound like a great hang."

She pursed her lips, and her brow furrowed. "Hmm. Now that you mention the tavern, my sister said something about taking me out for one of Boone's famous virgin daiquiris tonight. Maybe…I don't know…since we're leaving from the same place…you could give me a ride?"

Eli crossed his arms, hat still in hand. Then he uncrossed them and crossed them again.

Beth covered her mouth with her hand and laughed.

"Do you want a *ride*, Beth? Or do you want to go Midtown Tavern—the one and only nightspot in Meadow Valley—with *me*...together?"

He didn't realize how much he wanted it to be the latter until the words left his mouth.

She stopped fidgeting with the hair tie and instead hooked a finger into the belt loop of his jeans. "Eli...I don't know how to hide this. And I don't know if I want to anymore."

That was all he needed to hear.

He dropped his hat and grabbed her by the waist, lifting her onto his hips.

She yelped with laughter, then wrapped her arms around his neck.

"What are you doing?" she asked as he lowered his hands to the backs of her thighs.

"I'm giving you a ride back to the guesthouse. This is how we travel now, from here on out." Because how the hell was he supposed to hide the way he lit up when she walked into the room? How was he supposed to look away when all he wanted to see was her? And how could he be within arm's reach and *not* touch her when after three years of sleepwalking, just the nearness of her had finally woke him up?

Beth threw her head back and laughed again. "I was thinking something more like your truck for heading into town tonight."

He shrugged. "Trucks are overrated."

"You'll hurt your back…or pull a muscle…or *something*," she argued.

He might. This wasn't the most practical mode of transportation, but it was all he could imagine right now.

Beth. Next to him. Always. Even if always didn't mean forever.

"I guess we'll deal with that when the time comes," he replied, then buried the fact that the time *would*, in fact, come. "Remind me," he continued. "Does that guesthouse of yours have a shower I might be able to borrow?"

She buried her fingers in his hair and squeezed her legs over his hips.

"It does," she whispered. "And it's big enough for *two*."

———

"Wait there," Eli said, then hopped out of the truck and came around to the passenger door. He opened it for her, and she offered him her hand, letting him help her down.

Despite her oversize green sweater and the long skirt covering her boots, she still shivered.

"I'm glad you decided on the truck," she teased. "Is it always this cold at night?" she asked, but her eyes were bright in the moonlight, and she smiled as she looked up at him.

He laughed. It was just above forty degrees. "Pretty sure it gets a hell of a lot colder in New York come wintertime."

Her smile fell.

Shit. This wasn't how they were supposed to start the night.

"Hey..." He hooked a finger under her chin. "Forget I said that. It was just small talk, right? Stupid weather small talk. It doesn't mean anything."

He grabbed her cold hand, threading her fingers with his, and squeezed.

She squeezed back.

"Are we still doing this?" he asked, his pulse quickening not only at her touch but at what it meant for both of them to walk through those doors together.

She nodded. "We're still doing this."

He closed her door, filled his lungs with the cool, crisp air, and then side by side they strode through the entrance to Meadow Valley's one and only night spot. Together.

Boone saw them first. The guy was already smiling because when was he *not* smiling these days, but Eli swore the second his brother glanced their way, it was the happiest he'd seen him yet.

Maybe Eli should have gone easier on Boone when he'd first brought Cirrus home and talked about getting the ranch up and running again. But all he could see back then was the danger in rehabbing a practically feral horse, the supposed selfishness of Boone doing it behind his back. But that same "selfish" brother now stood behind a bar with a grin Eli knew was solely for Eli.

Boone nodded at his older brother's usual seat at the bar and raised his brows.

Eli shook his head.

"Bar or table?" he asked Beth as she scanned the room.

Delaney popped up from a large booth opposite the bar and waved.

"Shit," Beth said. "I forgot to tell her I wasn't exactly meeting up with the girls tonight."

Shit. The *girls*?

Eli's palms grew damp, and the air seemed to thin.

"I'll be right back." Beth dropped his hand and smiled nervously. "I'll just tell them we're going to sit somewhere else…and then answer all their questions. I should be back sometime before… um…midnight?" She winced.

"No." Eli squared his shoulders. It was time to rip off the bandage. "I'm going with you. But first…" If there were going to be questions, they might as well answer some right here.

He slid his finger into her loose blond waves, dipped his head, and kissed her good.

Like…*really* good.

His head spun. He felt her body start to go limp and caught her by the small of her back.

She melted into him, and the fact that they had an audience completely escaped his mind...until a voice sounded in his ear.

"So, Eli...what are your intentions with my sister?"

A month ago, the whole situation would have spooked the hell out of him. Then again, a month ago, Eli never would have been in this situation.

He smiled against Beth's lips, and Beth laughed.

They broke apart to find Delaney standing to their right, hands clasped under her chin and the biggest, broadest smile spread across her face.

"And, Bethy," she added, "what are *your* intentions with my friend? With your life? Tell me you're moving to Meadow Valley permanently, and make me the happiest person on earth."

Beth narrowed her eyes at her sister. "I thought your husband and daughter were responsible for that."

Delaney shrugged. "You moving here would make me an even happier happiest person. That's a level of happy most people never achieve. Think of the good you'd be doing, Bethy!"

"I'm here now," Beth told her. "Can that be enough for tonight?"

Delaney feigned thinking hard about the request, then finally relented. "Fine. We've got one of the big booths, so there's plenty of room. Come sit down." She hooked one elbow with Beth's and the other with Eli's.

FINALLY FOUND MY COWBOY   219

"Wait." Eli held up his hands. "Don't we need drinks? What are you and the rest of the table drinking?" he asked Delaney. Then he turned his attention back to Beth. "And one virgin daiquiri?"

Delaney gave him a playful shove. "Such a gentleman, but we're all good. Casey's at the table right now for her first night 'out' since Kara was born." She made finger quotes around *out* since Casey's parents owned the tavern and Casey's childhood apartment was right upstairs. "Her parents are upstairs with Kara for a couple of hours. She's not drinking, but she's keeping *our* glasses full!"

Eli nodded. "Okay then. Back in a few." He spun toward the bar but felt a tug on his sleeve.

"Hey, cowboy?"

He heard the hint of mischief in Beth's voice before he saw the same in her gleaming green eyes.

"Yeah?" God, he loved to see her smile, especially if that smile was for him.

"Skip the daiquiri, and get me whatever you're drinking."

His eyes widened. Delaney's did too. "But everything on tap has alcohol in it," he told her.

She gave him a nervous smile. "I know. But the reality is that I don't have to be up early for a rehearsal or audition or training session or anything, really. For one night, I want to see what all the fuss is about."

Dolly Parton's "Jolene" rang out from the bar's

music system, and Delaney suddenly twirled her sister while simultaneously calling out, "Woo-hoo! I *love* this song!" And just like that, the two sisters danced their way to the table as Eli stared after them, not wanting to turn away until Beth was out of sight.

When they finally disappeared into the booth, he turned back toward the bar and strode toward his brother, who looked as if he'd been watching the entire situation unfold.

Eli hopped onto a stool and slapped his palms on the bar. "I need your help, little brother." Then he pressed the heels of his hands to his eyes.

"Looks to me like you've got this under control," Boone replied. "If she's got you back on the horse and off your sad little barstool in the corner—not to mention putting on a pretty graphic display of affection for all my *paying* customers—then I don't think you're in need of any assistance at all, my friend." He tossed a dish towel over his shoulder like a veteran bartender, despite him only filling in when Casey's parents were short-staffed.

"Really?" Eli said. "Because I'm pretty sure I'm in love with her, and she's eventually going to leave and move to the other side of the country, so now I'm just waiting for the other shoe to drop."

Boone's face grew serious, and he produced two shot glasses from below the bar top, dropping one in front of Eli and one in front of himself.

"Tequila?" Boone asked, as if there was even a question.

"Tequila," Eli replied.

Chapter 18

BETH FELT LIGHT AND FREE, LIKE NOTHING could stop her. Every time a song she loved came over the speakers, she clanked her pint glass against Eli's or Delaney's or whoever's glass she could find, and she sprang out of the booth and onto the dance floor. When Shania's "Man! I Feel Like a Woman!" came on, that was it. The whole booth joined her... the whole booth other than Eli. But every time she looked in his direction, she found him staring right back at her.

"How many have you had?" Delaney called over the music.

"Three!" Casey answered before Beth had a chance to do so herself, which was fortunate since she didn't feel much like doing math at the moment.

"Since we *got* here!" Beth added but still didn't want to do math. "How long ago was that?"

Casey laughed. "Same number of hours as beers. So hopefully you're not in too much trouble."

The three women shook their hips, waved their arms, and dominated the small but respectable dance area.

Despite the lack of choreography, it felt *good* to

dance. Beth never wanted the music to stop. She readied herself for the next party bop, but when Shania finished her last word, the tempo slowed as Elvis's "Can't Help Falling in Love" took over, and Delaney and Casey exhaled with relief.

"I'm out!" Casey declared. She glanced down and cupped each of her own breasts in her hands. "These things are about to explode, which means either Kara is due to wake up screaming, or I'm due for a good old pumping session. Have fun, ladies!"

She kissed both women on the cheek and made a beeline for the back of the bar, which Beth assumed led to the apartment upstairs.

"I need a breather too," Delaney told her.

Beth deflated but only a little. It wasn't like they could party it up to Elvis, so she began following her sister back to the booth only to stop short when she found Eli standing just outside the dance area.

Delaney smiled and gave Beth a less than subtle wink, then slinked away.

"Want to step outside for some air?" he asked. "It's getting kind of warm in here."

She'd already discarded her sweater after her first trip to the dance floor.

Beth glanced down at the tank she'd been wearing underneath, then over her shoulder at the handful of couples slow dancing as Elvis crooned.

"How about you dance with me instead?"

She'd given him a pass on her time with the girls, but this was different.

Eli smiled and gently grabbed her hand, threading his fingers through hers. "Come on. It's a clear sky. I bet there are more stars than you've ever seen in Vegas or New York."

She nodded. "And they'll still be there after this song. But Elvis only has, like, two more minutes left."

Eli's smile fell.

Oh no. Did he not know how to dance, and she was basically asking him to humiliate himself in front of the entire town?

Yeah, right. A man as coordinated as him on a horse after not riding for three years *had* to have some moves—other than the ones he displayed earlier that day in the clearing.

"Mighty Dancer..." he teased. "I'll make it worth your while." He gave her a little tug toward the door, but she still hadn't budged.

Wait.

The song. It *had* to be the song. "Can't Help Falling in Love" was the perfect wedding song. Was it his first dance with Tess?

Her stomach sank. Their perfect night—their unofficial announcement that she and Eli were, in fact, *whatever*—and the King was going to ruin everything.

Beth forced a smile. "Sure. Let's go see those

stars. I'll meet you out there. I just have to grab my sweater."

His brows drew together. "Is everything okay?"

She nodded. "Yes! *Totes*! All good here, Doc. Now get out there and find us a primo stargazing spot, okay?"

She wriggled her hand out of his and practically ran past him and back to the table.

Totes? *Primo*? She needed to get a grip and accept the fact that being with a man like Eli meant being sensitive to the fact that *she* was not the only woman in his life.

When she got to the table, she downed what was left of her pint, squared her shoulders, and grabbed her sweater from where it lay in a ball on the booth.

Delaney glared at her, slack-jawed. "What the hell?" she asked. "I barely had one sip of that!"

Beth hiccupped and glanced from the empty glass she'd just set down to her sister's incredulous stare.

"That was yours?"

"Uh…*yeah*," Delaney replied.

"So I've had…" Beth started counting on her fingers, but her math skills were even fuzzier than they were before.

"*Four*. Bethy, is everything okay? I get wanting to let loose after, like, forever. But four pints would put me under the table, and I at least have some semblance of a tolerance. But you're a sweet little newborn party girl, and I think I need to officially cut you off."

Beth nodded. She wasn't about to argue. This fuzzy feeling wasn't fun.

Fuzzy feeling. Fuzzy feeling.

The more she said the words over and over in her head, the less they sounded like actual words.

"*Bethy.*"

Beth jolted to attention, eyes locked on Delaney's.

"Yes, ma'am!" She gave her sister a salute.

Delaney climbed out of the booth. "Okay, honey. I think it's time to go. Where's Eli? I need to make sure he's okay to drive you home."

Beth sighed. "He's outside because the slow song reminded him of Tess, so he didn't want to dance with me."

"He's out there already? Shoot. We'd better hurry." Delaney pulled Beth's sweater over her head, and after a minor struggle with the sleeves that had her slowly spinning like a cat chasing its tail, Delaney guided each of Beth's hands into its respective armhole in the garment.

Then Beth's sister grabbed her by the shoulders and gave each a firm squeeze.

"Whadaryoudoing?" Beth's question came out as one long word. "Sorry...*whad*are*you*doing?" She'd meant to separate the words this time, but all she managed to do was string them closer together.

"I'm *trying* to stand you up straight." Delaney groaned. "Oh, Bethy. This is what your twenty-first birthday should have been like, *not* your thirtieth."

Beth's eyes widened, and then her lips pursed into a pout. "*You* haven't wished me a happy birthday yet." She poked her sister in the shoulder with her index finger.

This time, her sister rolled her eyes.

"Wud?" Beth asked. "I mean *wud*? Wud? *Wud*? Omigod, why can't I say *wud*?"

"Because you're buzzing, honey. *Hard.*" Delaney threw her hands in the air. "You pounded *my* beer after downing three of your own. As for the big three-oh, it's only 10:30. You have to wait another hour and twenty-eight minutes for *my* birthday wish, but if you want to stay conscious until then, you need to say bye-bye to the brewskies. *Eli*, however, didn't want to wait."

Beth blinked, and her brain decided to take a break from spinning and swimming around her head.

"Eli knows? He didn't say... I mean, I didn't tell him."

Delaney cupped Beth's cheeks in her palms. "He wanted to surprise you."

Beth's expression fell. "But I don't like surprises."

Her sister pinched the bridge of her nose. "Don't remind me. I still have nightmares about getting pepper sprayed *in my actual face.*" Delaney opened her eyes and looked at Beth again. "You won't need pepper spray for this one, okay? But how about a quick glass of water?"

She reached for one of two water glasses on their table.

Beth had the wherewithal to regret not having downed one of those before instead of her sister's pint.

"Thank you," Beth told her and grabbed the glass with two hands.

The water was delicious. How was she thirsty after so much imbibing already? Water leaked out of the corners of her mouth as she guzzled until there was nothing left to swallow.

Delaney grabbed the glass back from her and set it down on the table. "Here's hoping that was evidence of you sweating off some of the alcohol on the dance floor."

Beth winced. "I overdid it, huh?" Her tongue felt funny, as if it perhaps no longer fit in her mouth like it was supposed to, but her words sort of sounded like words again, and she took that as a good sign.

"Understatement of the century," her sister replied. "Think you can get it together before I take you outside to Eli?"

Beth squeezed her eyes shut, willing the tavern to stop tilting and right itself. She let out a long, measured exhale before opening her eyes again. Her head still felt fuzzy, but the room stilled. She tucked her hair behind her ears and smiled.

"How do I look?"

Delaney sighed. "Like you had a few too many and danced your heart out. But beautiful, Bethy. Always beautiful. And happy. You look happy."

Beth waited for her sister to insinuate this happiness was tied to a place, *this* place, and pressure her to stay. But she didn't say anything else.

Beth *was* happy. Happier than she'd been in a long time. But a strange ache in her chest began to quietly pulse. It was as if the alcohol had unlocked something she'd forgotten was there, or maybe it had unleashed something new. Either way, her happiness blurred at the edges, unable to fully come into focus.

"Okay," she finally said. "Let's go out there. I promise to act surprised."

Delaney grabbed her hand. "You'd better," she warned, "or I'm in big trouble, and I need Eli in a good mood when I tell him on Monday that we just took in a pregnant goat at the shelter who is due any day now." She tugged her sister toward the door.

"Why do you need him in a good mood for a goat delivery?" Beth asked as they made their way to the front of the bar.

"Because the last one we had bit him right in the—" A gust of wind cut her off as Delaney pushed through the tavern door, and then there was Eli, standing in his navy crewneck sweater, hands shoved into the front pockets of his jeans as he rocked back on his heels.

He grinned when he saw her, the biggest, most beautiful smile she'd ever seen on any human. It knocked her off-balance, so much so that her sister had to grab her elbow.

"Someone needs another glass of water," Delancy said under her breath.

Beth didn't bother protesting. It wasn't as if her sister needed to know that something as simple as a smile had the same effect on her as one too many pints.

"I'm *fine*," she whispered and yanked her elbow back to her side.

She expected to be accosted by a sky full of stars, but instead of looking up, her eyes were drawn to the word HAPPY written vertically in yellow neon script down the side of a lamp post to her left. The one farther down the sidewalk to her right read BIRTHDAY in blue, and even though it was all the way at the end of the block and her vision wasn't exactly as crystal clear as it usually was, she knew the last one in pink said BETH. What wasn't so clear was the figure beneath her name that flashed on and off, seemingly dancing a circle around the post.

Dancing around the post.

Her breath hitched.

"Go ahead," her sister told her. "I'll go inside and grab that second glass of water."

Beth nodded absently and moved a few paces in the direction of the far post, slowly at first but then with increasing speed as she got closer until she was almost running by the time she made it there.

At first, she could only stare at the bright-pink outline of the ballerina as she seemed to pirouette around the post. Then she reached for it, fingers brushing over the tubes of bent plastic that formed each individual outline of the dancer as she spun.

Her throat tightened, and her eyes burned.

"According to your sister, I'm early." Eli's voice sounded softly behind her. "But I wanted to be the first to wish you a happy birthday."

She spun to face him, and there he stood, backlit by the bright windows of the Meadow Valley Inn, the empty porch swing softly swaying as if it had only been vacated moments before so the two of them could have the quiet street to themselves. He looked like something out of the pages of a Meadow Valley guidebook, if such a thing existed.

Come to our town, and all this could be yours... whether you planned on it or not.

Whether you planned on him *or not.*

"You did this?" she asked him, heart in her throat. "But how? When? I didn't even tell you..." She couldn't form a complete sentence, not when she was drowning in feelings she'd never intended to feel.

She rubbed her hands together and blew into her palms. Goose bumps blanketed her flesh beneath the sweater that had only minutes ago been too warm to wear.

Eli wrapped her in his arms and pulled her to his chest, resting his chin on her head.

"I did make you fill out that temporary employee paperwork for the clinic," he reminded her. "I might have sneaked a peek at your birthday when I photocopied your driver's license."

She laughed softly and burrowed into him, wrapping her arms around his waist. "Ah, yes," she replied. "Paperwork is always the start of any epic romance. But the lights? The dancer?" She leaned back and peered up at him. "I still don't understand. You didn't know until this afternoon that we were coming here together tonight, and I don't remember you sneaking off to town before we left."

He kissed her forehead, his lips lingering for several long moments before he brought his attention back to her observation and the unasked questions within.

"I had some help from Delaney and Casey. I came up with the idea last week but needed them to execute it." He shrugged. "And if we'd shown up separately like we'd originally planned, then it would have been your gift from them only."

Her mouth fell open. "You were just going to give them credit for your idea?"

He smiled, then hooked a finger under her chin and gently urged it back into position.

"Do you like it?" Eli asked.

"Of course I do. I love it, but—"

"Does it make you happy?" he interrupted.

"Well, yeah," Beth added. "But—"

"But *what*?" He cut her off again.

She slapped a palm over his mouth, his five-o'clock shadow tickling her fingers. His eyes widened, and she waited for him to protest.

"*But…*" She hesitated. When he made no move to interrupt again, she finally finished her thought. "But I wouldn't have as much fun thanking *them* as I will thanking *you*." Beth lowered her hand.

Eli's expression was unreadable. He cleared his throat. "Turn around again…please."

Beth obliged his request, spinning in his arms and then coming to rest with her back against his chest, his hands clasped around her middle.

The ballerina continued to spin.

"I know your sister likes to lay it on thick about you staying here for *her*, but she knows where your heart is, and she believes in you."

She wrapped her hands around his. "And what do you believe?" she asked, pulse pounding, happy she didn't have to look him in the eye.

She felt his chest expand and contract, expand and contract.

"I believe… Hmm… I believe in lazy mornings outside the chicken coop…"

Beth laughed. "As long as the feral ones stay *inside*."

"I believe in doing favors for friends, even if it

means a long car ride with a woman who wants nothing more than to tear me a new one."

She bopped him against the shoulder with the back of her head.

"*Hey.* You try being duped by *your* sibling into taking care of your mental health when you're *so* not in a place to do so...which is why you have to be duped."

He responded first by nudging her head with his chin. "I *was,*" he told her. "This morning."

She sighed. "Fine. But you were kidnapped for a morning. I was kidnapped indefinitely." Though she didn't feel much like a prisoner anymore.

"I believe in long rides to secret places..." he continued.

"You didn't used to."

"I didn't...but I do now."

Because of *her.* Beth knew that, yet at the same time she couldn't believe *she* had the power to push him forward. She could feel his heart hammering against her, and her own pulse raced to match its rhythm.

He dipped his head and whispered against her ear. "And I think, maybe, I might be starting to believe in second chances."

A spark of electricity ran down her spine.

Beth's head swam, and her belly felt like it was full of kindergarten butterflies at recess.

And what do you believe? Why did she have to ask

that? Or better yet, why did every single one of his responses have to do with her?

She knew why. It was the same reason why she'd ignored her filter—or maybe she could blame that on the pints—and asked in the first place.

Her stomach flip-flopped again, or maybe it was a cartwheel, or—

Beth's hands flew over her mouth.

Oh no. Oh no, no, no, no, no, no, NO.

This was *not* happening.

"Get my sister!" Beth cried through cupped hands.

"What's wrong?" He grabbed her by the shoulders and tried to turn her around, but Beth refused to budge other than to violently wave him away with a hand she desperately needed to stay where it was.

"Go!" she pleaded. "*Please*, Eli. I'm begging you. I don't want you to see me like—"

Both hands were on her mouth again. Her eyes darted left and right, then across the street where she found the beacon calling her home.

Beth tore away from his grip and sprinted across the street. She grabbed the black steel slats of the receptacle and leaned over the rim, and under the awning of Storyland, Trudy Davis's thankfully closed bookstore, she emptied the contents of her stomach into the sidewalk trash bin.

She whimpered.

"It's okay, Bethy," Delaney's voice crooned as a hand soothingly rubbed her back.

"Oh good…" Beth's voice echoed into the mostly—*thankfully*—empty bin. "Eli didn't see that."

Delaney whisper-shouted something to someone, which meant Beth's sister was *not* the only person at the upchuck receptacle with her.

"Oh *god*…" Beth amended, still bent over the dark, gaping hole. Somehow she knew that wasn't her sister's hand on her back. "He's still here? Okay. Great. Fine. This is where I live now, I guess. You wanted me to stay in Meadow Valley, right? Well… welcome to my new home. Please forward all my mail."

Chapter 19

"ARE YOU SURE YOU'RE OKAY TAKING CARE OF her?" Delaney asked as she stared at her dozing sister in the passenger seat of Eli's truck. "She can stay with me and Sam, but her upcoming hangover will *not* appreciate Nolan's six a.m. wake-up call."

Eli nodded. "I took care of two hell-raising younger brothers when they hit their teens." He glanced over his shoulder at Beth's head propped against the window, then back at Delaney. "This is nothing compared to the shit they pulled." He scrubbed a hand across his jaw. Ash—the youngest Murphy—was still pulling it. But he was beyond the reach of Eli and Boone's help now. Beth, for the time being, was still here.

"I got her all cleaned up in the bathroom," she assured him. "Even found one of those disposable minty toothbrush things in my bag along with some diaper wipes and a linty pacifier. Promise she only used one on her teeth."

He laughed. "Thanks for the disturbing visual of the other two possibilities."

She grabbed his hand and gave it a soft squeeze. "Thank you, Eli. Not just for tonight but for everything you've done this past month—helping me get her out of Vegas, giving her a place to stay, and apparently her very own horse to ride." She smiled innocently. "And for taking a look at Gladys next week when you make your rounds at the rescue."

His brow furrowed. "Who's Gladys?"

Delaney let go of his hand and started backing away. "She's an Alpine we took in the other day." She took another step back. "She's maybe, possibly, *definitely* pregnant and due any day now."

Eli's eyes widened, and Delaney grimaced.

"Thanks in advance! You're the best!" Then she spun on her heel and ran.

Eli's hands instinctively dropped to his groin as he swore under his breath.

Grumbling about a lack of incisors still being able to cause a pretty painful pinch, he made his way back to the driver's side of the truck and climbed inside beside Beth.

She snored softly on her next exhale, and Eli forgot about his newfound fear of pregnant goats and was immediately transported back four weeks ago to the stranger in the car next to him, one moment chewing him out and the next letting him see her—voluntarily or not—at her most vulnerable.

You couldn't hide behind bravado or false confidence in your sleep. Any walls built up during waking hours came crashing down. No matter how hard you tried, bits and pieces of truth were bound to slip. The effort was exhausting, and Eli was so damned tired.

He started up the truck and shifted into drive.

Beth stirred. "I'm sorry I ruined the night," she murmured as he pulled onto the street. She hummed a sweet sigh, and her head rolled back against the window. She was out again.

Eli exhaled. He grabbed her hand and lifted it to his lips, pressing a soft kiss against her knuckles.

"Not possible," he whispered. "Couldn't even if you tried."

Of course, the second part was a lie. She'd ruin *him*. She didn't need to try. It was a simple, inevitable fact. He knew that now.

Her hand still rested in his when he rolled to a stop in between the clinic and guesthouse. His gaze volleyed from one building to the other, mimicking the back-and-forth of the competing thoughts in his head.

In the end, he never made a conscious decision. He didn't even realize where he was going until he got there, Beth's hands unclasping from around his neck as he laid her gently on his bed.

Sweat beaded her brow, so he helped her out of her sweater and then tugged her boots off her feet.

"It hurts," she whimpered, but her eyes were still closed.

"Your ankle?" he asked.

"Everything," she sighed. Her head slumped to the side.

Eli lowered her skirt so she was only in her tank top, underwear, and socks.

His chest tightened.

She was so beautiful, so mighty, so—

"Shit," he hissed, then gently removed the sock from her left foot, and she whimpered again but never opened her eyes.

The swelling was minor enough not to be an emergency but significant enough to prove she'd overdone it, all on his watch.

The rational part of Eli's brain told him that Beth was her own person who knew her limits and made her own decisions. But he was there when they rode to the clearing. He was there when she proclaimed that every new song on Boone's playlist was her favorite, which meant she and Casey and Delaney *had* to dance.

But the smile on her face when she rode Midnight like a pro or let the music fill her from head to foot? It obliterated all logic.

He clenched his jaw as he propped her foot on a pillow, his fingers brushing over the raised scar running up from her heel. Thirty seconds later, he was already back from the kitchen with two instant cold packs from his first aid kit, a tumbler of water, and a banana.

He set the water and banana on the bedside table for when she woke up, then sat on the edge of the bed next to her.

"My turn," he whispered, cradling her head and lifting it just enough to place the first pack behind her neck.

He was back on the first day they met again, lying dizzy in the dark exam room as she placed cold compresses on his forehead and neck. He was so sure Midnight's resemblance to Fury would be his undoing, yet today he'd ridden beside the very same mare, not once even thinking about the latter.

"What have you done, Mighty Dancer?" he teased. He lifted the pillow with her ankle to his lap, then wrapped the second pack around her soft, swollen skin.

She sighed, a sweet smile spreading across her lips. Her eyes fluttered open.

"This was the best birthday ever," she whispered groggily.

Eli quirked a brow. "You sure about that?"

Beth's eyes fell shut again. She pressed a palm to her forehead and shook her head.

"It might be the worst too," she croaked. "I'm *never* drinking again."

He laughed. "Everyone says that."

"Yeah, but I *mean* it," she insisted. "I never, ever, ever want to feel like this again."

Everyone said that too, but he decided not to argue.

"Or let you see me like this again," she added.

He brushed a hand over her thigh. "I'd take seeing you like this over not seeing you at all any day."

She exhaled softly.

"Except for one part," she continued, struggling to open her eyes once more. "There's one part I want to feel again."

His pulse quickened. "Which part, Mighty?"

"Loved." Beth yawned, and she began to doze again. "I think this is the birthday where I felt the most loved."

He bent over and pressed his lips to her forehead, the words escaping before he had a chance to hide them away.

"You were," he said softly. "You are."

"Me too," she murmured, and then she was out like a light, leaving Eli in the wake of an admission she'd certainly forget by morning.

———

Eli could feel someone staring at him. He didn't believe in any sort of sixth sense, and science chalked the phenomenon up to confirmation bias. But still, he *felt* someone's gaze on him. He had to blink a few times when he opened his eyes in order to adjust to the sunlight streaming in from the bedroom window. And when he did, he found himself caught in the terrifying, beady-eyed stare of a white hen.

"Jesus!" he hissed, bolting up onto his elbow. "What the—"

"Shhh," someone whispered behind him. "We're playing chicken...for lack of a better term. No way I'm losing this staring contest."

Lucy, the supposed psychic chicken, had somehow made it outside the coop and straight to Eli's window.

Had Jenna come by to collect some eggs and somehow let Lucy escape? Had *he* forgotten to lock up the coop after his most recent visit with the chicks? His property was fenced in for this exact purpose, but still, he'd have to touch base with Jenna later that morning to make sure he shouldn't be worried about anyone wandering the property who shouldn't be.

For now, he decided to roll over to face the person he *thought* was the reason for his nonexistent sixth sense.

"Hey!" Beth exclaimed. "You broke her concentration."

Eli glanced over his shoulder to see Lucy strutting away back toward the coop.

"Doesn't that mean you won?" he asked, bringing his attention back to the woman in his bed.

She beamed. "You're right! I won!" She craned her neck to look over Eli's shoulder. "Take *that*, Henzilla!"

She brought her attention back to Eli, and he quirked a brow.

"*Henzilla?*" he asked.

She gave him a one-shoulder shrug. "If the name fits." Beth's cheeks suddenly went crimson, and she pulled the bedsheet up over her nose. "I'm in your bed."

He nodded. "*I'm* in my bed."

"Correction," she continued, "I'm in your *home*."

He was well aware of this fact too.

"Why?" she added. "You've never so much as offered me a peek inside. Now I'm in your bed having a staring contest with a chicken. And this?" She reached behind her and produced the sticky note he'd left on the bedside table. "Eat and drink as soon as you wake up," she read. "I did it. I ate the banana and drank the water, and I feel almost human again. Thank you, Dr. Murphy."

He smiled. "I promised your sister I'd take care of you. Seemed easier to do it here rather than at your place." His rational brain provided the simple, matter-of-fact answer. But he was stalling.

Even with half her face covered, he could see her expression fall.

"Oh…" She deflated. "Because Delaney asked you. I was pretty awful last night, huh?"

Eli shook his head. "No." He blew out a breath. "That was my safe answer. And you know what? I've been playing it safe for years, and what the hell has it gotten me?"

Last night, he acted without thinking, without talking himself into or out of a decision. But the truth was the simplest answer of all.

"I just wanted to," he admitted. "I wanted to fall asleep with you next to me and wake up with you in the exact same place. I didn't do it for Delaney. I did it for *me*." His eyes widened at the realization. "Huh. Guess that makes me a selfish asshole. Who knew?"

She laughed, finally letting the sheet fall so he could see her smile in all its glory.

"I like selfish Eli," she told him, then rumpled his hair. "Especially with bedhead."

"And morning breath?" He could definitely use a good brushing right about now.

Her hand flew over her mouth. "Oh my god!" she cried through her fingers. "And I...I got *sick* last night."

He tugged at her wrist, but she wouldn't budge. "Delaney cleaned you up in the bathroom at the tavern."

"Fine, but I just ate a banana and washed it down with lukewarm water. That can't be a pleasant addition to whatever is going on behind my lips. I should go. I *need* to go." Beth kicked off the bedding and flew to her feet, only to wince. She glanced down, and her eyes grew wide, then she plopped back onto the bed, not facing Eli. "I messed up. I'm supposed to continue with physical therapy and building my strength *slowly*, and I messed up."

He rubbed her back. "It's okay," he told her. "It's common in overuse after an injury. It's Sunday. You don't have anywhere you need to be, so stay off it for today, keep it elevated and ice it on and off throughout the day, and you'll be good as new tomorrow."

Her shoulders sagged. "Two months, Eli. I haven't been *me* for two months, and now I'm right back where I started."

He climbed out of bed and padded into the bathroom. He splashed some water on his face and brushed his teeth. Then he grabbed an item off the counter, another from under the sink, and hid them behind his back. He headed back into the bedroom, rounding the corner to her side of the bed.

"Lie back down," he told her. "Doctor's orders."

She stared back at him with glassy green eyes, and he had to fight to keep his smile in place, to make her believe everything would be okay. She fixed the pillows behind her so she could sit up, but she didn't fight him on his request.

He sat on the edge of the bed next to her, dropping the items on the mattress behind her. She instinctively shrank back, her hand flying over her mouth again.

"No kissing!" she cried. "You got to brush your teeth. *I* didn't."

Eli sighed. "I wasn't *going* to kiss you."

She dropped her hands. "Oh."

He bit back a grin. "Don't get me wrong. I *want* to kiss you. But it seems like you have some rules when it comes to kissing in the morning, so I brought you this." He produced item number one, and Beth's eyes lit up.

"Mouthwash!" She grabbed the bottle and hugged it to her chest. "This is the best morning-after-a-drunk-birthday gift I've ever received!"

He raised his brows. "Wasn't that your first drunk birthday?"

She nodded. "And *last*."

She excitedly opened the bottle and took a swig right from it, which was what Eli hoped she would do. He just figured she might *ask* first. He should know by now to expect only the unexpected from this woman who surprised him at every turn yet claimed to hate surprises herself.

Beth happily swished the blue liquid and even tossed her head back for a quick gargle. But when she straightened, she stared at him wide-eyed. She then looked down at the open bottle, to her left and also her right.

Finally understanding, Eli reached over her shoulder and grabbed the empty water glass from her nightstand and handed it to her.

Her shoulders relaxed, and she spat the now foamy blue liquid into the glass.

"Oh my god," she began with a happy sigh. "*Now* I feel human again." She glanced down at the contents of the glass in her hand. "But…ew. That's pretty gross."

Without comment, Eli took the glass and deposited it back where it had been.

Beth straightened, then closed her eyes and puckered her soft, pink lips.

Eli felt a stirring of movement in his boxer briefs, but he couldn't give her the satisfaction just yet.

"Not yet," he teased.

She opened her eyes, and her pucker morphed into a pout.

He found the pillow he'd used to prop her foot the night before kicked to the end of the bed. He grabbed it and gently elevated the swollen ankle again. Then he produced item number two, his bathroom first aid kit.

"You know," she told him, "for someone who works primarily with animals, you're awfully good at taking care of humans."

A month ago, his inner monologue would have warred with her, claiming he didn't know the first thing about taking care of *anyone* when it truly mattered. But aside from his recollection of that contrary voice in his head, it didn't speak to him now.

"This is where you say *thank you*," she stage-whispered.

Eli laughed. "Sorry. Lost in my head for a second." He cleared his throat. "*Thank* you."

From the first aid kit, he pulled another instant

cold pack and placed it beneath her ankle on the pillow.

"*Hey…*" Beth said. "I found one of those on the bed next to my head this morning." She pointed to her right. "And there's another one on the floor." Her eyes softened when she looked at him again. She grabbed his pillow and hugged it to her chest. "Wow. You really did take care of me last night. I'm so sorry I ruined your surprise and about…" She trailed off for a moment before continuing. "I would have been out there sooner *and* been a lot less inebriated if I hadn't downed that fourth pint like it was water."

His brow furrowed. "A *fourth*?"

Beth groaned and buried her chin and part of her mouth behind the pillow. "I asked you to dance, and you didn't want to, and speaking of getting lost in your head? Mine went right to the explanation. I mean obviously that song was special to you for reasons, and I should probably be more sensitive to stuff like that, but as far as I know I've never dated a guy who has been through what you've been through, and I've never cared enough about anyone else to even ask. But I care about you, Eli. And I'm sorry if—"

"I can't dance," Eli interrupted.

For several seconds, she just stared at him.

"Wait…*what*? How? Why? I don't—you've got *moves*."

He laughed, then scrubbed a hand over his unshaved jaw. "Tess was…" He sighed. "Tess liked what she liked and did what she did. She didn't care about first dances or a big wedding…or an even bigger white dress." He shrugged. "So we did a small gathering at the tavern with immediate family and a few friends, some pizza, and plenty of beer. I suspect her insistence there not be anything even resembling a dance floor at the party was her wedding gift to me, but she denied it. Claimed it was because her dad had a bad hip, and she didn't want him to feel left out."

Beth smiled, but the expression didn't quite meet her eyes. "Sounds like she really loved you."

He nodded. "But it also means we didn't have a first dance or any sort of special song." He slid closer to her, and this time she didn't flinch. "But next time, maybe before assuming the worst and pounding an entire pint, you can just ask?"

His chest ached, no longer at the fear of forgetting who Tess was but at Beth thinking she had any less effect on him simply because she hadn't been the one in his life first.

"Really?" She lowered the pillow.

"*Really*." He gave the pillow a soft tug, and she relinquished it willingly, which he took as an invitation to move even closer, close enough to slide his fingers into her hair and cradle her head in his palm.

She nodded slowly. "Do you miss her?"

He nodded right back. "We always miss the people we lose. It's the beautiful, shitty part of being human."

"You're so evolved," she said softly, no hint of teasing in her tone.

"I guess I am," he realized out loud. When had it happened, this evolution? No one notified him. There was no certificate sent in the mail. But somewhere in the past three years—or maybe only as recently as the past month—he'd learned that he could love, lose, heal, and start over. Huh. Who knew?

"You're like a full-grown adult," Beth added. "And I'm still this kid with stars in her eyes chasing a dream that doesn't seem to want to be caught."

He leaned in and kissed her softly. "You just took a detour," he whispered. *Eli* was her detour. He knew this. Yet right here, with Beth in his bed looking at him with those glassy green eyes, he dared to hope that maybe, someday, her road might lead back to him. But for now, she was here, and he wouldn't squander the time they had.

"A detour," she repeated. "Like I got on the wrong train or something, but eventually it'll take me where I need to be, right?" She kissed him back.

"Exactly," he replied. "And for the record, you ruined *nothing* last night. Except maybe that trash can on First Street."

Her cheeks flushed, but she didn't look away. "You've seen me at my worst, and you still want to kiss me." It wasn't a question but a realization.

Eli dipped his head so his mouth was a breath away from her ear.

"I want to kiss you *always*," he whispered.

She shivered.

Eli shivered too.

A current arced between them, and when their lips touched again, he knew there was no way he and Beth were leaving the house today, let alone this room.

"Happy birthday," he told her. "In case you don't remember me saying it last night."

"It was," she replied. "I mean it *is*. Happy. This birthday is *very* happy."

Chapter 20

"WHY DOES IT SOUND LIKE YOU'RE IN A POOL?" Delaney asked.

Beth repositioned herself, and the water sloshed again. "Sorry. I'm in the bathtub, and I knew if I didn't answer, you'd be worried."

Silence rang out for a beat. Then… "At…the guesthouse?" She didn't miss the insinuation in her sister's tone.

Because she was a terrible liar, when Beth didn't offer a prompt enough reply, her sister gasped.

"You're in *Eli's* bathtub? Are you alone? Oh god, tell me you're alone and that I didn't just interrupt my baby sister having bathtub sex!"

"Shhhh!" Beth cried, though she was ninety-nine percent sure Eli still wasn't home. Just in case, though, she didn't want her…her *what*? She waved off her own thought, remembering that she and Eli never put a label on this other than *whatever*, and this wasn't the time to start thinking about what *whatever* meant.

"Oh my *god*!" Delaney whisper-shouted. "You're *not* alone!"

"I am," Beth insisted at regular volume this time.

"Eli got a phone call about work and had to run out for a bit. But he drew me a bath first. With *bubbles*."

"Put me on video so you can see my jaw on the floor. *Eli Murphy* just has bubble bath lying around the house? A house that *you're* in and I've never been in, by the way."

Beth laughed, made sure she was covered in bubbles up to her neck, and switched the call from audio to video. As promised, Delaney's camera turned on to reveal a slack-jawed stare…and something orange caked on her cheek.

"Do you have food on your face?" Beth asked.

Her sister sighed. "You're living it up in a bubble bath while I'm over here with a toddler who thinks feeding Mommy a bit of her lunch means smearing it all over Mommy's face." She rubbed the dried mush on her cheek. "Guess I missed a spot."

Beth raised her brows. "Living it *up*? Did you delete last night from your brain? I'm nursing the world's worst hangover and a swollen ankle only one day after getting my cast off. Not that it's a pain Olympics. I know you work hard, mama bear. I just feel like I took two steps back when I should be moving forward."

She wiggled her toes beneath the water, wincing when pain pinched the back of her ankle and shot up her calf.

"You overdid it on the dance floor, didn't you?"

Beth nodded. "And riding earlier that day. But,

Lanes…" A smile spread across her lips. "Riding Midnight with both feet in the stirrups, like riding her for *real*? I don't know how to describe it. The only thing I can remember that might compare is…I don't know…maybe putting on my first pair of tap shoes and dancing around the tile entry of the motel lobby while Mom and Dad played the Radio City Christmas Spectacular on the TV."

Delaney laughed. "Weren't you, like, *four*? I don't remember anything about being four, let alone how something at that age made me *feel*."

Beth shrugged. "Do you remember when you fell in love with animals? Or Sam? Or what it felt like to see Nolan after she was born?"

Delaney sighed. "Okay, okay. I get it. Important moments stick."

"Exactly," Beth replied. "And it was an important day for Midnight too, you know? Her previous owners were ready to euthanize her, and there she was, galloping off the property and through the woods like a pro! I'm so proud of her!"

A big smile spread across Delaney's face, and the hairs on the back of Beth's neck stood on end.

"What?" Beth asked.

"What do you mean, *what*?" her sister countered.

A small pile of bubbles loosed itself from her protective armor and tickled the bottom of her chin. She swatted it away with her free hand, careful not to splash water onto her phone.

"I *mean* you look like you're scheming, and I already know your schemes tend to uproot my life without my full consent."

Delaney pressed a hand to her chest, her mouth agape in feigned indignation.

"It's how I ended up here in the first place. It's how I ended up at the doctor's office yesterday. And I'm not sure how yet to pin this one on you, but just to make it a solid three, I'm sure you had something to do with me tossing my cookies into a public trash can last night."

Only now Delaney's indignation didn't look so feigned.

"Do you really see being here while you heal as a punishment?" Her sister's smile was gone.

Beth thought. She tried to pinpoint the exact moment when she *stopped* looking at Meadow Valley as a place where she was stuck but instead as simply the place she *was*. For now.

"Come on, Lanes," she teased. "You know I wasn't being serious. But this isn't my life. It's the place where I'm coddled and taken care of, whether I want to be or not." She paused and waited for her sister's smile to reappear, but it didn't. "You found your dream here, and I'm *so* happy you did. You have your shelter, an amazing husband, and the cutest little girl on the entire planet. All facts, by the way."

The corner of Delaney's mouth twitched. "She really is the cutest, right?"

Beth nodded. "But I haven't found *my* dream yet."

Despite her choice in profession—which certainly wasn't easy—she tended to take the easiest route. All she'd ever wanted was to dance onstage at Radio City Music Hall, but when she got her first job as a Vegas showgirl and started making money…as a *dancer*…it was so easy to stay put. Despite the heavy costumes and grueling hours, Beth loved what she did. Then she was suddenly twenty-nine, a full decade older than some of the youngest Rockettes. If she didn't try now, then when? And what if she'd waited too long? What if she left something good for something she thought was great, but it wasn't?

"What are you thinking?" Delaney asked, finally breaking the silence. "Your brows are all pinched."

Beth let out a long breath, not sure what she would say until the words were out of her mouth. "What if I somehow, subconsciously, sabotaged myself? Like, what if when I was running up those stairs to the stage, somewhere in the back of my head a little voice was whispering, 'If you never make it to that stage, you'll never have to know whether you're good enough or not…whether *this* is what will finally make you happy in that way where you can't imagine your life any other way. If you never make it to that stage, you'll never have to decide.'"

Beth shivered. The water in the tub was turning cold.

"Oh, Bethy," Delaney said. "It's okay to be scared of the unknown."

Beth's vision grew cloudy, and she swiped at a tear. "Shit!" she swore, because the finger she used to wipe away the tear was covered in bubbles, and now the bubbles were in her eye.

"Are you okay?" Delaney asked, and Beth stared at her with one stinging eye squeezed shut.

"I think we need to cut this heart-to-heart short," she told her big sister, because it looked like whenever Beth was on the verge of some sort of monumental moment in her life, the universe tore her Achilles, had her upchuck into a trash can, or put bubble bath in her eye. Or maybe there was no universe messing with her at all, and it was just *Beth* sabotaging the big moments so she wouldn't have to fear the outcome.

"Okay," Delaney relented. "But I'm here when you're ready to talk again. And Eli, Bethy. Eli's there for you too, if you'll let him."

More tears leaked from her closed eye, but these were from ridiculous pain and *not* anything to do with Eli Murphy being another example of the easy path she couldn't keep taking, not when there was a universe—or self-sabotage—to finally prove wrong.

She ended the call, reached for the knob that

turned on the cold water, and stuck her face directly beneath it.

A short while later, despite Eli's protestations before he'd left, Beth dressed in her clothes from the night before and limped back to the guesthouse. She changed into jeans and the Betty Boop showgirl T-shirt her sister gave her before her very first show, and just to be safe she strapped on her air cast before heading out to the barn. She wasn't going to do anything foolish. She just needed to be with someone who wouldn't ask her questions when she was clearly still searching for the answers.

She pushed her sunglasses to the top of her head, using them as a headband to keep her damp hair out of her face, and she strode through the barn door.

"Hey there, Cirrus," she cooed as the white stallion poked his nose over his stall door. She gave him a soft pat, and he nuzzled into her palm. "Guess you like me more than Ace did, huh?"

He whinnied, and she wondered if *she* had been the one to give off bad vibes to Ace in the first place. Despite her excitement to ride, at that point in time she hadn't wanted to ride any horse but Midnight, and some part of her had let Ace know.

Speaking of Midnight...

Beth found her friend lying in her bedding, catching a midday snooze.

"Mind if I join you?" she asked.

Using the app Eli downloaded to her phone, she disabled the alarm and opened the stall door.

Midnight blinked one eye open and perked up when she saw her rider. She offered Beth an affectionate snort but didn't bother standing up.

"Don't get up on my account," Beth teased, waving off the mare's nonexistent gesture.

Midnight shook her head and snorted again before resting her head back on the stall's bedding.

"You feeling okay, girl?" Beth asked, making sure her section of floor was clean enough before lowering herself to the ground. "Maybe we both overdid it yesterday."

She nestled against the mare's side so that the two of them made a T, Beth's feet extending into the opened doorway of the stall. They were a carbon copy of the first day they met, yet so much had already changed in four short weeks.

"Is it weird if I ask for your advice?" Beth began. "I know you can't answer me," she added. "Not with words at least. But maybe what I need is someone to listen while I figure it out on my own, you know?"

Midnight sighed, and she probably would have sighed whether Beth was there or not. It didn't stop Beth from insisting to herself that if *anyone* understood her, Midnight did.

So she told her about the Rockettes and her first pair of tap shoes, about never missing the Radio

City Christmas Spectacular, about her fear of failing at her dream.

"Okay," she told the mare when she finally finished spewing her entire history. "What do you think? Am I up for this one final try, or should I take what the doctor says at face value and throw in the towel before I injure myself worse? I'm just warning you, though, that if you go with option B, I don't actually have a *plan* B, so I'm kinda lost."

Her throat tightened, and she felt the horse shift beneath her. A second later, Midnight's chin rested on her shoulder. Beth couldn't help but laugh.

"Fine," she relented as Midnight nuzzled even closer to Beth's cheek. "I found *you*. But you can't be my dream." She wrapped her arm around the mare's face and gave her a pet between the eyes, right on her white star. "Will friends do for now?"

Midnight puffed a burst of air from her nostrils, making Beth's cheek slightly damp.

"Ew, girl!" she cried out as she laughed at the result of asking a horse for advice. "You ever heard the phrase 'say it, don't spray it'?"

Her equine friend whinnied, and Beth supposed the closest she might ever get to the mare speaking back to her was a cheek peppered with horse snot.

Beth wiped away the barely there mess with the hem of her T-shirt, then soon found her eyelids growing heavy. She tilted her head forward, allowing her sunglasses to fall over her eyes, then let out a long sigh before settling in for a Sunday afternoon catnap.

"No matter where I end up, I can always come back here and see you. And do stuff like this, right?"

And Eli... Would he be here for her too once she figured out the mess that was her life? Did she want him to be?

Out of all her questions, that was the only one she could answer.

Yes. Whatever my future is, I want Eli Murphy to somehow be in it.

Because the possibility of a future without dance, without Midnight, *and* without him? That was something Beth couldn't fathom, even if she had no idea how it could work.

As she drifted off, she heard a voice mention something about rehabbing Midnight and placing her in a good home. Was it Eli? She couldn't remember. All she knew was that Midnight had already found a good home, which meant placing her should be a nonissue by now.

Yes. Perfect. If and when she ever returned to Meadow Valley, she'd find it exactly as she'd left it—and the people she loved exactly where she'd left them.

And then she was out, the only sound a hushed whisper in the distance, a sound she was sure existed only in a dream.

Chapter 21

"I THINK SOMEONE WAS SNOOPING AROUND THE property," Eli said to anyone at the table who would listen.

Sam and Boone both looked up from their sorry excuses for scarves, and he took their identical wide-eyed stares as proof of their envy at only his second attempt at knitting stripes.

"You're jealous, right?" he added. "That I'm this good on only my second Saturday?"

"You know what?" Sam responded. "I don't think I give as much of a shit about your snooping issue as I thought." He turned his gaze back to his own pile of yarn.

Boone laughed. "Who knew you had such a competitive streak?" he replied. "And *I'll* ask about the snooping while Callahan pouts."

"I'm *not* pouting," Sam grumbled.

He was totally pouting.

"I don't know," Eli continued. "Last Sunday, I woke up to Lucy staring at me through my bedroom window, and I always make sure the coop is locked at night."

"I'm not entirely convinced there isn't some sort

of sorcery at play with that hen," Sam added, still grumbling.

"Jenna's *not* a witch," Colt chimed in. "At least not in the sense you're thinking. I can attest to Lucy's abilities and assure you they are hers and hers alone."

Eli chuckled, aware now that this was a common—albeit good-natured—argument between Colt and Sam.

"Yeah, but even if you believe she's psychic, Lucy can't unlock a coop with those powers or abilities or whatever, can she?" Eli was only half kidding.

"No," Colt continued. "Last I checked, she wasn't letting herself in and out of the coop."

"Okay, but there's something else."

Eli sighed and set his needles on the table. The rest of the men did the same—even Sam—and gave him their full attention.

"Later the same morning, I got a call about a potential permanent placement for Midnight, someone who happened to be in town and wanted to see if we could meet."

Boone shrugged. "Isn't that what you wanted?"

Eli nodded absently. "It was… I mean it *is*. We met at that diner by the interstate."

"The one with the burnt out *N* in the sign?" Colt asked.

"That's the one," Eli replied. "He was a young guy—"

"So not *your* age," Boone interrupted with a grin. When Eli didn't smile back, his brother at least had the decency to look chagrined.

"Last name was Doyle. He was in this nice suit, had the papers all drawn up, and I don't know... It felt too quick. I hadn't even put my feelers out yet about placing her, so how'd the guy know I had her?"

"You're the only veterinarian for miles," Sam reminded him. "Any one of your clients could have passed on the news about Midnight."

Eli crossed his arms and leaned back against his chair. "He said his buyer didn't care about her lost passport or her injury as long as she was riding like she used to again." He paused. "That *like she used to* set off a warning bell. So I took the papers home and asked for time to look them over. And this morning, when I left to come here and Beth headed out to ride, the sensor on Midnight's door was loose."

His pulse raced. The other men stared at him.

It was Fury all over again. She'd been smart enough to outrun her would-be captors, but the storm coupled with her fear had proven to be a lethal combination, for the mare and for Tess.

"Eli..." Boone began gently, and Eli abruptly pushed back from the table and stood.

"Don't, Boone," he warned.

"Don't what?" his brother asked, holding up his hands.

"Give me a little credit, will you?" Eli told him. "I don't need you to tell me that I'm looking at the situation through an already warped lens. I'm not just basing this on a gut feeling. I know what I saw, and I don't think Midnight or Cirrus or Beth are safe."

"So you left them all on the property and came here?" Sam asked, though Eli could tell he was starting to put it all together. And when Sam sighed, Eli knew he already had. "They're all at my place, aren't they?"

Eli gave his friend a crooked grin.

"Cirrus is at your ranch, but Beth wouldn't leave Midnight. She's tied up in your backyard. The *mare*...not Beth."

Boone slid his own chair from the table and stood, clapping his hands together. "I guess that settles it," he announced.

"Settles what?" Eli wasn't sure he wanted to know where this was going because obviously his brother thought this was all in his head, and Sam now had a random horse on his property, and Eli realized he was spewing his worry about the horse in question, and holy shit... What if Boone was right? What if he was regressing back into that loop of Fury and Tess and not being able to save either one of them?

"We're cutting this session early so we can up the security on the barn," Boone told him.

And without one word of protest, the rest of them started packing up their knitting gear and assigning one another tasks.

"We got an extra baby monitor as a gift when Nolan was born," Sam said. "It's not even open. It might say *Hello Baby* on it or something like that, but it's one hell of a security camera. Even has night vision. We can set it up right inside the barn."

"Carter's on call at the station," Colt said. "But I bet he's got a ladder we can borrow to install that puppy high enough that no one would notice it."

"Are she and Cirrus chipped yet?" Sam asked.

Eli scrubbed a hand across his jaw. In all the craziness of letting not just one but *two* horses back onto the property, he hadn't thought far enough into the future of them *staying* on the property and needing to chip them. Usually that was a decision made by the owner.

"Shit," he mumbled.

"He was supposed to chip Cirrus a few weeks ago, but then Trudy came in with Frederick," Boone tossed out in his brother's defense.

"I should have rescheduled you," Eli admitted.

"Don't worry about it," Sam told them. "Ben's on the property. He's trained in the procedure and has chipped every stallion and mare in our barn. He can take care of Cirrus."

And Eli would take care of Midnight when they brought her home tonight…or back to Eli's property. Her *temporary* home.

He cleared his throat. "Thanks, everyone. I—just thanks."

They started filing out of the still empty bookstore café and down the stairs, but Eli grabbed his brother's arm once Sam and Colt were out of earshot.

"You think I'm crazy, right?" Eli asked him.

Boone shrugged. "I think you give a shit about Cirrus and Midnight...and *Beth*."

Eli nodded. "And you think I'm losing my shit, right?"

Boone clapped his brother on the shoulder. "If *you* believe something's up, then *I* believe something's up, okay?"

Eli's chest tightened, and he nodded. He didn't know how to navigate this, his younger brother taking care of *him* when for all intents and purposes, Eli had been a father figure to Boone since his younger brother's teens.

He tried to form the words, to thank Boone for what Eli never knew he needed from his brother, but nothing came out of his mouth.

"I know," Boone told him instead. "I know."

A few hours later, not one but *two* night-vision baby monitor cameras were installed, the sensors on Midnight's stall door were tightened (with Eli conceding that normal wear and tear could have been the culprit), and Cirrus was chipped and surprisingly happy with the change of scenery. According to Ben, he'd even taken a liking to his horse, Loki, and the two were currently grazing on the Meadow Valley Ranch property.

So Eli, Sam, Boone, and Colt finished off the job sitting on the arena fence, each with a bottle of beer in hand.

"It's five o'clock somewhere, right?" Sam declared, raising his bottle.

"We earned it," Boone added. "Baby monitors are no joke."

"Not when you mount them fifteen feet in the air with a ten-foot power cord," Eli admitted.

"Not a fan of tall ladders, boys." Colt took a healthy swig from his bottle. "Not a fan."

Maybe Eli had gotten bent out of shape for nothing, but he wasn't complaining about this—the four of them baking in the midday heat, cold brews in their hands. For years, he felt like he'd been crawling through a fog. But somehow, when he wasn't really looking, the clouds broke and who knew? There was a goddamn sun after all.

They were only a few sips in when Colt's phone chirped with a text.

"Shit," he hissed. "Jenna's car won't start, and we need to get the girls to their dance class in Quincy."

Boone's phone went off next, but his sounded more like an alarm. "Dammit!" he added. "Casey has a client in fifteen minutes. Daddy duty starts now."

Eli turned to face Sam, who had his head tilted toward the sun as he downed several sips of his beer.

"What?" he finally asked, rubbing his forearm across his mouth.

Eli shrugged. "Just waiting for you to get *your* bat signal."

Sam laughed. "Why do you think I'm downing this thing so fast?" He shook his almost empty bottle. "Nolan's napping, and Delaney is ovulating. Gotta head home to try for baby number two. Not sure if I'm ready for another newborn in the house, but the trying part is pretty enjoyable." He winked at Eli. "Might want to come by to pick up your mare and your girl."

Eli laughed. It all felt so normal. So perfect. So what his life was supposed to be.

His mare.

His girl.

None of it made any sense, yet at the same time, it made the *most* sense.

If he kept Midnight, did that mean Beth might stay too?

"I'm right behind you, Callahan." He hopped off the fence and grabbed each man's bottle, one by one, waiting until they each drained their respective brews down to the last drop. "Let me just get these in the recycle bin, and I'll be right over."

The four of them dispersed, and he brought the bottles inside, rinsed them out, and then headed toward the large bin behind the chicken coop. But he stopped short at the coop entrance, dropping the bottles into the grass.

The sliding lock to the coop door wasn't just loose. It had been completely pried off the wooden door. The chicks were still in their brooder, but he found several of Jenna's hens strutting around the fenced-in yard, Lucy included.

One by one, he snatched them up, carrying each like a football back into the coop, trying at the same time to account for them all. But for every two hens he brought back inside, one would escape again because there was no lock on the door.

Sam was going to wonder where he was. Worse, Sam was going to want to kick his ass if he missed out on *trying* for a baby because Eli didn't make it back on time. And while Eli had never really come to blows with anyone before, he didn't want his first time to be with a buddy who boxed for fun.

Eli finally had the brilliant idea to use the recycling bin as a barricade, and chasing down only three more hens, he finally had everyone inside. Only once he was inside his truck, the adrenaline waning, did he realize that he hadn't been making something out of nothing.

Someone was nosing around his property, his *animals*.

It might have been déjà vu, but it was also real as hell, and Eli wasn't going to let shit go down again the way it had before.

Chapter 22

"You want Bethy to stay the *night*?" Delaney asked. "Like, all afternoon and evening?"

Beth glanced around the front porch from Eli to her sister to Sam—who looked like he suddenly wanted to pummel Eli—and then back at Eli again.

"Okay, first of all," Beth began, "you say that as if you just found out I have lice and you now have to de*louse* me."

Delaney scratched her head and pouted. "Do *not* remind me. I'm still traumatized by your third-grade class's lice epidemic. Come to think of it, what did Mom ever do with all those stuffed animals she quarantined in giant garbage bags? Think they're still in storage?"

"Ew!" Both women cried in unison.

"Forget it, Callahan," Delaney said to her husband. "We're skipping this cycle. Two kids double our chances of lice coming home from school. I'm not ready for that yet."

Sam winced. "We can *not* be ready and still *try*..." he reasoned.

"You can stay, Bethy!" Delaney exclaimed.

Beth turned her gaze back to Eli, suddenly

realizing the ends of his dark hair were damp with sweat, his expression pinched and strained.

"What is going on?" she asked him. "And no way I'm being used as an excuse to keep you two from getting busy." She pointed back and forth between her sister and brother-in-law. "You all upped the security at the barn, right? So it's safe for Midnight to head back home?"

Eli blew out a breath and finally looked Beth in the eye.

"I haven't told you everything about that night." He paused.

"It's okay, Eli," she told him, hoping he could hear how much she meant it. She realized now that if he truly cared for her after what she'd given him this past month—which was decidedly *not* Beth at her very best—she had nothing to worry about when it came to Eli's past. This wasn't a competition with the love he'd lost. It was *whatever*. It was *them*. And Beth and Eli were something entirely different from anything either of them had known before. Did the timing suck? Yeah. It sucked *hard*. But here they were, right now, taking on whatever came their way.

"You know what?" Delaney began. "We'll leave you two alone to chat." She looked at her watch and then at her husband. "Nolan is down for at least ninety minutes. Let's go *try*."

Sam's face lit up, and he planted a smooch on his wife's lips right there in front of everyone.

She yelped with laughter and then shushed herself.

"Come on, handsome." Delaney grabbed Sam's hand. "Put another baby in me if you can."

"Challenge accepted, my beautiful, amazing wife."

He gave her a gentle tug as he stepped back over the threshold into the house.

Delaney stage-whispered to her sister and Eli. "He says that when I *know* there are mushed carrots in my hair!"

And then they were gone, two of the happiest people Beth knew, to hopefully grow their family from three to four. Plus Scout. Plus Butch Catsidy. Plus all the animals at Delaney's shelter, including the pregnant goat whose kid was due any day now.

Now it was just Beth and Eli on the porch, the two of them not quite a family but somehow also not quite *not*.

"Let's sit," Eli said, motioning toward the top step of the porch.

He held out a hand to help her, and though she didn't need it…though her ankle felt better than it had felt in over two months, she took it and let him guide her to the ground before sitting beside her.

He blew a breath and ran a hand through his damp, dark hair.

"Fury didn't just get loose that night," he began.

His voice trembled, and his jaw clenched. Beth

couldn't tell if it was due to fear, pain, anger, or some combination of the three. All she knew was going back to that night was probably the hardest thing Eli had ever had to do, and he was doing it for her.

"It's okay," she told him. "I mean, I know it's *not* okay. But I'm here, and I'm listening, and I'll do whatever you need, if you'll let me."

She rested a gentle hand on his forearm, and he slid his arm up until her hand met his and their fingers intertwined.

She gave him a reassuring squeeze.

"There were poachers on the property. It's all still kind of a blur…Tess and I hearing Fury's distress even on top of the storm, the two of us bolting out of bed and running out in the rain. She ran after Fury, and I took off after the assholes who came to take her." He paused. "Until the loudest crash of thunder shook the goddamn ground, and I heard Tess scream."

"Oh god." Beth squeezed her eyes shut. She didn't want to put him through this. She didn't know if she could relive the night with him. "Eli, you don't have to—"

"Yeah," he interrupted before she could finish. "I *do*."

He cleared his throat, and Beth didn't know if he was looking at her or still staring straight ahead because she couldn't open her eyes until he was done.

"I don't know how I found her. It was so god-damned dark, and the rain was relentless. And I knew. I fucking knew when I got there that it was too late. I think she did too, but she kept telling me she was fine, that she'd get up in a minute but that I needed to find Fury. She'd never forgive herself if anything happened to that horse." He let out a bitter laugh. "I used to tease her that she loved Fury more than she loved me, but I didn't care. At least when it came to humans, I was her favorite in that arena."

Silence stretched out for several seconds.

"You didn't go after Fury," Beth finally guessed.

Eli cleared his throat. "I did...but not until Tess was...not until..."

He didn't have to say the rest. He didn't have to tell her that he stayed with his wife until she was gone or that when he finally got to their almost stolen mare, she was injured too severely to save.

Beth opened her eyes because who the hell was she to let him go through this again...*alone.*

Eli's eyes were red, his cheeks streaked with tears.

"Hey...Eli..." She shifted to face him, took his wet cheeks into her palms. "*None* of it was your fault. You know that, right?"

He shook his head. "I should have gone after the horse with her. She had no business trying to mount Fury bareback in a fucking storm."

"And you did? It was an impossible situation that

likely would have ended badly no matter which decision you made. But if you dwell on the what-ifs and don't find a way to forgive yourself, you'll never really be able to move on."

He cleared his throat and shook his head, effectively shaking himself free from her grip.

"I can't change what already happened. I get that. But I'm not going to fuck up like that again."

Goose bumps pricked her flesh, and Beth wrapped her arms across her chest as if she was giving herself a hug.

"What do you mean...*again*?"

He stared at her for a long moment before continuing.

Beth was officially freaked out, and he hadn't said another word yet.

Eli set his hands on her knees. "They never caught the poachers. I lost everything, and they never had to answer for it. And now? I thought I had a potential placement for Midnight, but something felt off, you know? Something about it just gave me this feeling like Midnight wasn't going to be safe if I signed the deal. So I wanted to go over the paperwork, maybe get a lawyer's eyes on it, but—"

"You found a placement for Midnight?" Beth's voice trembled, and she felt the heat creep up her neck and into her cheeks until it filled her eyes with the familiar burning that came before the waterworks. "You're still getting rid of her?"

She grabbed his hands and gently pushed them off her knees.

"Beth…"

It was one word. Just her name. But she heard it all in his tone.

You knew this was the plan.

She was never meant to stay.

You were never meant to stay.

"Were you even going to tell me?" she asked, sniffing back the tears. Beth knew the mare didn't *belong* to her. Not in the technical sense. But she and Midnight belonged to each other in a way that no document or contract could explain. She knew it, and Eli knew it. But he still left her out of the conversation.

He nodded. "I'm telling you now."

His eyes were still red, and his dried tears left streaks on his dirt-smudged face. She only now realized that it was more than just his sweat-dampened hair. Eli was a mess.

How could she be angry after what he'd just put himself through? How could she fault him for what was always supposed to happen? Logic told her she needed to hear him out, but her heart wasn't listening to logic.

"Why?" She exhaled a shaky breath. "*Why* are you telling me now? Something happened."

"Yeah," he admitted. "It's more than Midnight's door. I think someone's been messing with the property, and I think whoever it is wants me to know that they can do it and get away unseen. So there's no way in hell I'm bringing you back there and putting you in danger. I've got the trailer. I'm going to take Midnight back to the property and wait."

Beth sprang to her feet. "You're using her and yourself as *bait*? Are you crazy?"

Eli stood too. "It's not like I can get the sheriff's department involved. I don't exactly have hard evidence." He held his arms out and tilted his head toward the sky. "It's gonna be a clear night." He met her gaze again. "And I've got the alarm and the security cameras installed. It's perfectly safe. The second I hear or see something, I'll make a call, and it'll finally be over."

Beth's heart raced. "This isn't the Wild West. You know that, right? It's California. I bet there's even a vineyard not too far off." He opened his mouth to respond, but she shook her head. She wasn't finished. "And you wouldn't be pawning me off on Delaney and Sam if it was 'perfectly safe.'" She made air quotes around the last words. "When people want to steal something valuable, they usually resort to violence to get it. Is she valuable? Midnight? Was Fury valuable?"

Eli waited a beat before asking, "Do I get to talk now?"

Beth groaned. "Yes."

He sighed. "Midnight is a Friesian, which is a rare enough breed as it is. That white star between her eyes, though? The appearance of a marking like that on a pure breed is even rarer. She and Fury could have been twins, and I know what Fury was worth, not that Tess or I would have ever sold her. So yeah. With Midnight being the horse she probably was before the injury, I bet she was worth a lot. And I'm guessing the reason why her owners were going to put her down was because the injury meant she wasn't."

Beth hugged herself tighter. Had the temperature changed? Why was she so cold?

Eli raised a hand gently toward her but let it fall. She could tell he wanted to touch her, to wrap his arms around her and fix whatever was happening here. She both wanted him to try and was also afraid she'd push him away. But it didn't matter because he stayed where he was, on his side of the porch steps, and somehow that made her gut twist even more.

Fury was a rare breed, and someone had tried to take her.

Midnight was the exact same breed, and even if Eli's physical evidence was almost nonexistent, if Beth were in his shoes, she'd suspect the same.

"Fine," she finally said. "If we're going to catch these horse bandits or whatever…" Ha. *Whatever*. They'd still never figured out what that word meant. "Then I'm coming too," Beth declared.

A muscle twitched in Eli's jaw. "The hell you are," he practically growled.

Beth scoffed. "You're kidding, right? Did you just hear yourself? You sound like the day you told me I couldn't ride Midnight. Are we back there again?"

"Maybe," he admitted, his own arms crossed now. "You didn't let me protect you then, and look where it got us. Now I *can*, Beth. So call me an asshole or hate me more than you already do for trying to find her a good home when the only human she truly cares about is going to eventually leave her anyway."

Beth flinched. "That's not fair, Eli." But it was, wasn't it? She was going to leave Midnight—and *him*.

He let out a mirthless laugh. "Fair? You want to talk to me about fair?" He shook his head, then pinched the bridge of his nose, the gesture she now knew meant that Eli Murphy had taken all that he could take. He would shut down soon, which meant he would also shut her out. "You're *not* setting foot on the Murphy property tonight. It's the only way I can keep you safe. Don't you get that?"

Beth clamped her jaw shut. She couldn't believe they were back where they started after all this time.

"Yeah," she replied, her tone clipped. "I *got* it, Dr. Murphy."

Then she spun on her heel, pushed through Sam and Delaney's door, and slammed it behind her.

Somewhere in the recesses of the house, a toddler shrieked, and her baby-making parents—even behind closed doors—audibly swore.

Chapter 23

Eli paced the stretch of concrete between Midnight's and Cirrus's stalls, though Cirrus was still at the Meadow Valley Ranch.

"You're kidding, right?" Boone barked in his ear. "Because I can't remember the last time you had such a batshit idea."

"So Sam ratted me out already?" Eli had barely been home long enough to get Midnight situated back in her stall.

"Of course he did. He'd have followed you home if he wasn't working the guest ranch tonight." Boone sighed. "What the hell is going on, huh? You're going all vigilante on a hunch when you're supposed to be the rational one, the one who plays it safe and keeps everyone in check, including yourself."

Eli ran a hand through his already wild hair. Three years...no...a decade at least of being rational and keeping everyone in check had finally reached its boiling point.

"Why?" he asked his younger brother. "Why does that job still fall on me after all these goddamn years? Dad got hurt, and the ranch became ours to run. Ash took off and never looked back. You and Casey…look, I know you had your shit, and that shop was your escape. But that left me and Tess with the clinic and the ranch, and we made it work. We never took on more than we could handle. We kept to ourselves and our quiet little lives while still keeping tabs on you and Ash, and we were happy. And where the hell did it get me?"

Even from the barn, he heard the sound of tires on gravel, the roar of an engine. Or was he hearing it *in* the phone?

He jogged out of the barn, not sure if he was moving toward whatever he heard or if the sound was simply moving toward Boone, wherever *he* was. Except outside, in front of the clinic, was Boone's motorcycle…with Boone on it.

Eli looked at his phone, then at his brother, still confused as the distance between them grew smaller.

"You were riding the whole time?" Eli scratched the back of his neck. "I didn't hear… I mean, what are you doing? I thought Casey had clients all afternoon and evening."

Boone pulled off his helmet and stowed it on the back of his bike. "Her mom is watching Kara. Told her that my big brother needed some help, and she didn't question me. But if you rat me out, I'm toast." His hair stuck out at odd angles in multiple spots. "What are *you* looking at?" he added, nodding at

Eli. "At least *I* was wearing a helmet. What's your excuse?"

Eli huffed out a laugh. It might have been the first time he smiled in days.

"Thank you," he told his brother, but his smile was short-lived. "So you came all the way here to, what? Lock me up while someone trespasses on my property and takes what belongs to me…again?"

Boone shrugged. "I guess it depended on how you reacted to me showing up. But hearing you refer to Midnight as *yours* changes things a bit, doesn't it?"

Eli's eyes widened. Had he really… Did he actually…

Shit. He did, didn't he?

"I wasn't going to keep her," Eli told him, hearing the realization in his own tone. "I didn't want her here in the first place."

His brother nodded. "I know."

"It's not because of Beth," Eli added.

The younger Murphy gave his brother a pointed look. Both men knew that was a lie.

"Fine," Eli amended. "It's not *only* because of her, and the *because of her* part doesn't even matter anymore because despite knowing she was always going to leave, she probably, most likely, *definitely* never wants to speak to me again."

Boone clapped his brother on the shoulder and let out a long breath.

"Let me guess. You told her to stay the hell away from the property while you try to be Dirty Harry? This isn't the Wild West, big bro."

Eli huffed out an incredulous laugh. "That's exactly what *she* said. Are you two conspiring against me now?"

Boone shook his head ruefully. "Actually, this is what it looks like when people are on your side. They show you that they *care*. Did you even call the sheriff's office?"

"Of course I did. But I've got nothing other than a broken chicken coop lock and a hunch. Pretty sure you need a lot more to warrant a stakeout."

Boone lowered his hand and crossed his arms. His expression softened to something more like somber. "You're right...about questioning your role in this family. When I was a messed-up kid, it was easy to let you take over for Dad because you had your shit together. You were brother, father, ranch manager, husband, doctor—all of it, and I never for a second questioned your ability to do it. But I also never questioned whether you *wanted* all that responsibility. And for that, big brother, the slightly less messed-up version of me is sorry."

Eli glanced back and forth from the barn to the clinic, his chest aching even as a weight felt like it was lifting from his shoulders. He'd never had the time or the chance to consider what he actually wanted. He just dove right in all those years ago, barely an adult himself, and made it work.

"I want it," he finally uttered, his throat tight. "I want this place to be what it was when we were kids. I want to keep the practice but maybe scale back to only three days a week in the clinic. And I want to catch the sons of bitches who made me believe for more than three years that I was happier and safer without a whole part of my life that made me *me*."

Boone's grin returned. "Well then, let's catch us some horse poachers." He threw an arm over his older brother's shoulder, and together they strode toward the clinic and Eli's home just beyond. "And what about the girl?" Boone asked as they dropped down at Eli's kitchen table to formulate a plan.

Eli cleared his throat. "What about her?" he asked, a loaded question. He'd sabotaged the hell out of whatever he and Beth had become. Was it for her own safety? Of course it was. Could he have gone about the situation in a better way? Maybe, but hindsight didn't change anything. What was done was done, and the most important thing was that Beth stayed safe, that she made it back to New York where she clearly belonged, and that when she came back someday to visit her sister, she *might* stop by for a ride with her favorite mare. Because of course Midnight was *hers*. And whether or not he was truly ready to be a ranch owner again, he'd do it for Midnight, for Beth, and for the chance she might forgive him someday.

Boone leaned back in his chair and clasped his hands behind his head. "You know, I seem to remember someone giving me some really good advice before I almost married a really great woman who just happened to be the wrong woman for *me*. It went a little something like this... Whoever you choose as your partner through all of it—especially if you're a lucky enough son of a bitch for her to choose you right back—make sure it's someone who not only loves you at your best but can also still find that hidden ray of light when you're at your worst. That's when you know, you know?"

Eli's eyes grew wide. "Did you *memorize* that?"

His brother beamed. "Stuff gets a little jumbled in here sometimes..." Boone tapped his temple with his index finger. "But that really hit me, you know? It stuck like goddamn crazy glue. I hear it every time I look at Casey and still can't believe we found our way back...or when I hold my daughter. Some of us are only lucky once, Eli. But you've got another shot, and I don't want to see you piss it away."

Eli glanced toward the open door of his bedroom, to the place where he knew the scent of Beth's shampoo still lingered on her pillow. He knew now that his heart had the capacity for not one but *two* great loves of his life and that if Beth chose *him* like he'd already chosen her, he was the luckiest son of a bitch there was.

"I'll tell her," Eli promised. "I'll tell her how I feel after we make it through tonight." Because somehow he knew it would all be over by morning.

For the guy who'd always been Mr. Rational, he was betting everything on this hunch.

Boone slapped his palms on the table. "All right then! First order of business… You look like absolute shit. Get yourself in the shower and regroup. If anything is going to happen, it won't be until after nightfall."

Eli laughed. When had his little brother grown so wise? Or maybe it was that Eli had grown so weary. Maybe, finally, they were ready to tread on common ground.

"Noted," Eli said, then nodded behind him. "The monitors are on the kitchen counter. Make sure the cameras both have night vision turned on and that they're still pointed at the right angles."

Except as he glanced toward the monitors, he caught sight of something stuck to the refrigerator door with a magnet, and even from the other side of the counter, he could read what it said.

Boone, none the wiser, offered his brother a two-fingered salute. "You got it, boss. Now *go*." And he shooed Eli off toward the shower. And Eli decided to pretend it wasn't there, plain as day, that before he'd even gone to Delaney and Sam's that afternoon to make sure they kept Beth safe, she'd already had one foot out the door and on a plane to the other side of the country.

———————

Eli checked his watch: 9:32 p.m. It felt like it had taken forever for the sun to set, but it was finally dark, and pitch-dark at that, save for the star-speckled sky which—while pretty to look at—did nothing to illuminate a property that had purposely left all artificial lighting off.

"This is good," Boone told him as they settled onto the breakfast barstools of the guesthouse, their eyes adjusting to every light inside being turned off. "It'll hopefully give our *friends* more confidence."

Eli nodded. He'd insisted they wait out their confrontation in the guesthouse because it was closer to the barn. Whether or not Boone knew the truth—that Eli wanted to make sure Beth hadn't somehow snuck back in while he'd been shower-ing and regrouping—he didn't question his older brother's plans.

Each Murphy brother held a baby monitor in his hand, the cameras pointed at the stretch of ground Eli had been pacing before Boone had shown up, the screens dark unless triggered by motion in the barn.

"Reminds me of the time we camped in the clearing," Boone said softly.

"When Ash insisted we bring walkie-talkies so *Mom* wouldn't be so nervous about us being gone?" Eli asked.

He was pretty sure he detected a nod from Boone in the dark. "He was so scared." He chuckled.

"In his defense," Eli began, "he *was* only seven."

A beat of silence stretched between them.

"He'd probably have gotten a kick out of this if he were here," Boone finally added.

Eli sighed. He couldn't remember the last time all three Murphy brothers were together. Hell, he was pretty sure neither of them had seen Ash in years.

"I miss him too," Eli admitted. "But I've tried to reach out—"

"And you only get a response from his tour manager? Just because he's a rich and famous country rock sensation doesn't mean he wouldn't enjoy a good old-fashioned stakeout with his brothers, right?" Boone let out a knowing laugh, but somehow Eli could tell he wasn't quite smiling. "Maybe we need to try harder," Boone added.

"Yeah," Eli told him. "Maybe we do."

Suddenly Boone's face lit up, his monitor's small screen flickering on. At the same time, Eli's phone buzzed on the counter, a notification from Midnight's stall door sensor.

"We got motion!" Boone whisper-shouted.

"Shit!" Eli hissed, realizing part of him was

hoping the would-be thieves would simply give up and let him get back to his life. But where would that leave him? Always looking over his shoulder? Always wondering if there'd be any sort of justice—or, at the very least, closure—for what happened to Tess and Fury.

Both men sprang from their stools, Boone ready to block the barn door with his bike and Eli ready to sneak in from the rear. But just as quickly as the sensor alarm had gone off, it suddenly stopped.

He checked his phone. The alarm had been disabled.

"Dammit!" he growled. "Beth is in there!" How—after *everything*—could she be so reckless?

Boone swore as well, and the two men took off out the door of the guesthouse.

A clamoring of shouts sounded from the barn.

"She's got the mare!"

"Rope her!"

"Yah! Midnight, *go*!"

The mare squealed, and before Eli and Boone could even think to block any entrance to the barn, Beth and Midnight burst into the arena, jumped the fence, and took off in the pitch-dark toward the woods. And whoever else was in the barn took off after them on a motorbike that would quickly outrun a scared horse trying to find her way in the dark.

"Give me your keys!" Eli demanded, and Boone stared at him, jaw agape.

"That wasn't the plan!" Boone replied.

"Fuck the plan, Boone! I left Cirrus at the guest ranch, and those assholes are after Beth. I'm not letting history repeat itself."

Boone must have realized there was no arguing with him because he stuck his hand in his pocket and produced the keys.

"Do you even know how to ride?" the younger Murphy asked as his brother snatched the keys.

"You showed me once," Eli called over his shoulder.

"Jesus, Eli! That was, like, four years ago! And... and you need a license!"

Eli didn't have time for technicalities. "I'm sure it's just like..." He stopped in front of the vehicle and muttered the rest to himself. "Like riding a bike."

He was about to turn back to his brother to tell him to call 911, but Eli already heard sirens way off down the road.

Beth. She'd not only gotten to Midnight in time, but she'd somehow managed to call the authorities before she gave chase.

Eli affixed his brother's helmet, hopped on the bike, and slipped the key into the ignition. He surprisingly remembered how to shift into gear, and with a small but noticeable lurch forward, he was off.

Boone yelled something at him as he passed, not

that Eli could hear him. He was sure it was something along the lines of *Be careful!* or *Break my bike, and I break your face!* But he guessed it was likely some happy medium between the two.

All that mattered to Eli was that Beth and Midnight made it home safe. So he rode, following the waning light of the motorbike ahead of him, his own headlight becoming increasingly dim in what seemed to be a growing fog.

It was like riding through a cloud, which would have been difficult enough in a truck with *two* headlights and four strong wheels balancing on the unsteady ground. But Eli wasn't in his truck. And he sure as hell wasn't practicing what he preached about not being reckless. Because the woman and the horse he loved were out there, and he was furious and terrified and determined to bring them home safely, no matter the cost to his own safety.

Such a hypocrite, a voice murmured in his head. But he couldn't make out the voice.

"Tess?" he said aloud to himself. "Beth?" Or was it his own voice realizing what he should have known from the start…that there is no such thing as *safe* when it comes to the people you love.

The grass quickly grew thick beneath his tires, and if he could see past the fog in front of his visor and now starless sky, he'd probably notice white knuckles gripping the handlebars of his brother's bike.

In the waning reach of his headlight, he swore he spotted a blurred figure ahead, one that looked like a woman on a horse. At least that was what Eli hoped he saw. But the vision was there and gone as the world around him plunged back into the foggy darkness.

The lights of the other bike bobbed ahead of him, but other than that, he could see nothing. Finally, he reached under his chin and yanked the helmet off, tossing it somewhere in the grass below.

It was still difficult to see but now only because it was dark and not because he was squinting through foggy glass.

He heard a male voice yell something indecipherable, and then he detected the unmistakable sound of a woman's scream.

"Beth!" he called out, but the thick air seemed to swallow his voice. He twisted the throttle as far as it would go, then without a second of warning, the front wheel of the bike hit a divot in the grass, and Eli instinctively pulled on the brake—*hard*—which he realized too late was not the right move. The back wheel flew up behind him, and he was weightless.

Until he wasn't.

His back smacked the damp earth a millisecond before his head. Every ounce of air escaped his lungs in a searing, painful rush.

Eli gasped. Or at least he tried to, but taking in

even a mouthful of air felt like trying to swallow a knife. He thought it might kill him, yet he knew if he didn't breathe, that *would* kill him. So he forced one sip of air and then another, all the while realizing that the longer he lay there, the more danger Beth was in.

Finally, he no longer felt like he was suffocating, until he tried to sit up. A growl tore from Eli's throat, one that was coupled with the sharp, searing stab of pain in the right side of his chest and back.

Had he fallen *on* something? Was he bleeding?

Eli's pained breaths came in short pants, and his vision was clouding again, which was weird because the fog wasn't as bad down on the ground. But he felt oddly cold. And Beth and Midnight were still out there. And once again, he'd failed at protecting what was most important to him.

"Eli!" The woman's voice sounded like she was shouting from underwater, but he swore it was Beth's.

"Beth?" He tried to call out, but each utterance…each breath only made whatever was poking through his back and chest poke harder. He knew what it was now, but the knowing wasn't going to make it any easier to breathe.

"Oh my god, *Eli!*" She dropped to her knees next to him. A second later, a bright light shone in his eyes. "Your lips are *blue.*" Her voice trembled as she spoke.

"I…messed up…again." He sucked in shallow breaths between the words.

Beth lowered the small flashlight but left it on. He could see her now. She was okay. But Midnight? The men in the barn?

She shook her head, and he could see her cheeks were streaked with tears.

"This is my fault." She hiccupped. "I should have told you I was coming, but I was so *mad* at you for not letting me help and for thinking I could possibly leave you and Midnight to do this alone. And now…"

A horse whinnied in the distance, and Eli saw flashes of red and blue in his peripheral vision.

"Midnight's okay?" He groaned, coughed, then gritted his teeth against the ensuing pain.

She nodded. "The police are here, and there should be an ambulance on the way." She swiped a fist under each of her eyes as she sniffled. "They got the bad guys," she added, and it looked like she was trying to smile.

"How did you know?" he asked weakly.

She let out a tearful laugh. "Who else would Midnight let in her stall without making a sound? So I army-crawled under the door and waited with her until it was time to run."

Despite every part of him screaming not to, Eli pushed himself onto his left elbow. His whole right side protested against the movement, which he made painfully clear with a hoarse but definitive "*Fuck!*"

"What are you doing?" she cried.

He tried to reach for her with his right arm, but he couldn't lift it, not unless he had any plans to pass out soon after. Actually, he was pretty sure he was going to pass out even if he kept still.

"Tell the EMTs it's a right pneumothorax. That means collapsed lung... Most likely from a cracked rib." He coughed and winced. "Or *ribs*," he amended.

"Oh my god!" She threw a hand over her mouth, but Eli shook his head.

"Not...your...fault." He coughed again. "I was an asshole."

Beth dropped down into the grass beside him. "Lie back down," she ordered him, voice trembling.

Eli didn't need to be told twice.

He swore as he tried to gingerly lower himself, his head falling in her lap. As much as it hurt to simply inhale, it still somehow felt so good to lie here like this, touching her, even if he was barely hanging on to consciousness.

"You *were* an asshole..." Beth choked on something that was part laugh, part sob. "But, Eli..."

He shook his head. Or maybe he didn't move at all. It was getting to the point that he couldn't tell. "I'm gonna be okay. It's not as bad as it looks." Except it *felt* as bad as it probably looked. Eli wanted to comfort her, but somehow the shallow breaths he took between words coupled with the fact that his only expression at the moment was a wince probably wasn't doing the job. "But first I think I'm gonna black out for a few minutes, so remember...pneumothorax, ribs, not your fault..." Was he forgetting anything? "You...you did *good* tonight. You're so strong, Beth. I should have given you more credit."

"*Eli*..." His name sounded like a plea, or maybe it was a promise.

"Just stay until they come," he added. "Is that okay?"

He could see bright lights in the distance moving closer.

Then he felt her hands in his hair, her trembling lips against his forehead.

"I'm not going *any*where," she whispered. "Even when they get here, I'm staying with you. Is *that* okay?"

He laughed, then pressed his left palm to his right side.

"Yeah," he whispered. "I love you. So I think it's okay if you stay."

The blackness started at the edges of his vision, and before he could gauge her reaction to what he thought he might have just said, someone turned out the lights.

Chapter 24

WHEN THE AMBULANCE ARRIVED IN THE MIDDLE of the muddy field, Beth was still in shock about so many things. *Too* many things.

"Beth!" someone called, and she looked up to see Captain Carter Bowen of the Meadow Valley Fire Station and, if she remembered correctly, Eli's friend. Beside him stood another uniformed paramedic whose name tag read *JT*. The stretcher on which they'd soon carry Eli away stood beside them.

"He…he…" Her voice shook.

Carter dropped to a squat next to where Eli still lay unconscious with his head in her lap. "It's okay," he said calmly. "I know Eli well enough that we can skip some of the general health history, but whatever information you can give me will help us get him the treatment he needs as quickly as he needs it. Was he awake when you found him? Did he tell you anything to tell me?"

Right. Right. Right.

"His lung!" Beth told Carter. "And his ribs. On his right side. He said it was a pneumo…a pneumo…"

"Pneumothorax?" Carter asked, and Beth

nodded earnestly. "Good, Beth. You're doing great. And he thinks it's due to his ribs?"

She nodded again. "His lips...the color... Is he not breathing? Are you going to give him oxygen? Can you fix him?"

The other paramedic was on the ground fitting a metal contraption to Eli's height before splitting it in two and placing one half of the device on his right, the other on his left.

Carter gave her a reassuring smile. "We're going to do our best to get his oxygen levels back where they need to be. You see this?" He hovered his open palm above Eli's chest, and Beth was able to detect the slight rise and fall.

"He's still breathing," she said through her own shuddering breath.

"Yep," Carter confirmed. "That's a good sign, and we're going to make things even better, but we need to get him to an emergency room as quickly as possible so he has the best chance of avoiding complications. Do you have someone who can—"

"I'm riding with him!" she blurted. "I can do that, right? Eli said I could. I mean, I know I'm not immediate family, but he said he loved me, so that counts for something, right?"

He was probably delirious with pain when he said it and probably had no idea *what* he was saying, but Beth didn't care.

"You're caked in mud," Carter reminded her

as he and his partner connected the two halves of the metal stretcher-type thing beneath Eli's back. "Looks like all those bikes tore the earth up pretty good."

A horse whinnied nearby but was cloaked in darkness.

Beth sucked in a breath. "Midnight!"

She'd heard the revving of the motorcycle engine, a crash, and then the eerie silence that followed. She wasn't sure what made her turn around and ride back toward the men who were chasing her. It could have been one of *them* who'd crashed. But somehow she knew, the same way she was sure that if she hadn't come back tonight—despite Eli's protestations— she might have lost them both. All she remembered was hopping out of the saddle and telling Midnight to stay, hoping like hell that she would.

And then the police were there, and Midnight was *fine*, but Eli...

"I'll take care of the mare!" a male voice replied. Then out of the corner of her eye, Beth saw Boone leading her horse out of the dark. "And I'll give the deputy as much information as I can, but she's probably going to want to talk to you as well, Beth."

Beth nodded. "Later, though, right?"

"Yeah," Boone confirmed. "Later is good. Go take care of my brother, and when he wakes up, tell him he's going to help me fix that bike." He gave her a half smile.

Despite his attempt at levity, Beth could see the worry in Boone's eyes.

"I'll tell him," she replied. "And, Boone, I'm sorry. I never meant for anything like this to happen."

Carter and JT lifted Eli from the ground and onto the transport stretcher. The sudden absence of his head in her lap made her throat tighten.

"You saved the horse," Boone told her. "That was all any of us were trying to do."

"Yeah, but—"

He interrupted her by extending a hand and pulling her up from the muddy grass.

"You can't change what's been done," Boone explained. "You can either learn from it and move on, or you can stay stuck in the 'yeah, buts' or what-ifs until you forget that moving on is even an option."

His lip twitched into the promise of a grin.

All Beth could do was sniffle and nod as she wondered whether Boone's advice was meant solely for her or if he was referring to his big brother as well…or even himself.

"You ready, Beth?" Carter called from over her shoulder.

Boone shooed her toward the ambulance that now had his brother closed inside.

"Thank you," she told him. "For being here for Eli tonight."

Then she spun toward the emergency vehicle and let Carter usher her to the passenger side door.

"I can't ride with him?"

Carter shook his head. "JT's driving, and I'll be in back giving Eli everything he needs. I need room to work, and it's safer for you up here, but I promise if he wakes up, the first thing I'll tell him is that you're right up front, okay?"

What was she going to do, tell Carter that she was terrified to have Eli out of her sight, that even though she had *zero* medical capabilities, she was so scared of *not* being directly by his side in case something happened? How was she supposed to just go through life from here on out *not* knowing at any given moment if Eli Murphy was okay?

And when Eli woke up—because of course he would wake up—how the hell would Beth explain that after her stunt with Midnight, she was on her way to New York in less than two weeks for the audition she wasn't expecting to have until next spring?

All the questions made her head spin, so she lowered the ambulance window to suck in gulps of the cool Northern California night, to breathe in the scent of the place she'd never wanted to come to and was now devastated to leave.

Something tugged at her hair, and Beth yelped, bolting upright in…her bed? *No.* A chair? She squinted, eyes adjusting to the dim flicker of the fluorescent light above the hospital bed.

"Sorry," Eli whispered groggily. "My fingers must have gotten tangled in your hair."

Beth's hands instinctively went to her head where clumps of her hair were still matted together with bits of mud. Then her eyes caught the small dark circle on the edge of Eli's bedsheet where she'd been *drooling* while she slept!

"Oh god!" she exclaimed, and Eli winced. "Sorry!" she whispered, forgetting about the concussion, which was the icing on the cake of the two fractured ribs and—as Eli figured out himself—a collapsed lung.

Her eyes adjusted, and he came into focus. Other than one tube—which she learned was called a cannula—delivering extra oxygen through Eli's nose and another one traveling out beneath the sleeve of his hospital gown—the one draining fluid from his chest—he still looked like her Eli. So why did she feel the hot threat of tears behind her eyes?

"You should go home," he replied, his voice hoarse. "I'm sure Midnight is worried about you. And the guesthouse has a really nice shower."

She sucked in a sharp breath, suddenly realizing what it was. He was awake. *Eli* was awake. And did he just crack a joke?

"What?" Beth asked, choking back a sob. "You're not a fan of this look?" She gestured to her navy sweatshirt with the word HOSPITAL embroidered on it in white. She at least had to hand it to the gift shop for providing a much-needed dose of humor to her evening. Or was it morning? She pulled her phone out of the still damp back pocket of her jeans, noting the 2:06 a.m. time on her lock screen before the battery used its last bit of juice.

"You're a little blurry," he admitted. "But I'm positive you're still the prettiest one in the room." He coughed and winced again. "I mean *any* room," he managed to add.

"Eli…" Beth's voice shook on the second syllable of his name. She was seconds away from losing it, so she had to get the words out before they didn't sound like words anymore.

"Wait," he whispered, then patted the sliver of room on the mattress to his left. "If you're not going to leave, then I need you to come closer."

Her breath hitched, and she sat there frozen for several seconds. Eli responded by pressing both palms against the bed and shifting his entire body to the right, a swear escaping his lips as he did.

"Are you *crazy*?" she hissed, springing from her chair. "You're not supposed to be moving!"

A muscle in his jaw twitched, and he fisted the sheet at his sides.

"You're right," he ground out through gritted teeth. "Won't be doing that again. But now that there's more room..." He gave the bed another pat even as beads of sweat broke out on his forehead.

Instead of taking Eli up on his invitation, Beth darted for the bathroom, returning a few seconds later with a cool, damp washcloth. She folded it in half and laid it gingerly on his forehead. He closed his eyes and sighed, his shoulders relaxing.

Only then did Beth gently climb onto the bed, careful to cause as little movement as possible before awkwardly leaning on her right elbow to face him. She had to use every muscle in her core to keep from toppling onto the floor.

Eli's brow furrowed. "I might not be able to see straight right now, but I can still tell you look ridiculous." He slid his arm out from where it was pinned between their bodies and reached behind her to lift the bed rail and lock it into place. "Now lean back," he said. "And put your head here." He nodded toward his left shoulder.

Beth let out a breath and let the bulk of her weight fall against the rail, then rested her head softly on his shoulder.

She watched his chest fall as he exhaled, marveling at the sight of something she once took for granted. And when she tilted her head up to look at him, she found him smiling back at her, the big, beautiful Eli smile she used to think didn't exist. Knowing now that *she* had the ability to put that expression on his face felt like a superpower she never knew she wanted until it was in her possession.

"I should have listened to you and stayed away," she whispered.

"I should have never shut you down like that," he whispered back.

She inhaled the unmistakable sterility of high-powered cleaners, the scent of iodine and soap, and somewhere beneath it all something inherently Eli, and for the first time since her adrenaline-induced escape from the barn on Midnight's back, Beth finally felt like she could breathe.

"I get it now," she continued, her barrage of *I'm sorries* and *Please forgive mes* replaced with the simple truth that up until this very moment, she'd never completely understood the man beside her. But tonight, she did.

"Get what?"

She was half on her side, half on her back, not sure where to put her arms. She couldn't exactly wrap them around a man whose body was broken on one side, and letting them simply lie straight at *her* sides just felt weird. Where was the manual for what to do with your freaking arms while lying in a hospital bed with the man who loved you but didn't know yet that you loved him back?

It was then that his left arm, which must have still been on the bed rail, wrapped around her torso like a safety belt, and she held on to it for dear life.

"I get why, when I first got here, you never wanted me to ride Midnight in the first place. And I get why you were such an asshole about letting me be there tonight." She forced a laugh, then tilted her head toward his. "You were thrown off a *motor*cycle."

A shallow laugh escaped his lips. "Is that why I feel like hell?"

Beth swallowed. "I was *so* scared when I saw you just lying there. And I know you're eventually going to be okay, but god, Eli. I don't know what I would have done if I lost you like…"

She couldn't say it.

So he surprised her yet again when without missing a beat, *he* could. "Like I lost Tess?"

She pressed a palm to his cheek, careful not to tug his oxygen tube, and nodded.

"All I kept thinking about the whole ride here," she continued, "was how I couldn't even stand to be in the front seat of the ambulance because it meant I couldn't see you, and I just wanted to keep you safe, which was ridiculous when *I* was the reason you were in that ambulance in the first place."

He pressed his lips to her forehead, and a feeling of warmth and safety better than any blanket spread over her from the spot where his lips made contact all the way to the tips of her toes.

"I just wanted to keep *you* safe," he echoed. "But we're human. That makes us strong and stubborn.

I couldn't have stopped Tess from mounting a spooked horse in a storm any more than you could have stopped me from coming after you on a bike I had no business riding." He buried his face in her hair and sighed. "I spent *three years* blaming myself for something I couldn't control and thought the only way I could fix the past was to keep a tight grip on the present. But I think the evidence speaks for itself that I can't protect myself from getting hurt no matter how hard I try." He laughed, then coughed, then once again swore.

She skimmed her fingers along his hairline, then pressed her palm gently over the damp washcloth. "And you can't keep me from sometimes going against better judgment and jeopardizing my own safety. I push boundaries."

"I stay safely inside them. Well…until tonight."

She smiled easily now, and god, it felt good to be like this with him, even if it was less than optimal circumstances.

"Maybe it's not about being safe," Beth said. "Maybe it's about trust. Like, we have to trust each other to try—I don't know—not to hurt ourselves or each other."

He nodded, then let out a shaky breath. "I think it's more than that." He squeezed her, she guessed, as best he could with one arm and let out a sigh. "I need to learn how to let go and know that I'll be okay." Eli cleared his throat. "I know about New York."

Her breath hitched, and she buried her face in his shoulder, squeezing her eyes shut. If she never moved from this position, she'd never have to face him. She'd never have to leave. And she'd never have to chase a dream she might be destined never to actually catch.

Except if Beth didn't move, her muscles would grow stiff, and she'd be stuck.

If she never left, she'd never know for sure if she was choosing Eli or choosing to run in the opposite direction of her fear.

And if she never chased the dream all the way to the finish line, she'd always wonder.

Beth propped herself on her elbow and finally looked at him.

His glassy blue eyes nearly did her in, but she had to see this through. They both did.

"All my life," she told him, "since I was four years old, I've wanted *one* thing—to perform in the Radio City Music Hall Christmas Spectacular as a Radio City Rockette. That was it. *One* thing. One silly little thing. Until now."

"It's not silly, Beth. Not silly at all." Despite the inherent sadness in his eyes, Eli smiled that private yet undeniable smile she knew was only for her. "But…has something changed?" he asked with mock innocence.

She nodded with a grin. "I came to this town, and I met this…*horse*…"

Eli groaned and let his head thud lightly against his pillow. Probably not the best move for a guy with a concussion.

Beth laughed. "I'm *kidding*. I mean, I *love* Midnight, but I haven't spent the past few weeks considering whether to give up on New York just so I wouldn't lose her." Her lips twitched, the smile on her face suddenly feeling like the biggest and boldest lie she'd ever told. Because how could she leave him…and how could she not?

"I love you," Eli blurted, and Beth's eyes grew wide. He let out a nervous laugh. "I love you," he said again, more surety in his tone. "And it's the most terrifying thing to say or think or feel. For three years, I convinced myself that what happened the night I lost Tess and Fury was *my* fault. I should have known what to do. I should have protected them. I should have, should have, should have…"

He squeezed his eyes shut, and Beth wasn't sure if it was the pain from his memories, the physical pain, or both. But she could tell he had more to say, so she did her best to remain patient even though he'd just said what he said, and she was desperate to say it too.

"So," Eli finally continued, "I wore my loss as this badge, like it was my penance not only to display it but also to preserve it. But that badge turned into—I don't know—a suit of armor, I guess. I shut everyone out, and they *stayed* out. But *you* didn't."

"It's because I'm mighty," she told him, her whole body both abuzz and lit from within. If she opened her mouth and a firefly flew out, she wouldn't even be surprised.

"The mightiest," he added.

Beth knew she was strong, but somehow having Eli see that in her during a time when she felt her weakest made her believe it even more.

He was a closed door and a closed book, and there might have even been a dead bolt or two keeping everyone out. But *Beth* had found a way in.

"And also," she added, wondering if she should tell him. Or was it simply the time to let him have his moment?

No. She shook her head. From here on out, there would be nothing unspoken between them. Hell, there'd be nothing between them *period*.

Except maybe around three thousand miles.

"I already kind of sort of knew," Beth admitted, then winced. "That…you love me. You sort of told me right before you passed out, but maybe you didn't mean it then? I mean, you'd just been thrown from a motorcycle and were probably in a ridiculous amount of pain, so I doubt you even knew what you were saying. And you were concussed!" She let out a nervous laugh. "You probably don't even remember saying it, right?" Oh god. *Stop talking, Beth.* But she couldn't stop, nor could she escape, because she was trapped in this tiny bed with him spewing words *she* probably wouldn't remember thirty seconds from now. "I don't know," she continued. "It felt like cheating to accept that declaration, so I tried to forget it. But you went and said it again, and now I think that maybe you really did love me before tonight. And just in case you think that *I'm* the only one mighty enough to claw her way through someone's emotional armor, I'll have you know that before *you*, I never just said all the things I was feeling when I felt them. But I feel *so* much with you, Eli. Maybe too much, and when you say things like you love me—*twice*—I don't know... I mean, I can't... It's just... How do I..."

From the strained look on his face, she guessed it took Eli the entirety of her jumbled emotional eruption to lift his right arm and press his palm over her mouth.

"Sorry!" she exclaimed, her voice muffled behind his hand. "I'm hurting your head, aren't I?" She was certainly hurting her own.

"No," he whispered. "I mean, yes, my head is still throbbing, but that's not why I stopped you." He lowered his hand, letting it fall softly against his chest.

"You wanted to put me out of my misery?" Beth asked with a nervous smile.

"You looked like you needed the assist," he teased. "But I was also hoping you'd put me out of *mine*." He paused. "I...don't remember what I said after the accident. I don't remember much about the accident at all." Another pause.

Beth's stomach sank, and her expression fell.

"But," he went on, "if I said it, I meant it. I've loved you for weeks already, Beth. Maybe longer. So whether or not I remember saying it has no bearing on it being true. There's just one problem with this whole scenario."

Her eyes widened. "It's because I didn't tell you about New York, isn't it? I can explain, Eli. I wasn't keeping it from you. It all just happened so fast that—"

He covered her mouth again, his amusement quickly turning to a look of exasperation.

"I've apparently told you I love you three times by now, so just answer my question." His voice was a low whisper. "Do…you…love…me…too?"

Ohhhh. Had she not mentioned that part yet?

Beth nodded.

Eli dropped his hand, releasing a relieved breath.

"I love you, Eli." She brushed her lips over his.

"That's one," he told her.

"I *love* you, Eli." With another soft kiss, she told him again.

"That's two." He grinned.

"I love you. I love you. I love you," she continued. "That's—"

But before he could finish, she covered *his* mouth with her palm.

"I win," she said. *Not* that it was a competition. Then she dropped her hand.

"Nah," Eli replied. "Pretty sure I just won the entire jackpot."

Yet eventually, they were both going to lose. Beth wouldn't think about that now, not when she had him safe and sound in this bed, loving her and letting her love him back. Tonight or this morning or whatever time it was, she had *everything*.

Her dream.

His love.

And a hope that someday those two things wouldn't have to exist so far apart.

Chapter 25

"ARE YOU SURE ABOUT THIS?" BOONE ASKED, sealing the box with one last strip of packing tape. "This is a big step."

The last time Eli had heard Tess's voice—whether it was really her or his own subconscious pretending to be her—was that first night in the hospital when Beth said she loved him. *Five* times.

You'll be okay this time.

That was all the voice said. And somehow, after that, he knew from then on it would be gone.

Eli nodded.

He'd packed up and donated Tess's clothes and other belongings a year after she died. But the smaller things—a picture he'd left on a shelf or a grocery list he'd left hiding under a magnet on the fridge—those had taken longer.

"I used to be afraid I'd forget if I didn't have all these reminders. Does that sound crazy?"

Boone hoisted the box onto the high shelf in the clinic's hallway storage closet. Then he turned back to face his brother and shook his head. "Not crazy at all. Sounds like you were a good husband who loved his wife." He gave his brother a smile that could only be described as bittersweet, and Eli let his chest tighten and then release before closing the closet door.

He *would* be okay this time.

"Where's Beth?" Boone checked his watch. "Because your rideshare leaves in thirty minutes. After that, surge pricing kicks in." He winked, and Eli laughed, which ten days after the accident still hurt like a son of a bitch. But the pain was worth it.

Laughing felt good, and Eli vowed to let more of it into his life.

"Considering I paid for the rental, I don't think that authorizes the driver to up the rates," he teased, playing along. "And Beth's in the barn with Midnight," he added. "I just want to give them another minute alone before barging in on their moment."

Eli glanced out the clinic's front window to the midsize sedan he'd rented for the ride to the airport. He couldn't drive while he was still taking medication for the pain, and he sure as hell couldn't climb in and out of his truck, even just as a passenger. Sitting in a car for ninety minutes probably wasn't going to feel great, but hell if he wasn't going to spend every last minute with Beth before she got on that plane.

"It's an audition for a swing spot," she'd told him. "Which means I might never even get onstage. Auditions are usually in April, but a swing dancer dropped out, and a girl I used to dance with in Vegas who made it to Radio City a few years ago… she gave them my name."

Beth had shrugged, but the smile that lit up the entire room as she told him the story was evidence enough how huge this opportunity was for her.

"Anyway, rehearsals don't start until October, so I can work hard on PT and getting stronger until then and…I don't know. Then we'll see. But I should probably get through the audition first."

He'd only ever seen her dance on the Midtown Tavern dance floor. And even though he was pretty sure a Christmas Spectacular would include little to no Dolly Parton or Shania Twain, somehow he knew she'd be the most spectacular dancer on the stage.

Boone pulled his phone from his pocket and glanced at the screen.

"Traffic alert on the route to Reno," he said. "We should probably hit the road sooner rather than later."

Eli sighed. "Yeah. Okay. I'll go grab her."

As he made his way slowly to the barn, his body stiff and sore, he thought back to almost two months ago when he'd acquired an office manager who practically hated him on sight and an abandoned mare he wanted nothing to do with.

Now both Midnight and Cirrus were about to become the founding representatives of the

Murphy Horse Rescue and Rehabilitation Ranch. When he was healed and given the green light from his doctor, he planned to make riding a part of his daily life again—horses, though. *Not* motorcycles.

"Am I interrupting?" he asked when he found a familiar pair of feet sticking out from beneath Midnight's stall door.

The mare's head rested solemnly on Beth's shoulder, and Beth's eyes were red-rimmed, her lashes wet.

"I'm not going," Beth declared with a sniffly pout.

Eli laughed. "Of course you're going." Even though it hurt to say the words, he also knew that he would never truly be happy if Beth wasn't. And Beth couldn't be happy in Meadow Valley. Not now. Not yet. But he wasn't closing the door on someday.

She sat up, kissed Midnight on the white star between her eyes, and stood, dusting the bedding off her jeans.

"I'd have offered you a hand..." Eli started, but Beth shook her head.

"You shouldn't even be out here. Or riding with me to the airport. You need to rest and take care of yourself."

He took her hand, led her the rest of the way out of Midnight's stall, and then closed the door softly behind them. He kept walking until they were in the arena, the sun already baking the dirt.

"What are we doing here?" she asked, her confusion, for the moment, replacing her tears.

"I'm thanking you," he told her.

"For what?" Her brow furrowed. She still wasn't getting it.

"For this." He held his arms out as wide as he could to gesture at the surrounding arena. "You gave back to me something I never knew I missed. And because I have Midnight and the clinic and the ranch, I'm going to be okay. And so are you."

She threw her arms around him, burying her face in his neck.

It hurt like hell, but Eli didn't care. He held her as tight as he could. He'd let her go eventually. He'd let her figure life out the same way he was beginning to. But just like boxing up his memories of Tess didn't mean he had to forget, saying goodbye to Beth today didn't mean he had to say goodbye for good.

"I love you," she whispered against him. "I love you. I love you. I love you."

She always said it like this now, the three in a row. And Eli swore he'd never tire of it. It was his favorite song even if it lacked any sort of tune.

A knot formed in his throat, and even though he'd said the words before and meant them more than ever now, he was afraid if he opened his mouth, the only word that would come out would be *stay*.

So he kissed her, tasting the salt of their mingled

tears. He kissed her and kissed her and kissed her and hoped that she *knew*.

———————

"I'll circle until you text me," Boone told him, glancing over his shoulder after they pulled up to the sign denoting Beth's airline.

"You're coming in with me?" Beth asked, eyes wide. She wasn't crying anymore, but her green eyes were still glassy pools, like they were waiting for him to be out of sight before spilling over again. He wasn't ready to let her do that. He wasn't ready for any of it. Just a few minutes more.

"I'm going as far as they'll let me go," he told her. Then he glanced back at Boone. "Thanks, bro. Text you in a bit."

Before he left, Boone dutifully fulfilled his role as driver, lifting Beth's case out of the trunk. She checked in curbside with the skycap, which left nothing else to do but walk her to security.

So Eli followed her inside, and for several awkward, quiet moments, he combed the recesses of his mind for what to say to make any of this better.

Suddenly Beth just stopped, right there in the middle of people rushing to get to the TSA line.

"What's wrong?" Eli asked. "Did you forget your ID?" Was it wrong for him to *hope* she forgot her ID?

Beth crossed her arms and stared at him. "Did you know the female ferret will die if she doesn't mate once she goes into heat?"

Eli's eyes widened, and before he could stop it from happening, he barked out a laugh.

"Shit!" he hissed, grabbing his side.

"Sorry!" Beth cried. "I thought we needed a tension breaker."

He shook his head, still pressing his palm against his tender ribs. "We did." He allowed himself a softer, gentler laugh this time. "God, we really did. I just wasn't expecting... You remembered that?"

She cupped his cheek in her hand. "Oh, sweet Dr. Murphy," she began with what he hoped was feigned condescension. "A girl never forgets the first time a guy tells her about the female ferret's insatiable libido."

He turned his face into her palm and kissed it. "I know you're making fun of me right now, and I don't care," he told her. "Because what you're *really* saying is that I made a lasting impression on you from day one, and I'm okay with that."

"The *lastingest*," she said, both hands clasping around his neck.

"The *mightiest*," he replied, placing a hand on each of her hips.

And then he saw it, over her shoulder, the real reason for her sudden halt. Less than twenty feet away stood the entrance to the TSA security line.

And of course, on today of all days, there *was* no line. Passengers instead moved swiftly through the roped-off, zigzagging walkway.

"We made good time on the drive," he said softly. "You're not in a rush, right?"

She shook her head. "But if I don't go, I *won't* go."

"And you *have* to go." He wasn't asking because there was no question. "Because you're going to nail this audition, and you're going to make it onstage this Christmas. There's no way this isn't happening for you, Beth. The universe isn't that much of an asshole, and I believe in you too much for it not to be true."

He realized they were *that* couple now, the one you saw every so often while traveling, unwilling to let go of one another and not giving a shit who stared as they walked by. Eli might have rolled his eyes had he seen such a couple before today. Not anymore.

She sucked in a breath. "You *always* believed I could do this. Even when my sister tried to convince me that my doctors knew me better than I knew myself."

"*Always*," he said without hesitation.

"If you ask me to stay..." But she trailed off. Both of them knew he'd never put her in that position.

Eli shook his head. "It's not our time, Mighty. Not yet." The *yet* was the important part. Neither had asked the other to wait, and he was pretty sure neither of them would. But he needed her to know that when it came to the two of them and whatever the future might hold, she didn't have to ask. His heart was hers, and he gave it willingly.

"I love you," she told him, and every time the words left her mouth, he still couldn't believe they were meant for him. "I love you. I love you. I love you."

He blinked and felt the wetness on his lashes, then her lips on his cheek as she kissed away the rogue tear. And once again, the words lodged in his throat.

"It's okay," she whispered. "I *know*."

And then they shared one final, lingering kiss.

He savored the taste of vanilla and mint, the familiar scent of her hair, and the feel of her in his arms.

And then, because they'd both agreed *not* to actually say goodbye, she squeezed him gently and turned and walked away.

Shit.

Why the hell couldn't he say it?

Then he remembered his fail-safe. His *just-in-case-I-screw-this-up* plan B.

He reached for the item in his back pocket, unfolded it, and held it up high over his head, broken ribs be damned.

Turn around, he willed her before she was out of sight. She'd never hear him if he tried to yell now, and even if he managed, it would probably undo any healing he'd actually done in the past ten days.

Turn. Around.

And just when Beth was about to zig her last zag, to hand her boarding pass to the TSA agent and then walk out of his line of sight for good, she stopped.

Turn around, Beth. I'm still here. Turn around. Turn around. Turn—

She turned around, and the biggest, most beautiful smile spread across her most beautiful, blotchy, tear-streaked face as she read the sign in his hands.

Eli didn't know why he'd saved it, but when he found the plain white sheet of paper on his office desk, the one with BETH SPENCE written across it that he'd used to identify himself as her airport driver the day she arrived in town, he shoved it in a drawer just in case.

Now, in the white space that surrounded her name, he'd scrawled *I love you* wherever he could fit those three little words.

He said the words now as she stood there, facing him, laughing *and* crying.

"I love you. I love you. I love you."

For as long as she stood there, he kept repeating the phrase. And after she mouthed the words back, the TSA agent beckoning her to continue through the line, she finally disappeared out of sight.

I win, Eli thought, carefully refolding the paper

and stowing it back in his pocket. Even though right now it felt like he'd lost, the words still played on a loop in his head.

I win.

————

Boone arrived back where he'd left Eli and Beth a few minutes after Eli texted. Eli glanced back at the door to the departures entrance one last time before lowering himself into the rental car.

"You okay?" Boone asked as they slowly pulled out of the drop-off lane.

"No," Eli admitted.

But he would be.

Chapter 26

BETH HAD ONLY RECEIVED A FORTY-EIGHT HOUR notice that she'd be going onstage, on Christmas Eve, no less.

"There's no way you can make it, right?" she'd asked Delaney. "Tickets are probably so expensive. I'm sorry I didn't know any sooner. I—"

"Bethy!" her sister had interrupted. "You're a *Rockette*! On Christmas Eve! I don't care if I have to sacrifice Nolan's—or the yet-to-be-named baby number two's—college tuition. We. Will. *Be*. There."

And by *we*, Delaney had meant her and Sam. Her sister had already enlisted Sam's mom to watch her niece.

Even her parents had gotten the front desk at their Vegas motel covered for the night. They were going to take the red-eye back to Vegas as soon as Beth's performance was over.

"Did you tell Eli?" her sister added, never one to tiptoe around a sore subject.

Of course she'd told Eli. At least she'd told her texting app, and she saw that the message was delivered. Their communication had been good at first.

At least once a week, they'd schedule a video chat to fit both of their time zones. It wasn't the same as seeing each other in person, but it wasn't the worst. Because it was Eli. *Eli.* The love of her life.

Except once summer ended and rehearsals began—six hours a day, six days a week, *plus* Beth's continued physical therapy—their calls became fewer and farther between. She would go back to her tiny apartment that she shared with one other dancer and pass out only to wake up to a missed call from Eli. When she called him back, she often caught his voicemail more than the man himself.

Soon missed calls turned to sporadic texts, and then it happened. A week went by where they had no contact at all. And now that one week had turned into three. It hurt to think of Eli getting over her, but it had been six months, and she also wanted him to move on, to find happiness with someone who could actually *be* there for him the way he'd been there for her.

"I told him," Beth finally replied. "I'm sure he's too busy to come. But there will be three tickets at will call. Just in case."

———

Beth was finishing touching up her makeup for her final number, "The Parade of the Wooden Soldier," where she was dressed as, well, a toy soldier. Just as she finished filling in the red circle on her second cheek, the phone on her makeup table buzzed with a text.

Eli: Always knew you'd do it. Be the mightiest tonight.

The only time stamp on the message was from when she texted *him* to tell him about the show. So was the text new? Meaning he'd just responded to *her* text from almost *two* days ago? Or was the shitty reception backstage only now pushing through a message that came hours earlier? And why did it matter?

It mattered because if he got the message in time, the one offering him a free ticket to the show, would he have come? Had he been out there the whole time?

Her phone buzzed again.

Delaney: You. Are. AMAZING. Proud sis out here!

Hands shaking, she fired off a quick reply to her sister.

Beth: Did you just send this?

The telltale three dots appeared on the screen and, soon after, Delaney's reply.

Delaney: YES! Wanted to give you a quick boost before your final number. Luv u!

Okay. That settled it. Eli's text must have been immediate as well. That was the easiest and most logical conclusion. He was just wishing her luck and probably mixed up the time zones, not realizing the show was almost over instead of almost starting.

If he was *here*, he would have told her. Or Delaney would have. Because her sister knew better than to surprise her, especially in a high-stress situation. And Beth was pretty sure having not connected for almost a month meant she and Eli were past the point of surprising each other as well. At least *Beth* knew she'd be terrified to just show up on Eli's doorstep as if he'd been counting the minutes until she returned. So what if *she'd* been counting the minutes until she got to see him again?

"You ready, Beth? It's almost our cue."

One of the other toy soldiers tapped her on the shoulder.

"Yeah!" she replied, making eye contact with the other dancer via her reflection in the mirror. "Be right there."

Okay, then. Eli wasn't here. He'd have texted sooner if he planned to come.

After the holiday season, Delaney offered her an open invitation to come back to Meadow Valley for as long as she wanted, especially with baby number two due in late spring, but Beth still hadn't made up her mind. Being a Rockette was her dream, but it was only a three-months-a-year gig. She hadn't quite figured out the other nine. She didn't think she could be in the same town as Eli and not be *with* Eli. Not yet. But maybe once the baby came, they'd both be in a better place. Maybe they'd even be friends.

Beth swallowed the knot in her throat.

One more number on what should be the best night of her life. She needed to be *in* the moment. To not forget this as it might be the only time she took the stage this season.

She closed her eyes and allowed herself one more steadying breath before rising from her chair, smoothing out nonexistent wrinkles in her costume, and heading to her spot in line.

———

Tears streamed down Beth's cheeks as the curtain closed on the line of thirty-six toy soldiers sitting in their perfect, trainlike formation after having just fallen in slow motion when the toy cannon went off. The "Toy Soldier Dance," as she called it when she was a kid, had always been her favorite, and tonight Beth *was* a toy soldier—a toy soldier *Rockette* no less—at Radio City Music Hall, on Christmas Eve.

Even in her wildest imaginings, she couldn't

have dreamed up this kind of happiness, of fulfill-ment, of pride. She said she would do it, and she *did* it, even when they told her she couldn't.

Sure, there was a slight limp in her step once she got offstage, but there was only one week of shows left. Even if she took the stage again between now and then, she'd likely have time to recuperate and ice her ankle before and after.

For now, since Beth wasn't in the finale and it *was* the holiday, she wanted nothing more than to be with family. So she scrambled out of her cos-tume and into her purple hoodie, matching purple leggings, and her warm gray fuzzy boots. Then she snuck out the stage door and was immediately greeted by a huge group hug from her mom, dad, and visibly pregnant sister.

"Bethy!" Delaney squealed. "You did it! We're so proud of you!"

"So proud!" her mom echoed through sniffles and tears.

Her father, the strong silent type who didn't often wear his heart on his sleeve, simply swiped at the dampness under his eyes and kissed her on the forehead.

Sam swooped in for a hug after everyone else had their fill.

"Nice job out there, kiddo," he told her, then shivered despite his puffy down jacket. "But I'm ready to get *inside* again if that's okay with you."

Beth laughed. "I am with you there. My Vegas blood isn't warm enough to compensate for winters like this." She zipped her own long puffy coat even higher. "Do you guys really have to go?" Beth asked, turning back to her parents.

Her mom stroked Beth's overly lacquered hair that was held into a tight bun not only from an excessive amount of hair spray but also bobby pins that felt like they'd embedded themselves into her scalp. But Beth didn't care. She was a Radio City Rockette on Christmas Eve.

"We wish we could stay. But a twenty-four-hour business is a twenty-four-hour business," her mom replied. "I promise, though, that if we can plan ahead for the next one, we'll make it a longer trip, and you take us to that place with the cheesecake you love."

"Junior's!" Beth exclaimed. The restaurant was a Times Square tourist trap, but Beth didn't care. Not when they had a banana cheesecake that reminded her of the banana bread pancakes someone made for her once upon a time.

"Junior's," her dad replied. "It's a date, Bethy."

And then after another group hug, her parents piled into a taxi to head to the airport, leaving as quickly as they'd come.

"You okay?" Delaney asked once they were gone.

Beth had been running on adrenaline for the past two days as she prepared for her numbers.

Now that she'd finally done it and done it *well*... Oh, who was she kidding? Beth kicked some major lifelong-dream *ass* tonight, and she wasn't about to downplay it, even in her head. But the adrenaline was beginning to wane, which meant real life was creeping its way back in.

"Actually," her sister continued before Beth had a chance to respond, "I'm beat. This whole being a mom while also being pregnant is a tougher gig than I thought. Catch you in the morning for brunch?"

"What?" Beth asked, incredulous. "You're ditching me?"

Sam, the brother-in-law she counted on to be the levelheaded one in the relationship when Delaney got all flighty, shrugged and put his arm over his wife's shoulders.

"Guess I have to get this one back to the hotel for bedtime. We'll call you in the morning. You were great, Beth."

"The best, Bethy!" Delaney added, and then they both pivoted in the other direction and strode off toward their hotel.

"What the hell just happened?" Beth asked, each word forming a small cloud of condensation as she spoke into the frigid air.

A throat cleared behind her, and Beth froze where she stood.

"I think they maybe wanted to give us some time to talk alone."

Beth's whole heart caught in her throat, every single emotion sweeping over her like a wave.

Fear... Was this closure? A final goodbye?

Joy... How good would it feel to see him in the flesh again, even if it was just this one last time?

Anger... How *dare* anyone surprise her when that either meant pepper-spraying both the surpris*er* and the surprise-*ee,* or Beth bent at ninety degrees over an outdoor trash can, tossing all her cookies?

Love... Everything Beth felt for Eli was still there. If she turned around and saw him, she might burst into a million pieces.

Heartbreak... Ditto her thoughts on love.

"You gonna look at me, Mighty Dancer?" he asked, breaking the audible silence. But did he know that inside Beth's head and heart, it was absolute and utter chaos?

"Are you really there?" she asked, just to be sure. "Or is this my subconscious making me think I can actually have *all* the things I want at the same time."

She threw a mittened hand over her mouth. Winter and exhaustion certainly did a number on her external filter.

When he didn't respond, Beth feared he actually was a hallucination, so she spun on her heel and had to immediately take a step back so she didn't knock right into him and the most gorgeous yet jumbled bouquet of flowers she'd ever seen.

"I realized I never asked you what your favorite flower was, so when I finally found a florist who was still open, I had him give me one of everything he had left."

The man before her was an Eli Beth had never seen. For starters, he had a *beard*. It was short and neatly trimmed, every color of warm, rich brown she could imagine with a few flecks of gray. And where she'd always imagine his Stetson or his gorgeous, perfectly overgrown hair, he wore a gray knit cap to counteract the New York chill. But those bright blue eyes…she'd recognize them anywhere, especially when they crinkled at the corners due to the smile Beth knew was meant only for her.

It was a nervous smile, for sure. But it was *Beth's* nervous smile, and she couldn't believe it was here. That *he* was here.

"All of them," she finally uttered, voice shaking. "All the flowers you brought are my favorite."

"I like your…uh…" He pointed at her face, and Beth realized she hadn't bothered to wash off her makeup.

"Oh my god!" she gasped. "I'm still a toy soldier!"

Eli's face grew serious. "Beth, you were unbelievable tonight. I knew you'd be good, but I didn't know what it would be like to *see* you do what you were born to do. I can't believe I almost didn't…"

He trailed off, but Beth didn't need him to finish. He wasn't going to come.

"This *wasn't* a surprise, was it?" she asked. "Delaney didn't know you'd be here because you weren't planning on being here." The reality felt like a punch to the gut…him showing up at the last minute, the ridiculous bouquet of flowers. It was a goodbye and apology wrapped all in one. And could Beth blame him? She'd been all but unreachable for the past month.

He shook his head. "And I got here so late that they'd given away my ticket. So I had to sit a little farther back. Delaney and Sam didn't even know I was here."

Beth nodded. The cold was starting to seep into her bones. She needed to remind herself that this was her *best* night, and nothing was going to erase that. Except…

This was *almost* her best night. The only thing missing was sharing it with her favorite human. Her person. Her *Eli*.

"I *miss* you," they both said at the same time.

"What?" Beth asked. "You're not here to"—she swallowed—"end this for good?"

"What?" Eli echoed. "*No.* Is that what you want?"

Beth's eyes widened. She hugged her big puffy coat against her chest because despite being a dancer who had full control of her body onstage, this was one of those times when she had *no* idea what to do with her arms again.

"No!" she cried. "But you just said you weren't

going to come. And clearly those are *Sorry-I'm-dumping-you-after-you-just-had-your-stage-debut* flowers. I can't think of any other explanation."

Eli let out a nervous laugh. "I was supposed to neuter Trudy Davis's new beagle this morning, which meant I never would have made it on time. But Trudy had to reschedule for next week, so I canceled the rest of my less pressing appointments and hopped on the first plane out here. I didn't want to tell you I *couldn't* come until the very last minute. But by the time it *was* the last minute, I realized it could have been a courtesy invite and that you might be better off without me here, so I wished you luck." He groaned. "This all played out a lot better in my head, but I can see now how it might have looked from your perspective."

"Put the flowers down," she said softly.

"What?"

"Eli, put the flowers down." The words came out as more of a command this time.

He glanced from left to right, then over his shoulder. But there was only the sidewalk and, a half block away, a fire hydrant.

"Put them on the ground, *please*. I promise they'll be okay. I just really need you to not have anything in your hands right now, okay?"

His eyes widened, and recognition—along with *her* Eli smile—bloomed on his beautiful, bearded face.

He dropped the bouquet on the ground and barely had time to open his arms before she launched herself into them.

He hoisted her onto his hips, and she hooked her ankles tight. And then she kissed him and kissed him and kissed him until his beard rubbed her chin raw, until he finally lowered her to the ground, though he didn't let go of her for even a second.

"You have a beard!" she whispered through tear-soaked laughter. She tore off one of her mittens with her teeth so she could run her fingers over the coarse hair that made him look wholly new but also still exactly like the man she loved. "And Trudy got a new beagle?"

Eli nodded. "He's actually a beagle–dachshund mix. She named him Noodle." He laughed, then rubbed a thumb across her chafed chin. "As for the beard, maybe it wasn't the best idea."

"I love it!" she exclaimed, then decided that wasn't convincing enough. "I love *you*, Eli. I know this has been hard, but I want to make it work. If you do, I mean."

He stared at her, eyes clear and blue and sure. "I love you, Mighty Dancer. And I'll endure New York winters for as long as I have to if it means we're in this for the long haul."

Her breath caught in her throat.

"What is it?" he asked.

She shook her head, but then she decided to tell him anyway.

"Back when I first got to Meadow Valley, and you were adamant about me not riding Midnight…"

Eli's jaw tightened, and he nodded, but he didn't interrupt.

"Delaney said something to me that has always been in the back of my mind. She said that everything gets easier with time but that some things stick with us for the long haul. I knew she was partially talking about my injury and what it might mean for my career. But I also knew she meant you." Her throat tightened. "The years before we met were so different for each of us, and I get that for better or worse some part of your loss will always be with you. And that's okay. I guess I just feel lucky that you have enough room in your heart to love me too, and maybe I didn't realize it until tonight, but I really needed to hear that you and me? Us? That *we're* your long haul too."

Eli kissed every one of her tears as they fell, and when she looked up at him, she saw that his lashes were wet too.

"Thank you," he told her softly.

"For what?" she asked.

"For loving *all* of me, even the messy parts." He dipped his head so his breath tickled her ear. "And not that it's a competition," he whispered, "but I love you, Beth. I *love* you. For the long haul and infinite days after that. I love you." He kissed her. "I love you." He kissed her. "I love you." And for good measure, he kissed her again. "Pretty sure I won that round."

"We both won," she told him, and she felt his lips part into a smile against hers.

"Then I guess we'll call it a tie."

That night, they lay in Eli's hotel bed, her naked body aligned perfectly against his. Her head rested on his chest as he traced lazy circles with his index finger on her back.

"I was thinking," she began, eyes growing heavy with sleep. Or maybe it was just that this whole night felt like a dream. "That I might like to learn more about rehabbing horses. I mean, I need to earn a living on the off months, right? So I was wondering if you might know of any ranches in your area that need horse trainers." She kissed his chest. "Of course, this ranch would need to train *me* how to train the horses, but I'm a quick learner."

She heard his sharp intake of breath, then felt it as his lungs expanded beneath her.

Beth tilted her head up to catch his gaze.

"Are you serious?" he asked. "You want to come *home*?"

The way he said that last word—as if he'd been

waiting for her to ask that exact question for six months—made her realize that this, right now, was her best night. Her best moment. The happiest she had ever been.

"Yes." She climbed over him, pressing both her palms to his bearded cheeks. "I want to come *home*."

Epilogue

By the time Eli had Holiday—a brown Arabian recovering from a ligament tear in her right rear ankle—tacked and ready to go, Beth and Midnight had already exited the arena and were galloping toward the late-summer woods.

"Show-off," Eli mumbled as he led the mare into the arena and then through the back gate. He mounted her, gave her neck a quick pet, and then tapped his heels against her flanks. "Yah!" he called, and Holiday erupted into her first trot and soon a gallop since her owners had brought her to the ranch. This would likely be her final ride before she went back home, and Eli wanted it to be a good one.

In the distance, he caught a flash of Beth's long wild waves, of Midnight's black coat shining in the sun. He loved how well she knew the way to their secret spot, loved that whenever she wasn't working or training for the following Christmas performance, she was on the back of a horse, usually Midnight, riding as far as they could go for as long as they could ride.

Beth knew her injury would cut her time in the

dance company short, but she hadn't let it stop her from achieving her dream. And Eli knew the years she spent splitting time between New York and California would be tough on them both but that Meadow Valley would *always* be home.

By the time he and Holiday made it to the woods, he was grateful for the shade to protect him from the unforgiving heat. Beth made sure they packed uncarbonated water this time, and they even included some cut-up apples and carrots to give Midnight and Holiday a proper feast while he and Beth rested under their favorite tree.

When he reached the clearing, Beth already had Midnight tied off to her regular tree, the blanket spread out on the grass, and... His brow furrowed. Was that a bottle of champagne?

He hopped off of Holiday, got her tied off and situated with a few snacks, and then made his way nervously to where Beth waited for him, two plastic flutes already filled.

"What is all this?" he asked, still confused as she handed one of the flutes to him. Only then did he notice the bottle lying against the trunk of the tree.

Sparkling Grape Juice.

He stumbled backward a couple of steps before righting himself again. And for more than the first time since his mighty dancer came into his life, Eli Murphy was speechless.

"So here's the thing," Beth began. She stepped

toward him, hooking her finger into the belt loop of his jeans. "It would seem that the Spence women are immune to contraception." She laughed as she referred to Delaney and Sam's surprise pregnancy with Nolan.

"But we used..." he stammered.

"I know," she replied.

"And we were so..." Eli added.

"We *were*," Beth continued.

"The new season." His heart sank. "You auditioned for a principal role in the company." And she'd made it too. In only three weeks, she'd be heading back for six weeks of rehearsal before the holiday show season began in November.

She nodded. "Now hear me out, okay? Another dancer in the company found herself in a similar situation a few years ago, except it was twins. And she was able to dance through her fifth month, which meant she made it through the whole holiday season. She even came back the next season, but I don't know. Maybe two is enough for me." Eli's mouth fell open, and Beth laughed. "It's not going to be twins for *us*," she continued. "I mean, it *could* be, but what are the odds, right?" She laughed again, but this time he heard a tremble, as if she wasn't as steady in her resolve as she'd thought.

"What's wrong?" he asked, finally remembering how to speak. "Do you feel okay? Do you need to sit down? Should you even be riding in this heat?"

"Aside from throwing up three times already today, I feel great!" She sniffled. "But I probably should have *asked* if you even *want* to be a father before popping the cork on the sparkling grape juice."

Did he want this? Did he *want* this?

"You're telling me that not only was I somehow lucky enough for you to fall in love with me, but now I also get to be a father?"

He'd been forced into the role of caretaker for his two younger brothers long before he was ready and able to understand the privilege of being any-one's actual father. When he lost Tess, Eli thought he'd also lost that part of his future as well. But Beth continued to give him gift after amazing gift, and she wasn't sure if he wanted this.

"Hold this?" he asked gently, handing her back the plastic flute of sparkling juice.

She let go of his belt loop and accepted his offering.

Then Eli dropped to his knees, slid her T-shirt up from where it rested on the hem of her jeans, and pressed his lips to her not-yet-swollen belly.

"I want *everything* with you," he said, looking up at her through glassy eyes.

She sniffed back her own tears, then looked from her right hand to her left.

"Dammit!" she cried. "Why did I pour the juice *before* I told you? I don't even think I can drink it. The smell is making me nauseous."

Eli laughed, rose to his feet, and grabbed his flute, tossing back the contents in one swift gulp. Then he grabbed Beth's and did the same before tossing both empty glasses onto the picnic blanket.

"A baby?" he asked, wrapping his arms gently around her.

She nodded. "A *baby*. And, Eli?"

"Yeah?"

"I want everything with you too, just in case that wasn't clear."

"I know," he told her. And he did. It might have taken him some time to realize he deserved a second chance like this, but now that he had it, he was grabbing on tight and holding on for as long as he could. "But…" he added, "I don't want you quitting your dream for this. As much as I'd love you home for good, I'm not asking you to give it up. We'll make it work." He knew now that this was true.

She nodded, the tears falling freely now. "I want to make it through this second season, and then I want to move on to my new dream."

Eli tried to clear his throat, but it was no use. His heart was stuck where his words should be, but somehow Beth knew. She always knew when he needed her to fill in the blanks.

"I want to raise a family on this ranch," she told him. "And teach our kids to ride horses and to dance. I noticed there's no dance school in Meadow

Valley, and yet the population of small humans seems to be growing exponentially. I might need to do something about that."

Eli spun her in his arms so they were both facing the woods that led back to the field and from there back to the ranch. He rested his hands on her abdomen, already impatient to watch it grow. All he ever used to see was everything he'd lost, and while that loss would always be there, he was finally able to open his eyes to everything he'd found and the possibilities yet to come.

"You know I'm going to insist on weekly doctor appointments while you're in New York," he whispered against her ear.

Beth laughed. "I'd expect nothing less from you."

"And you need to be careful riding. Midnight's carrying double the precious cargo now."

God, he loved her, and he loved the baby he'd have to wait months to meet. He loved and he loved and he loved, and how the hell could this day or this moment or this *life* get any better than it was right now?

"And I'm going to fly out every other weekend. Maybe even *every* weekend," he continued.

She clasped her hands over his and shook her head. "You can't miss all your Saturdays with the boys at Trudy's café. And we rehearse on Saturdays anyway. How about once a month, and you stay for an extra-long weekend?"

He kissed her neck. "Okay, but we're never leaving the hotel room while I'm there."

"Good," Beth replied. "Because I won't have energy for anything more than *sleep*."

He stilled. Right. Of course. The baby was going to change a lot of things for them. He'd adjust.

"Eli?" She guided one of his hands up and beneath her T-shirt, snapping open the front clasp of her bra. "I'm not tired *now*."

"Marry me," he growled into her ear.

"Definitely," she replied. "And remember how that whole contraception thing doesn't really work on me? Why don't we pretend to make a baby on purpose and see how that goes?"

Okay, so maybe *this* was how life topped itself for today. But that was the thing. There would be moments like this when the happiness he felt seemed unfathomable, but there would also be moments like the one in the airport the first time he and Beth said goodbye. What mattered was that between here and there, they would figure it out together, his mighty dancer and him, their ranch, her dancing, his clinic, their *baby*, and today…no condom.

———

That night, Beth turned to him in bed. "I want to tell you something," she started.

"Tell me anything."

She kissed his clean-shaven cheek, which she said she'd tolerate for the summer, but she expected the beard back by winter. Every holiday season, she wanted to remember what he looked like when he showed up in New York and told her he was in this with her for the long haul. She even made him promise to take her back to Rockefeller Center every Christmas Eve—while she was still dancing and even after she wasn't—to tell her again. He had no problem agreeing to that.

"Last year, on that day with Trudy and Frederick?"

"Yeah?" he said softly. It felt both a million miles away and like it just happened yesterday.

She ran her fingers through his hair. "When Trudy and I were alone, she tried to explain to me what it was like loving a pet. She said that it was a wonderful thing to love them and have them love you back, but you enter into the contract knowing that you'll outlive them. And I didn't get it, you know? I didn't get why you'd enter that kind of contract knowing that it not only had an expiration date but one that ended in grief." Her breathing hitched, and Eli realized she was crying.

He swiped his thumbs beneath her eyes. "It's okay," he told her. "Whatever it is, it's okay."

Beth nodded. "And then she told me...she said, 'If I give up the possibility of pain, I'd also be giving up the possibility of joy. Years of it, which is what

I've had with Frederick.'" She pressed her hands against Eli's chest. "This... *Us.* It hurt a lot in the beginning. And then again in the middle. But it so easily could never have happened at all, and that's the scariest part. I sometimes wonder, *What if I'd never gotten hurt? What if I'd turned down Delaney's invitation? What if I hadn't been brave enough to kiss you that day in your office?* I think of all these questions where the answer is us maybe never falling in love and never having to go through the parts that hurt. But being with you also brings me more joy than I ever imagined a person could experience. It's the most wonderful, terrifying thing to get to love you, Eli Murphy, but I get what Trudy was saying now."

"That I'm your pet?" he asked with a half smile.

She gave his shoulder a playful shove. "Eli..."

"Sorry, sorry." But he was still smiling. "I get it too," he admitted.

And from the look in her clear green eyes, he knew she trusted that he did.

He wouldn't give up the years of joy he had with Tess just to escape the pain of loss. And did it terrify him to be this happy with Beth, to love her and the baby he'd only known about for mere hours *so* damned much? Of course it did.

But Eli Murphy didn't live in the land of *what if* anymore. He couldn't predict the future nor prevent the painful moments from happening.

But he could be in it right now, in *this* moment, and not take a single second for granted.

"Not one second, Mighty Dancer," he whispered. "I wouldn't trade a single moment I get to spend loving you. And loving you and loving you and loving you and loving..."

Yeah, Eli Murphy was pretty damned sure that tonight and *every* night thereafter, he won.

Acknowledgments

Thank you so much to my editor, Deb, for loving the Murphy brothers as much as I do. So thrilled to finally be giving Eli his long-awaited HEA.

To my agent, Emily, I'm always grateful for more projects for us. Thank you for championing this midwestern girl's dream of creating heroes on horses who trade sunglasses for cattleman hats.

Lea, Megan, Jen, and Chanel...I miss your faces. It's been too long. Thankful for our ongoing Messenger and Slack chats, but I need a conference style, adjoining-hotel-room retreat with all y'all!

S and C, my two favorite humans, I love you 3000 x infinity. Let's travel the world and dream up more stories.

M and W, thank you for the dedicated bookshelf and always preordering. D and I, thanks for making me feel mildly famous with the hostess at The Buffalo!

And always, my wonderful, supportive readers, thank *you* for letting me do this thing I love. It means the world that you love it too.

About the Author

A corporate trainer by day and *USA Today* best-selling author by night, A.J. Pine can't seem to escape the world of fiction, and she wouldn't have it any other way. When she finds that twenty-fifth hour in the day, she might indulge in a tiny bit of TV to nourish her undying love of K-dramas, superheroes, and everything romance. She hails from the far-off galaxy of the Chicago suburbs.

ajpine.com
Facebook: AJPineAuthor
Instagram: @aj_pine
TikTok: @aj_pine

Also by A.J. Pine

THE MURPHYS OF MEADOW VALLEY
Holding Out for a Cowboy

HEART OF SUMMERTOWN
The Second Chance Garden

HOLDING OUT FOR A COWBOY

First in a brand-new, compelling cowboy romance series from USA Today bestselling author A.J. Pine.

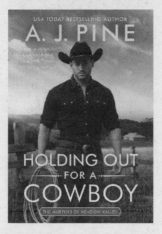

In high school, Boone Murphy and Casey Walsh were the couple most likely to tie the knot, until tragedy tore them apart and upended Casey's future. Now, more than a decade later, the beauty school dropout runs Meadow Valley's family tavern and steers clear of the cowboy who once stole her heart. What Casey doesn't know is that she is the only reason Boone hasn't left behind his life in Meadow Valley. He's never stopped loving her, and if she would give him a second chance—this time, he'll never let her go.

"A fabulous storyteller."
—Carolyn Brown, *New York Times* bestselling author

For more info about Sourcebooks's books and authors, visit:
sourcebooks.com

LOVE DRUNK COWBOY

Was it her blue eyes...or was it the watermelon wine?

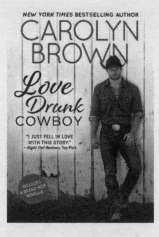

After high school, Austin Lanier left Oklahoma as fast as her feet could carry her. Years later, when she learns she's inherited her grandmother's watermelon farm, she just wants to sell the place, slip on her stilettos, and run back to corporate America. That is, until drop-dead-sexy cowboy Rye O'Donnell shows up next door and tempts Austin to trade her heels for cowboy boots...

"Fresh, funny, and sexy...filled with likable, down-to-earth characters."
—*Booklist*

For more info about Sourcebooks's books and authors, visit:
sourcebooks.com

EVERY BIT A COWBOY

She swore she would never fall in love again,
but then she met Knox Garrison.

No matter how swoony the cute cowboy is, romance is the last thing on Carley Chapman's mind. But it's hard to ignore Knox Garrison and the spark of attraction she feels every time he's near. When a water line break floods her building, she's forced to move her salon out to the Horse Rescue ranch, and Knox shows up to help. But things get even more complicated when Carley's no-good ex comes sniffing around and Knox "fixes" the problem by telling him they're engaged...

"Filled with humor, heart, and real love."
—Michelle Major, *USA Today* bestselling author

For more info about Sourcebooks's books and authors, visit:
sourcebooks.com

COWBOY TOUGH

Sparks fly in this opposites attract cowboy romance
from bestselling author Joanne Kennedy.

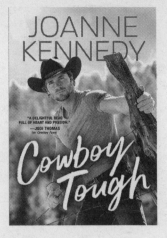

Mack Boyd might be able to ride a wild stallion to a standstill, but
he won't ever say no to his family. When his mother asks him to
help manage the family ranch, Mack arrives just in time to prepare
for an upcoming artists' retreat and to meet Cat Crandall, a pas-
sionate art teacher who can't be more different from him. But when
the ranch is threatened financially, can Mack and Cat set aside their
differences and work together?

"Full of heart and passion."
—Jodi Thomas, *New York Times* bestselling author,
for *Cowboy Fever*

For more info about Sourcebooks's books and authors, visit:
sourcebooks.com

TANGLED IN TEXAS

It took thirty-two seconds to end his career,
but it only took one to change his life.

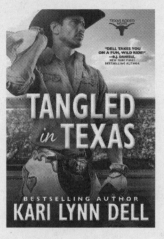

One moment Delon Sanchez was the best bronc rider in the
Panhandle and the next he was nothing. Knee shattered, future in
question, all he can do is wonder what cruel trick of fate threw him
off that horse and into the path of his ex, Tori Patterson.

Tori's finally come home, intent on escaping the public eye.
It's just her luck that Delon limps into her physical therapy office.
Seeing him again, Tori can't remember what made her choose foolish pride over love…or why the smartest choice would be to run
from this gorgeous rodeo boy as fast as her boots can take her.

"Real Ranches. Real Rodeo. Real Romance."
—Laura Drake, author of the Sweet on a Cowboy series

For more info about Sourcebooks's books and authors, visit:
sourcebooks.com